An Hour to Kill

Also by Edward Wellen
Hijack

An Hour to KILL

by
Edward Wellen

St. Martin's Press
New York

AN HOUR TO KILL. Copyright © 1993 by Edward Wellen. All rights reserved. Printed in the United States of America. No part of this book may be used or reproduced in any manner whatsoever without written permission except in the case of brief quotations embodied in critical articles or reviews. For information, address St. Martin's Press, 175 Fifth Avenue, New York, N.Y. 10010.

Library of Congress Cataloging-in-Publication Data

Wellen, Edward.
    An hour to kill / Edward Wellen.
      p. cm.
    ISBN 0-312-09307-1 (hardcover)
    I. Title.
PS3573.E4566H68   1993
813'.54—dc20   93-3520
                                                                                                    CIP

First Edition: June 1993

10 9 8 7 6 5 4 3 2 1

For Barbara and Jerry Schreiber

AN HOUR TO KILL

CHAPTER
1

Mal spotted Woolf in the darkness beyond the glassed-in section of the promenade. Mal followed him out onto the deserted afterdeck, into the gale-force wind that made the sensible and the queasy take cover.

The deck shoved up and then dropped away underfoot and the moment merged with all the déjà vus of Mal's uncle Phil staggering carefully in at dawn, trying to anticipate the heave of the floor. *A lorn boozer,* Uncle Phil said of Uncle Phil.

Hell with Uncle Phil, Woolf was butting through wind buffets right up to the bulwark rail. Mal had to smile; looked like the guy was going to feed his dinner to the fishes.

With alarm, Mal caught on to the stupid bastard's real intent.

Woolf started to climb over the rail, the wind fluffing the surround of his tonsure and flapping his sport shirt.

Mal could reach him in time only with a shout. "Hey! You're forgetting something!"

Woolf's head jerked around. "Who the hell said that?"

Mal, holding the rail along the superstructure, leaned out of the shadows. "Me."

"Who the hell are you?"

"A guy who can tell you why you don't want to do it."

"What makes it your business?"

"Look, the wind is tearing our words. Climb back down and I'll tell you. Don't worry, I won't make a grab."

Mal could almost feel the guy's stare. A toss-up for a long minute: to jump or not to jump.

Then Woolf climbed down off the rail. But he held it, ready to hurdle. "Shit. It would've been all over by now." He sounded somewhere between sore and sullen. "Okay. So tell me why not."

"Because there has to be a body."

Mal said it so seriously that—after initial surprise—Woolf laughed.

The laugh died into a thoughtful grunt. "You got something there. If I vanish into salt air, it could take my ever-loving heirs seven years to settle my estate. I couldn't care less. But shit, man, you know how long it took me to nerve myself to the jumping point? I'd have to work up the nerve all over again." He shivered all at once. "Goddammit, let me buy you a drink. I know I sure could use one."

"Likewise."

Woolf let go of the rail and skidded downhill to Mal and caught hold beside him. Woolf stuck out his free hand. "The name's... Max Schaf." The voice sounded strained but carried a politician's rote frank heartiness; the flesh felt clammy but delivered a politician's preemptive quick-release grip.

"Harry Pace." The name *he* was traveling under.

"Great, Harry."

Mal saw that Woolf failed to remember him from the lifeboat drill on the *Queen Mab*'s first day out. They had drawn the same boat station, and Mal had certainly sized up Woolf at the time, but Woolf's obvious preoccupation had kept Woolf from registering Mal. And since then, Woolf had holed up in his cabin, living on room service while he thrashed out whether to stonewall the federal investigation or to spill his guts. Some vacation, this Caribbean cruise his doctor had ordered to avert breakdown and elude the media. Some vacationer, Borough President Al Woolf traveling sans mustache and sans toupee as "Max Schaf."

Woolf looked around. "I guess we go back through the glass section to the stairs."

"Never mind the stairs." Mal steered him to another door. "I found a shortcut. It's a way just the crew uses. It goes straight down all the way to the engine room."

Actually, it didn't go straight down; it corkscrewed. But you could see that the shaft had doors so that you could get off at the decks along the way.

Mal ushered Woolf in. "Hold tight and watch your step."

Woolf started down the twisting stairs. "You know, I feel born again." He sounded manic. "I'm glad you happened along when you did."

Mal was busy taking plastic gloves from his pocket and pulling them on. "I'm glad you're glad."

Woolf started to look around with a big smile. Mal gave him a hard neck chop and then a shove. Woolf ended up in a heap a dozen steps below. Mal swung swiftly down to make sure the guy was dead. The guy was dead.

He had *told* Woolf there had to be a body. Mal's client needed to know that Woolf hadn't faked a suicide, needed to know that Woolf wasn't still around in some new identity, needed to be sure that Woolf couldn't still bleat if the Feds caught up with him. Mal's client needed to *know* that Woolf was dead.

One ear cocked for footsteps, Mal patted the body down and found the nothing he expected: no wallet, no loose change, no house keys, no car keys. A suicide would not take that stuff with him. But he did find something he had not expected: the stateroom key.

Mal weighed it in his hand—a key like his own with the stateroom number stamped on a heart-shaped tag. Why would a would-be suicide have this on him? Habit? Unconscious insurance in case he changed his mind at the last?

Well, Woolf was not a suicide. Woolf was an accident. Mal shoved the key back into Woolf's pant pocket. He got up to get the hell out of there.

Something clicked in his mind and he stopped dead. Woolf's suicide try had implications that meant complications. With suicides went suicide notes.

Mal retrieved the key.

On his way to Woolf's stateroom, Mal ran into Sigrid, the thirtyish, stacked Norwegian stewardess who handled this section.

Mal had been about to open Woolf's door but spotted Sigrid coming and moved on to his own door. But with Woolf's key still in his hand, he didn't even try it in the lock. Especially as he also still had on the plastic gloves. He did his best to hide his hands with his body.

The encounter called for a smile, so he stretched his mouth. The wind must have put a glow onto his face.

Sigrid dimpled. "I see you enjoy the cruise."

He nodded. "It's extra nice when you've found someone to enjoy it with." He winked.

She giggled. "Good for you. That's the whole point."

He knew she was wondering why the fuck he didn't unlock his door. "An older broad has a lot to offer," he said with a leer. "But so does a younger one." He looked her up and down.

He had guessed right. Sexism turned her off. Suddenly, she was all business. "I'm sure. Have a nice evening, sir." And she was gone.

The bedclothes were rumpled. The wastebasket held an empty fifth. Three Elske Line No. 10 envelopes stood propped up on the built-in dresser.

He read the addresses—all in Brooklyn—as he snatched them up. One to the D.A., one to an Esq., and the third to a Mrs. Millie Schaf.

He ripped them open.

The letter to the D.A. named names, including Mal's client Guido Palmieri, and placed places, including motels and diners and pizzerias used as payoff venues. The letter to the lawyer had to do with a holograph codicil to Woolf's will, leaving big sums to charity. The letter to Mrs. Schaf—"Dear Sis"—was both maudlin and practical; the practical part told her where to find keys to a safe-deposit box registered in the names of Max Schaf and Millie Schaf.

Mal shook his head. Had Woolf really thought that the letter to Millie would remain sealed and that Millie would get a crack at the safe-deposit? Woolf should've fixed it up with her beforehand. Guy's mind sure was fucked up.

He kept the letters but tore the envelopes to bits and flushed the bits down the john.

Then he searched the dresser drawers and the closet. He turned up Woolf's passport and wallet. The wallet held Woolf's driver's license and his credit cards and a half grand in cash. The bills were neither fresh nor in sequence, so Mal helped himself to half the half grand. He left the passport and the wallet in plain view on the dresser. He double locked the door behind him.

A trip to the writing room for an envelope large enough to hold the three letters. He stuffed them in, stuck the flap firmly, printed his L.A. mail-drop address, stuck on more than enough stamps, and posted the envelope in the purser's office, the way Woolf should've done if he'd been thinking straight.

Now only one thing tied him to Woolf: Woolf's stateroom key. Sure, he could ditch it anywhere within reason for someone to find, and they would think Woolf had dropped it. But what if it somehow really got lost, kicked down a scupper or whatever, or got picked up by one of the sneak thieves there surely had to be aboard? Mal hated loose ends. Neater to restore Woolf's stateroom key to Woolf's person.

* * *

A painting in the writing room showed the *Queen Mab* with what the little brass plate called "A Bone in Her Teeth," the curl of white water at the bow. Well, right now the sea had the *Queen Mab* in *its* teeth and was shaking her.

Mal moved up and down with the corridor on his way to the steel door that had the Bakelite sign AUTHORIZED PERSONNEL ONLY on it; he hauled himself along by the handrail to keep from caroming off the walls. He reached the door, took hold of the pull, braced himself, waited for the cusp of the moment, and then swung the door open and himself in.

A drop of something hit his nose. Mal leaned away, flicked the wetness off his nose, glanced at a pinkish wash on his fingertip, looked up through the mesh stainless-steel treads of the spiraling stairs. The body was moving. Not because the ship was shifting it. Purposefully.

The movement stopped. Then a head leaned out, burnished darkly blond in the recessed light.

"Nei, så morsamt, Mathiesen!" The man's voice echoed hollowly.

Mal pulled back out and shut the door.

Faintly from within, "Mathiesen?"

Mal moved away fast. *Boy, for a minute there* . . .

So they had found the body already. That crewman had been swabbing the steps, mopping up the blood that had trickled from Woolf's mouth.

Way it stood now, with no identification on the body and no one reported missing, it would take them a while to give the corpse a local habitation and a name. Mal figured the only two people aboard who knew "Max Schaf" by name as well as by sight were himself and Sigrid. Mal pictured a lineup in reverse, stewards filing past to I.D. the body.

As advertised, the midnight buffet was sumptuous. It surprised Mal to see at this hour and in this weather so many passengers capable of eating as if there were no tomorrow. Mal stuffed himself with the best of them. Took him five minutes to gobble all he needed.

And also as advertised, the ship's hospital was open around the clock.

Mal stopped short of the door to thrust a finger down his throat. He held it there till he gagged and the food he had gorged on started back up.

Both hands over his mouth, he staggered into the room in a blind rush.

The nurse looked up from a chart, dropped it, leapt to her feet, and rushed Mal to a sink. She had a warm, moist towel ready when he finished heaving.

As he wiped his face he studied the layout. This room served as both clinic and dispensary. On one side, a door led to the doctor's office. On the other, a half-open door showed four hospital beds in a night-lighted room. A pajamaed woman snored on one bed; the others were unoccupied. *Shit. They had Woolf's body elsewhere.*

The nurse handed Mal a clipboard with a form on it to fill out. He wrote down lies while he tried to think how to get Anne-Marie Kielland—the name on her tag—to tell him, without knowing she was telling him, where the body was.

A crewman—Mathiesen?—saved Mal the trouble by wheeling in a gurney. It was empty but for a rumpled sheet. The way Nurse Kielland and the crewman exchanged glances Mal wasn't supposed to guess the meaning of told Mal the gurney had taken Woolf's body to cold storage. Kielland pointed to a corner of the room. The crewman rolled the gurney there and left.

Nurse Kielland glanced at the form Mal had filled out, took Mal's pulse and temperature, looked into his mouth, made a few notes, and told him he was healthy as a fish. Mal hoped that was Norwegian for sound as a dollar. Though these days, the dollar . . .

A Dr. Sommerfelt came in, threw Mal a vague smile, exchanged looks and shrugs with Nurse Kielland, and washed his hands while she presented him with Mr. Harry Pace's seasickness.

Dr. Sommerfelt dried his hands. "No problem, Mr. Pace. I can give you an injection."

Mal frowned. "Will it knock me out?"

Sommerfelt made a judicious mouth. "One might say so. But you will wake up feeling fine."

"I'd rather not. I like to stay on my feet."

The doctor shrugged. "As you wish." His gaze swept Mal. "Ever had glaucoma? Metabolic, liver, or kidney disease? Obstruction of stomach or intestine? Trouble urinating? Skin allergy? Taking any other medicines?"

Mal shook his head to all.

"And you're not elderly and not pregnant. So what I will give you instead should be quite safe." He brought a prescription pad within writing distance. "Nurse, please apply a Transderm Scōp. I'll prescribe the patient more, though the one should be effective for seventy-two hours."

The doctor scribbled something on the pad and handed the sheet to Mal. "You can get this filled at the drug counter in the gift shop."

Mal thanked him. Dr. Sommerfelt nodded and disappeared into his office.

Nurse Kielland turned to unlock a cabinet. Before she was done, Mal had slid Woolf's stateroom key under the rumpled sheet on the gurney. He let the point of the heart-shaped tag peep out.

The nurse rubbed behind Mal's left ear with a dry tissue. She removed the backing from a corn-plasterish disc and stuck the disc firmly behind Mal's ear near the hairline. "Do not touch it for three days." She went to wash her hands.

"What does it do?"

She turned and stared at him. "It stops nausea and vomiting connected with motion sickness."

"I mean *how?*"

She shook her head, then, brightening, let him read the writing on the package.

What it did, the disc time-released scopolamine through the skin. This reduced the activity of the nerve fibers deep in the ear that help people keep their balance. Mal read on warily. Side effects included dryness of the mouth in two-thirds of the users, drowsiness in one-sixth, temporary blurring of vision if the drug got onto the hands and rubbed off into the eyes—which explained the nurse's hand washing. Infrequently, the manufacturer admitted, the drug might cause disorientation, memory disturbances, dizziness, restlessness, hallucinations, confusion, difficulty urinating, skin rashes or redness, and dry, itchy, or red eyes. *Jeezus.*

Mal handed back the package. Nurse Kielland returned it to the cabinet. As she turned again, her glance fell on the gurney. The red point of the heart-shaped tag caught her eye. She made a face. She must've thought it was blood, Mal thought. Then she went over and pulled out the key.

Absently she asked Mal to excuse her, then stepped lively to the doctor's door, rapped, and went in.

He heard their voices, and then the doctor made a phone call, but it was all in Norwegian. Then the nurse came back, looking surprised to see Mal still there. Easing him out of the clinic, she told him it would take a little while for his queasiness to go away but that he would soon be fine.

"As a fish?"

"Exactly."

He did feel some queasiness, so he left the patch in place to see if it helped.

* * *

It didn't hurt. Both Mal and the weather were fine when the ship pulled into Nassau Harbor.

Mal got up early and took a turn around the promenade deck, more interested in what had happened aboard ship than in the view of Nassau.

The captain and the ship company's home office must have been worried about liability, because sometime during the night someone had painted ABSOLUTELY NO ADMITTANCE on the door Mal had ushered Woolf through. As though it had been there all along.

Mal watched an ambulance pull up onto the dock and a stretcher go down to it.

By midmorning, with passengers chafing to step ashore, everyone aboard knew that Brooklyn Borough President Al Woolf (of New York City political scandal) had been among them and had died in a fall down stairs he had no business being on. Then the chatter of sight-seeing and shopping swamped that topic of conversation.

Mal joined the lemming swarm but was not of it. Once ashore, he drifted away on his own and called his contact in Brooklyn from a pay phone in town.

He did not mention the envelopes Woolf had left behind. He could have scored points for doing away with the incriminating letters, but the mob did not like it when you knew too much. They might thank him for shielding them from all kinds of heat, but they might also feel threatened—and when they felt threatened, they hit out. He took it as a given that the instant they thought he was too well informed—even if they had always looked on him as a stand-up guy who would never squeal or put the bite on them—they would put out a contract on *him*.

So he just said he found Nassau cooler than he thought it

would be. That meant Woolf was dead. And the guy at the other end laughed and said not to worry and told Mal to buy himself a sweater, his credit was good. That meant the balance due Mal for the hit would go into Mal's numbered Cayman Islands bank account.

Then, just making conversation, the guy in Brooklyn asked, "What you gonna do now?"

"Buy that sweater and a couple of pairs of slacks."

The guy laughed, and they hung up.

Mal turned away from the phone slowly. He found himself shaken. He had surprised himself by coming out with the truth, telling the guy something about himself that was none of the guy's business. Mal never, *never,* spoke about his personal life—at least not truthfully.

Must've been the scopolamine in the patch talking.

He peeled the fucking thing from behind his ear, balled it up, and flicked it into the gutter. *Jeezus.* He stared at his hands. Now he had to find soap and water.

None of their business how he lived, what he did with his money. He had broken his own rule that no one—absolutely no one—should get a line on him. No one needed to know how he got release.

He had no drinking buddies; he didn't drink and he didn't buddy. He released by splurging on clothes. He had been pisspoor as a kid. Not even an urn to urinate in—Uncle Phil's elegant way of putting it. Those days, he had worn hand-me-downs, once-elegant rags handed down from Uncle Phil. So these days he bought nothing but the best.

And this day, right now, he followed the information sheet the ship handed out and hunted down the fanciest men's shop in Nassau and, after using its john to wash his hands thoroughly, treated himself to the most expensive sweater and slacks in stock, paying cash. The place was busy and he didn't want to hang around for the shop's tailor to take a half inch off the slacks, so he gave the address of his L.A. mail drop, took his sweater, and left.

Then he visited another few shops, picking up some ties and shirts and shorts, had those shipped too, glanced up at an old fort on a hill, and went back to the ship.

CHAPTER 2

Miami's front pages featured a chopper's failure to fly through the trompe l'oeil open-space mural on the wall of the Fontainebleau. Pilot error. Or pilot substance abuse; crack vials turned up in the wreckage.

For word of Al Woolf's freak death at sea, Mal had to turn to the burying place of week-old news. Snowbird Brooklynites, whether they had voted for Woolf or not, saw him as their man, cut down by Fate—their man, whether on the take or not. Now only his alleged sidekicks would know for sure. Today's bone for them, the dropping of grand-jury hearings on Guido Palmieri.

The Woolf hit had been a rush job, and Mal had whizzed through from airport to pier. Now, on his way back, he could take Miami in.

He still had a good two hours before he had to catch a No. 20 bus at the corner of Northeast First Avenue and First Street for the ride to Miami International Airport.

Do him good to stretch his legs. He believed in traveling light and had only a carryon to tote. He slung it over his shoulder and set out on a stroll, a tourist among tourists and Miamians.

Through dark glasses he picked out the street people who were undercover cops. The few he spotted did not worry him. As long as he did not wear a sweatshirt with HIT MAN on it, their eyes would pass him by. The law would be out in force and in earnest at night, when passion and crime were too. Midday was a kind of reverse sun block, a dulling daze of heat that screened the emotions *in.*

Food smells stirred hunger. He considered eating Chinese—Szechuan restaurant coming up—but monosodium glutamate always gave him migraine, the sweats, and heart palpitations.

He let the human tide carry him past dim sum and Szechuan duck. Miami had changed in fifteen years. Now Jesse Jackson could call it Jaimetown, if Jesse didn't mind breaking up the Rainbow Coalition. *Bueno,* when in Jaimetown . . .

He followed Southwest Eighth Street to Little Havana, where it became Calle Ocho. A window menu lured him into a restaurant for paella, coffee, and crema catalána.

He could have checked his carryon but parked it instead under the small table the maître d' found him in the no-smoking area. A busty waitress brought him a glass of ice water and took his order.

While he chewed ice and waited, he eyed the other patrons. Only one to watch out for was a young Hispanic male a couple of tables away, sitting alone, though the table was set for two. Mal experienced a moment of clear-air turbulence, a sense of wrongness. The guy's shirt had the sleeves torn off to show his biceps. A good guess the guy was on anabolic steroids. And, to go by his look of irritability, abusing them. A guy to stay away from.

The waitress brought Mal's dishes and Mal gave the food his attention. *Ah. The goods, the real thing.*

Then cigar smoke swirled across his food.

The macho Hispanic sat employing his cigar—deep hollowing of his cheeks on the inhale and Dizzy Gillespie-ish puffing of his cheeks on the exhale—while looking around daring anyone to object.

Mal dropped his gaze to his plate before their eyes could

meet. Took two to tangle. Mix it up with a guy in a 'roid rage, could miss his flight.

Finish up and get the hell out. He ate faster, softly blowing the smoke away from each forkful. Downed the paella before too much smoke had settled on it. Took up the dessert spoon for the caramel custard.

Now the guy was rapping his heavy signet ring on the table. The waitress came running, listened to his loud, rapid Spanish, and then hurried to the ladies' room. She came back to the guy's table after a minute, looking scared. She shook her head apologetically and gestured helplessly.

He gave her a long, hard stare and his face darkened. He mashed out the cigar on the tablecloth, knocked his chair over getting up, and brushed the waitress out of his way.

Mal saw her dip a napkin into the guy's abandoned water glass and rub at the tablecloth, then right the chair. But that was at the outer edge of his eye. He focused on the guy.

The guy strode to the ladies' room, went in, and, after some shouting inside, came out hauling a young woman by a slender wrist. He pulled her to the place setting opposite his, shoved her down into the chair, and sat again in his own chair. He picked up his mashed cigar, eyed it, dropped it to the floor, and lit up a fresh cigar. The young woman sat stonily, not even pretending to eat.

Mal slowed his spooning. He checked out the young woman, feature by feature. A looker, a knockout, despite the overpowdered bruise on her left cheekbone. Not that her looks made her all that special. Whenever Mal felt horny between jobs, he called up this high-class Hollywood madam who ran a string of disease-free hookers—and many of them could match this broad's looks. Some said they were in films, and Mal could believe them.

This broad, though, had jenny squaw, a term Mal had picked up from Uncle Phil, who admitted—or boasted—he had stolen it from Thackeray. So what the fuck did she want with a guy that beat on her? Maybe just that. Kinky sex, S/M. You could see the tension between them, but she wasn't making a scene, wasn't screaming for the cops. So there had to be something in it for her. Some sex partners picked fights for the fun of making up. Or maybe she was a hooker, after all. No rings on her fingers, so whatever the nature of their union, it was not blessed by the Church.

She turned away from a puff of smoke and her gaze met Mal's. Mal thought he saw a flash of mute appeal in her face, but if that's what it was it lasted only a fraction of a second. Her face was blank as she turned away.

"Hey, *comierda,* what you looking at?"

The guy was talking to him.

Mal played deaf. He pulled back his gaze and concentrated on tearing open a sugar packet and pouring the sugar into his coffee.

But that didn't sweeten the guy's disposition. "Hey, I'm talking to you." He drowned his cigar in his water glass, shoved himself to his feet, and started toward Mal.

Without stirring except to move the sugar in his cup with his spoon, Mal got set to grab his table knife. He would feint for the eyes, and when the guy pulled his head back Mal would go for his throat and then pick up his carryon and walk fast out through the kitchen.

Right then the broad took her chance. She eased up out of her chair and sidled toward the entrance.

The guy must have caught it with the corner of his eye. He was quick. He swung around and, pushing a laden table out of his way and knocking a couple of diners off their chairs, got to the door before her.

He clamped his hands on her shoulders and propelled her backward to their table and slammed her down onto her chair.

All the fight went out of her. She slumped forward.

The guy glared around.

Nobody met his eyes. Nobody had seen anything. Nothing had happened.

A smile fattened the guy's face. He sat down and lit a fresh cigar. He sprawled at ease, hooking one arm over the back of his chair and blowing smoke rings at the broad.

People who were in the middle of their meals began asking for their checks. Mal watched the discreet stampede and figured it was a good time for him to get the hell out too. He signaled for his check and left a 15 percent tip for the waitress, neither undertipping or overtipping, so she would have no call to remember him. Then he picked up his carryon, slung it over his shoulder, and palmed the table knife just in case the guy got in his face.

But the guy seemed to have forgotten all about him and Mal reached the cashier's desk at the door without having to use the knife. So Mal pocketed it while taking out his wallet.

While he waited for his change, he said to the cashier, "Surprises me nobody called the cops." Actually, it didn't surprise him at all. He just wondered what she might have to say.

The cashier flushed, and her mass of frizzed red hair bounced like springs escaping a mattress. Her glance jumped to the guy's table while her husky voice stayed close to home. "You don't know who he is?"

Mal shook his head.

She turned down the gain on her whisper. "Felipe Díez."

Now Mal understood. Díez was a big name in southern Florida. "Anything to Ramón Díez?"

"Younger brother."

Mal nodded and turned away. He would have liked to ask about the broad, but he had already drawn too much notice to himself. Not getting tumbled to rested on not pushing yourself on people.

He pocketed his change, leaving his hand in the pocket to

keep the coins from rattling against the knife as he walked out into the blast of day.

He stopped to stare back in through the restaurant window at the twosome. He knew he was well out of it. Mal stretched his mouth at the thought of how near he had come to going up against a Díez. Who needed it? And for what? Nothing to do with him. She had to be one screwed-up broad to take up in the first place with a guy she must've known would beat up on her. Even to think about her was to waste time and misplace sympathy. Her own fault. She should've known the guy was poison. Way these things went, she would wind up not just battered but dead.

He started to go. He stopped. He looked at his watch. What the hell. He had an hour to kill.

CHAPTER 3

One hour tops—that's what he'd give the whole thing, because it wasn't worth missing his flight over.

He looked at his watch. Like they said in the war films and the caper films when they synchronized: *Mark.* If Felipe and the broad remained inside the restaurant more than fifteen minutes from *now,* it was all off. If he had to follow Felipe and that took him more than fifteen minutes away from the bus stop, it was all off.

Be simple if he were packing a piece. When Felipe came out, drill him, walk away, ditch the piece. But he wasn't packing a piece because he had to pass through airport security.

All he had was the table knife. Knifing could be messy. And with something as dull-bladed and blunt-tipped as this sorry excuse for a knife, real messy. Tough to walk away or grab a cab, blood all over him.

Which brought up: How had his buddy Felipe and the broad reached the restaurant in the first place? More to the point, how did they plan to go? On foot? By car? He'd need wheels to follow wheels.

He sauntered past the restaurant to its parking lot and eyed the dozen cars there. He stretched his mouth. Wheels.

Now he had options. He could run Felipe down with a car and take off in it, weapon and getaway in one. He could knife Felipe and take off in a car. If he couldn't hit Felipe on the spot, he could follow Felipe to a better spot. Uncle Phil had a gag about a leopard's spots: "Who says a leopard can't change its spots? Fucking leopard makes fucking leaps. First it's on this spot here, then it's on that spot there. Right, Mal?" Right.

Mal spotted what he would have given odds was Felipe's car—a purple Cadillac.

The lot had no attendant he could see. Mal strolled toward the purple Caddy. *The* way to do it: be waiting in the backseat. But a decal on the driver's-side window warned of an alarm. He thought he could beat it, but he just might not, and he'd feel plenty foolish if he set it off and drew rubberneckers. Plus this just might not be Felipe's car after all, and he'd feel *really* plenty foolish if he crouched in the back of the purple Caddy while Felipe and the broad drove away in another car or maybe in a taxi.

Bottom line, Mal had to be at the wheel of some other car, ready for whatever.

He picked out a heap at the far end of the lot. Faced the right way for a good run at Felipe if Felipe rounded the Caddy to help the broad—and not out of old-fashioned courtesy, to be sure—into its passenger seat. Could be tricky to hit Felipe without hitting the broad. But if he had to hit her too, he had to hit her too. People who kept the wrong company couldn't complain if they got hurt. They *might* complain but they wouldn't have the *right* to complain. Go along with that, Uncle Phil?

He made for the heap. Someone had tossed bread crumbs onto the blacktop. He walked through pigeons to the scattered applause of wings. A cardboard accordion sunshade advertising a service station filled the inside of the heap's windshield. No decal on the window, and no alarm when he tried the door handle. Locked. But the knife blade pried the windscreen open enough for finger purchase and he wrenched it wider and reached in and lifted the door lock. He climbed in and hotwired the starter and got the engine running. Needed a tune-up and sounded like a gas guzzler, but at least it ran. The fuel gage showed the tank three-quarters full. He smiled sourly. Clouting a heap was a simple matter, but it could be a dumb move.

Guy he knew boosted a car in New Orleans and got as far as Tampa, where a cop stopped him for a bum taillight. Then the cop found the guy had an expired driver's license and no papers for the car. So they had him for GTA and crossing state lines. Then they found cocaine hidden in the spare in the trunk. So now they had him for transporting a controlled substance. Then they found a gun under the seat. So *now* they had him for armed trafficking. And because this was Florida, that meant a life sentence. *Fuck that.*

One eye out for Felipe or anybody else, Mal tossed the car for cocaine and guns and found none—though he would have appreciated the gun—and only then took possession. He snapped the knife blade popping the trunk lid open, so he grabbed with pleasure the long thin screwdriver he found in the trunk. It had it all over the knife as a weapon. Next best thing to an ice pick. Some of his cleanest hits had been with ice picks.

He gouged holes in the reversible accordion sunshade—on the inside it said, NEED HELP/PLEASE CALL POLICE—so as to be able to see the outside world and sat watching and waiting.

Papers in the glove compartment said that this 1970 Chevy belonged to a Sisto Favilla; probably one of the restaurant staff.

The quarter hour was up. Mal gave Felipe one more minute. And one more.

That was it. Mal put his hand to the door opener.

But here the fucker came, one paw wrapped around the broad's arm. Way they looked, he wasn't restraining a spirited dame but keeping a zombie moving. Felipe headed the two of them straight for the purple Caddy.

Mal let up the hand brake and put the car in gear. But one option was already gone.

He would not be able to run Felipe down, because Felipe did not come around to the passenger door but shoved the woman into the Caddy through the driver's door. Felipe pushed her over and got in.

Mal pulled the cardboard sunshade from the windshield, folded it, and tossed it into the back of the heap. He followed the Caddy into traffic.

Felipe drove the way Mal figured he would, leaning on the horn, cutting in and out of lanes, jumping lights.

Mal pushed the heap to keep up but the Caddy pulled away.

Way it had been heading, it could only be making for the Rickenbacker Causeway, so Mal hung on.

And cursed his cussedness when traffic seized up near the tollgate approach. He opened his door, set a foot outside, stood up to see over the unmoving cars ahead. He braced himself for the sight of the purple Caddy passing through the tollgate bottleneck and pulling out of sight, aborting this crazy chase.

But the purple Caddy *was* the bottleneck. It stood empty, with its two front doors winged out. And now Felipe came back to it, dragging the broad.

Mal's mouth stretched. She must've jumped out when the line slowed for the toll. Nice try.

Felipe threw the broad back into the Caddy, scowled around at the horns before he got in himself, then got rolling again, passing through the tollgate.

The line moved. Mal forked over a buck when his turn came. They crossed Biscayne Bay to Virginia Key, headed across Bear Cut for Key Biscayne. Soon, fluorescent-orange traffic cones narrowed the roadway, guarding newly poured patches in the far-right lane. Everybody crept along, packed together. The Caddy stayed a dozen cars ahead while Mal's hour ate itself up.

Mal checked his watch. *Shit.* He made up his mind to turn around and head back first chance after they hit Key Biscayne. It was all off.

Then the Caddy suddenly swerved right, bowling traffic cones over, and rolled along the new surface.

At first, Mal thought Felipe meant to bypass the traffic and then cut back in, but then the Caddy braked abruptly. Hard to tell from here just what, but something went down in the Caddy's front seat. The two figures looked locked together.

It was on.

Mal swung the Chevy through the traffic cones and rammed the Caddy. A nice solid crunch to leave a nice deep dent in the left rear fender. Then he backed up three feet and braked. He slid out on the passenger's side and leaned back in to paw through the glove compartment with his right hand. The screwdriver was ready in his left hand. He was a lefty. The Chevy should shield the action from the passing traffic.

He heard quick, hard footsteps, then felt a heavy hand on his shoulder.

Mal made to shrug it off. "Just a minute; my insurance papers."

The hand pulled him out and turned him around.

Felipe, looking disbelieving but pumped up with rage, loomed over Mal. Mouth set, spoiled; eyes used to staring others down. "What the fuck's wrong with you? You see what you did to my car?"

Mal glanced at the dent, then met Felipe's glare. "I see. So what, *comierda?*"

Felipe's disbelief and rage redoubled, and Mal watched him struggle to see straight. Felipe's eyes got Mal in focus and placed the face. "You. At the restaurant." He balled his fist and drew back his arm. "Man, you are dead."

The screwdriver blade came up in a swift smooth arc to enter under the breastbone.

Felipe's body didn't know it was dead, and it tore free of the screwdriver blade and staggered backward.

Mal was on it before it could fold. He walked it as far as the Caddy and then let it fall to the road on the passenger's side, hidden from traffic. So far, so good. To the drivers passing by, the whole configuration spelled only another rear-ending. Mal buried the screwdriver in Felipe again, to make sure, left it there, and used Felipe's loose shirt to wipe the handle.

He pulled the signet ring off Felipe's finger and rolled the body for Felipe's wallet. Not because he wanted the damn stuff but to make this look like a bump-and-rob.

Still, when he remembered the broad and jerked his head around and saw her watching from inside the Caddy, he felt his face flush.

Reflexively, he ducked his head and turned halfway to keep her from getting a good look at his face.

For her sake as much as his own. If she got a good look at his face, he would have to do her too.

But then, instead of doing the smart thing, hopping into the heap and burning rubber, he did a stupid thing. Something in him *wanted* her to see his face. So, while the smart part of him hollered at him not to be a fucking fool, he stayed put, facing her squarely, eyeing her levelly.

Another bruise on her face drew his gaze, but it was her eyes that held him. They looked red and swollen, but fierceness shone through.

For a sinking second he thought the fierceness was aimed at him. Shit, he should've known what every fucking rookie cop knows: that when you step into a domestic brawl, the victim is apt to turn on you.

Then she looked from Mal to Felipe and back to Mal and the fierceness gave way to a shaky smile.

That took a load off his mind. Quickly, he shook his head

and pushed out his lower lip and waved one hand dismissively at the loot that the other hand shoved in his pocket. Ring and wallet meant zilch. He was no thief.

Her eyes flickered. Had she remembered him from the restaurant? Her face showed nothing. She turned her head and opened her compact and began to powder the fresh bruise on her cheek.

For the benefit of her compact mirror, he made an okay with his thumb and forefinger; then he got back behind the wheel of the Chevy and bulled his way back into traffic.

On Key Biscayne he hit a parking place in Crandon Park, hastily wiped down the Chevy, and traded it in for a station wagon that he hot-wired. He headed back toward the causeway.

Not surprised to find commotion at the spot. But hadn't counted on delay this side of the divider, even though if cops did their job they would be screening for front-end damage. Least of all, looking for an encounter.

Cop cars and an ambulance had joined the purple Caddy at the scene. Cops on both sides tried to goose traffic along, but rubbernecking governed. So Mal snailed by—and while he looked across at Felipe's woman, she looked across at him.

She sat on a gurney while a paramedic took her blood pressure and a pantsuited black woman with a gold badge clipped to her lapel talked and took notes. Felipe's woman looked past the paramedic and the female homicide dick, straight at Mal.

Saw him sitting there for what seemed an hour and didn't give him away.

Safe in the airport bus, he was still shaking his head at his stupidity. If the mob guys found out he had done this one for free, they would have themselves a good laugh on him. Not only that, he had left behind a witness who could make him, who could at least give the cops a good description if they leaned on her.

But the cops had nowhere to start. He was not local. As happened with all his hits, he was just a shadowy figure that came in and did it and went right out. He had no criminal record—his juvenile files had been sealed while he was underage, destroyed when he became an adult. He had no m.o.—unless it was to let the means fit the opportunity. He had ditched the station wagon a couple of blocks from the corner of Northeast First Avenue and First Street after wiping it down. And he intended to steer clear of Miami for years to come.

As he boarded his plane, he felt his face spread in a stupid grin. He felt *good*.

Every now and again he looked down at the sun-kissed clouds covering the country and r-e-a-l-l-y stretched his mouth.

CHAPTER
4

Detective Sergeant Carol Shanley, Metro Dade P.D., found the woman just too damned calm. Not the false calm of shock—the real calm of control. Sad thing was, Marita Garcia's story just didn't hold up. Sad because Shanley's first assignment on joining the force had been at the Rape Treatment Center at Jackson Memorial Hospital, and Marita surely had the look of the women Shanley had seen there.

Still, she was too composed for her own good. Shanley feared there could be hidden damage from the rear-ending or delayed shock from witnessing the crime, but Marita wouldn't even take the paramedic's advice and go to the hospital for X rays and observation.

Insisted quietly she felt fine and just wanted to get back to her quarters. Said she was enrolled at Florida International University, majoring in sociology at the University Park campus, Southwest Eighth Street at Southwest 107th Avenue, and lived off-campus in a university-residence apartment.

Shanley promised to see she got home. First they would drive to headquarters for the typing up and signing of a statement and for Marita's help in putting together a sketch of the perp, while Shanley's partner, Jack Vogelsang, set about tracking down the perp's car.

Right there was one of the discrepancies: Marita said the

car that bumped the Caddy was dark blue, while paint scrapings on the dented fender said rusty black.

Even so, Vogelsang bought Maríta's story. As he told Shanley when they stepped away from Maríta, "Black, dark blue. Same thing to a shook-up eyewitness. You know how unreliable even the *best* eyewitness is."

He made sure the forensic investigator from Crime-Scene Search bagged a scraping of the scraping. But all the same, he said, "All what this is is a bump-and-rob. You'll see."

Shanley felt in her gut that they would both see that what this was was something more.

She probed, offhand, one eye on the road, one eye on the tilted-down rearview mirror to watch Maríta's face, as she drove Maríta to headquarters.

How long had she known Felipe Díez? Since coming to the States from Colombia six months ago. She had a green card? Yes; here it was. Mind letting the police hold on to it long enough to photocopy it? No. How well had she known Felipe? Well. Had Felipe given her the bruises? Yes. Why did she stick with him? A shrug. Where had they been coming from? A restaurant, El Abrazo, on Calle Ocho. Good food? A shrug; she hadn't been hungry. Where were they heading? Felipe's brother Ramón's place on Key Biscayne, for a ride on Ramón's boat. That would be *the* Rámón Díez? She supposed so. She supposed so? A shrug.

Maríta had just finished working with a police artist to put together a sketch of the perp and was making chicken wings and a big Coke disappear, hungry after all, when Vogelsang strutted in, shepherding three Hispanics, two women and one man. Shanley had an eye on Maríta and saw she made at least the two women. And *they* grew excited when they saw *her.*

Vogelsang told Shanley he had the perp's car in custody and that it came from the parking lot of a restaurant on Calle Ocho—

Shanley nodded. "El Abrazo."

Vogelsang scowled. "That's right. And these folks work there. The guy who looks like he could bust out bawling is the chef, and he's upset because it's his car and its front is banged up and the trunk lid is sprung and there's a parking ticket under the windshield wiper. How I got onto it, I asked for a check on all stolen older-model black sedans. This guy had just called in his Chevy was missing. So I put out a call and a patrol car spotted it in Crandon Park. Coincidentally, a station wagon missing from the same parking area turned up right here in Miami, in a bus stop, no less. Woman with the prematurely orange hair is the cashier; one with the cleavage is the waitress. They say a guy was in the restaurant same time as Díez and the girl, there was some kind of almost run-in between Díez and the guy, and on the way out the guy asked the cashier about Díez."

Shanley handed Vogelsang the sketch worked up by Maríta and the police artist. "Ask them if this is the guy."

Vogelsang showed it to them. The women shook their heads right away. The chef had not seen the man in the restaurant, but he grabbed the sketch for a good look anyway. Shanley guessed he wanted to see who had stolen his car.

Shanley had an eye on Maríta. The young woman's face looked flushed, but her lips were set.

Vogelsang pulled his chin, then his face cleared. "So the perp in the sketch is another guy altogether. The guy in the restaurant had nothing to do with it."

Shanley hesitated. "Even if they aren't the same guy, the guy in the restaurant could've helped set it up. Won't hurt to let the cashier and the waitress work up a sketch of the guy *they* saw."

Vogelsang's turn to hesitate, on principle, as he always did when responding to a suggestion of Shanley's. Then he nodded. "Sure, why not."

It took the cashier and the waitress about ten minutes to agree on the likeness the police artist shaped.

Shanley showed it to Marita and watched her closely.

Marita gazed at it and said she had a vague memory of having seen this man in the restaurant.

But she held to her story that *her* sketch showed the man she saw stab Felipe with the screwdriver they found in his chest.

Marita's blinking registered high on the Nixon scale, Shanley thought. *Shit, she's lying her head off.*

Vogelsang told Shanley that forensics had dusted the Chevy for prints and come up with nothing—or as good as nothing, just partials of the chef, and the chef had a solid alibi for the time in question; he had been sweating in the kitchen. No prints on the screwdriver they took from Felipe's chest. The chef had to admit the screwdriver looked like his; he kept one just like it in the trunk. In the trunk, the cops had found institutional-sized packages of rice and saffron, slashed open and contents spilled. What they were doing there in the first place was between the chef and his conscience—and between the chef and his boss. What the car thief had been looking for was anybody's guess. The cops had also found in the trunk the two pieces of the knife that had snapped in jimmying the trunk lid. The chef and the waitress and the cashier all identified the handle's pattern as that of El Abrazo flatware. The chef had not jimmied his own trunk with the knife; someone else had taken the knife from the restaurant and wiped it clean of prints.

So when Shanley suggested to Vogelsang that they circulate both sketches, Vogelsang hesitated less than usual and said that that was his idea too. And Shanley watched her partner cast a cold eye on Marita García as Shanley ushered her out.

* * *

While giving Marita the promised ride, Shanley limited her probing to glances at the rearview mirror. Marita knew more than she had said and other than she had said. Marita had to be shielding the perp. Shanley felt this close to reading Marita her rights but felt far from ready to hold the woman even as a material witness. She had to learn *who* Marita was. A look at her living quarters could help. Meanwhile, as the car stopped and started in Saturday-evening traffic, Shanley let silence weigh on Marita.

Marita shared an apartment in a coed section of the residence. It was on the third floor of the building, and she and Shanley walked up. They passed a few students, who glanced at Marita's face and at Shanley, but everybody was cool. Cool must be in everybody's curriculum, Shanley thought.

Shanley saw Marita to the apartment door. There, Marita said she felt fine, thanks. But Shanley didn't leave.

"You look pale." The honest truth—the bruises really stood out—but Shanley was used to telling truths dishonestly. Rather, ulteriorly. "But even if you're fine, *I* could use a glass of something."

So Marita had to be polite and invite her in.

Marita fumbled with the key, but her roommate was inside, heard them talking at the door, and let them in.

Right away the roommate put Shanley off. She acted eager to please, eager to help, and all the while the eyes asked, *Are you a threat? What can you do to me?* and *Are you anybody? What can you do for me?* Caucasian, twenty, five-six, 140, green eyes, heavy features, long, curtaining brown hair.

Marita gestured them at each other. "Sergeant, this is Kathy Frakes. Kathy, this is Sergeant Shanley."

Kathy's eyes widened to measure Shanley, then narrowed to see through the civvies. "In what, Sergeant? The Army or the Marines?"

"Metro Dade P.D."

Kathy swiveled to face Marita. "Something happened? What happened?"

Marita moved toward a cooler. "I'll tell you later. Let me get the sergeant a soda."

Shanley wanted to hear from Kathy before the roommates talked over what Kathy knew. "Did you know Felipe Díez?"

"*Did?*" Kathy's eyes were getting a real workout.

Marita came back with an open can and a glass.

Shanley took them. "Thanks." She moved to Kathy's other side so Kathy could not look for cues from Marita without being obvious about it. "He's dead. You knew him?"

"Well, I met him a couple of times when he came here to pick Marita up, if that's knowing."

Shanley poured and drank.

"Did he ever say, or did you ever hear, that he had a run-in with anyone?"

Kathy's eyes had a field day on that. "You mean he was *mur*dered?"

"*Did* you hear about any enemies he might've had?"

"I don't know about anybody in particular. I guess he could be too macho for some tastes and rub people the wrong way, but I don't know any names."

"Did you ever advise Marita not to go out with him?"

"Oh, no." Kathy's eyes turned to Marita and dwelt on the bruised cheeks; her voice turned sickeningly sincere. "He loved Marita."

Shanley's next stop was the morgue on Bob Hope Road. The attendant told her they were autopsying Felipe Díez's body right now. He handed her a disposable pale-green hooded jumpsuit and a matching face mask and deodorant to spray on the face mask. Shanley suited up and went into the autopsy room.

The pathologist was speaking into a neck mike. He

switched off when he saw her come in. She introduced herself, told him she was on the Díez case, and stretched out her gloved hand. He looked at it and made no move to take it. His eyes radiated distaste; then he pulled his face mask down to show a nasty smile.

That burned Shanley up; a sizzle in her ears kept her from hearing all he said. She knew the word *nigger* was in there, and that was enough.

She got in his face and backed him to the wall. "You rather I file charges of racial and sexual harassment or you rather I knee you where you live?"

"Hey, I didn't mean anything personal."

"You going to behave professional-to-professional?"

"Of course."

She pulled up his face mask and smoothed a wrinkle of his jumpsuit. "You're not bad-looking for a white boy." One of her dishonest truths.

And now she let herself see for the first time the reality of the naked body on the stainless-steel table. She held herself grimly while the pathologist finished up. Afterward, there wasn't all that much for him to tell her. The screwdriver killed Felipe, and Felipe had been on anabolic steroids.

Shanley went out, holding her breath till she could reach the comparatively fresh air of the anteroom. She got out of the jumpsuit and trashed it, sidestepped a WET FLOOR sign, and skirted the swish of the attendant's mop. She reached the other side of the door and breathed.

Vogelsang grinned at her. He perched half-assed on the attendant's desk. *Louse.* No sense both of them going in, but somehow Vogelsang never was the one to go in.

"No surprises?"

She shook her head. "We ought to get the next of kin down here to identify him for the record."

"I'll make the call."

Don't strain yourself. "Good."

Vogelsang didn't move his butt. His brow wrinkled. "Let's look at the ways we can go." He ticked them off on his fingers. "Bump-and-rob is for real, the perp knocks Felipe off. Bump-and-rob is for real, there's a struggle for the screwdriver, the perp drops it but gets away, and the García woman sees her chance and grabs the screwdriver and ices Felipe. Bump-and-rob is phony, the García woman is a coy duck, she's in it with the perp. Bump-and-rob is phony, the perp uses it to settle a private score. Bump-and-rob is staged, cover for a hit in a drug-cartel power struggle." He looked at Shanley. "What one do you like?"

Shanley shook her head. "I don't like any of them."

Vogelsang stiffened. "You got a better idea?"

She sighed. "No. I think you covered the possibilities. I just don't *like* any of them."

He nodded slowly. "Yeah. It's going to be a big one and a bad one. I can see us trying to work it out with the chief on our ass because the media is on his ass."

"And with the assistant D.A. on our ass because Ramón Díez has him in his hip pocket."

Vogelsang grinned and waggled a finger at her. "Anh-anh. You shouldn't go spreading well-founded rumors about Byron Oziel, Esq." He heaved his ass off the desk. "I'll go make that call."

CHAPTER 5

Benny Sánchez gave a guilty start when the call-waiting signal came on the line.

He had found himself alone in the house for a few minutes and right away had dialed a 900 number and was listening to a dirty-talking babe—who had described herself so he could *see* her—tell him what she would like to do to him and what she would like him to do to her—and he could see and feel that too.

So when he heard the call-waiting signal, his first thought—or even before that, his first reaction—was to hang up and put distance between himself and the phone. *Who, me? Phone? What phone?*

But Ramón knew he was in the house, had *sent* him to the house for music tapes to play aboard the boat. So if this turned out to be an important call and Ramón missed it on his account . . .

Benny put the receiver back to his ear and switched from the babe to the waiting call and said, "Yellow." Smartass yuppies said hello like that and Benny said "Yellow" because he thought he was being funny when he aped them and because he knew he was really thinking, Yellow was for caution and caution was Ramón's obsession because every fucking line tying the house to the world had a tap on it and because most calls were lemons anyway, wrong number or somebody wanting to sell you something.

His mind was aswarm with all that thinking about yellow so what the guy at the other end said had to fight to get front and center.

Benny asked the voice to say again.

The voice asked if this was the residence of Ramón Díez, next of kin to Felipe Díez.

"Who wants to know?"

The voice said it was Detective Sergeant Jack Vogelsang, Metro Dade P.D.

Benny's scalp tightened. "Can I take a message?"

He listened to the message, then asked the dick to repeat it. He was not hard of hearing and not always slow in processing, but the message was heavy and he wanted to be fucking sure he had it right. He hung up slowly and breathed, *"Jesucristo."* Not for the news, but for the messenger who would bring the news to Ramón—for himself, because he had no one else to wish it on.

Angel was out chauffeuring Ramón's woman, Lázaro was working on the boat, Raquél had her half day away from the kitchen, and Hernando was patroling the grounds with the dogs.

Maybe if he waited, Angel and the woman would be back soon—though when the woman went out shopping . . .

Benny stalled as long as he dared, five minutes.

He silently called on his *tocayo,* his name saint, San Bernardo, swallowed hard, and sweating even before the unconditioned air hit him, slid the glass partition open and stiff-legged across the patio and past the pool and down to the dock.

Ramón, brown from cocked captain's cap to wide-planted sandaled feet, stood on the landing stage, watching Lázaro polish the *Medallion*'s brightwork. *Medallion* might be an inside joke, a play on Medellín, but the boat was no joke; it was a real yacht.

Benny walked heavily to let Ramón hear him coming. Ramón did not like to be crept up on, hated *any* surprise not of his own springing.

Ramón turned slowly. He lifted an eyebrow. "Where are the tapes?"

What tapes? Shit. The music tapes. Well, the message would make Ramón forget the tapes too.

Benny worked one corner of his mouth, then the other. He saw no way of breaking it to Ramón nice and easy. Benny stopped just beyond Ramón's reach, in case Ramón felt like taking a swing at him.

Here went. "I just now heard from the morgue."

Ramón paled. "They took her there? It's over?"

Benny's mind blanked behind blinking eyes. *She? Oh. Oh-oh.* Quickly, "Not your mother, your brother."

Some color came back, but nowhere near all of it. "Felipe? You're telling me Felipe is dead?"

Yeah, the carajo *got his.* Benny tried to look sad. "They want you to go there and I.D. him."

"How did it happen?"

"They say it went down on the causeway. They're not sure yet if it was an accident accident or if the other guy rear-ended him on purpose. Either way, when Felipe got out to look at the damage, the other guy stabbed him."

"They get this other guy?"

"Not yet."

Ramón's eyes darkened till they looked like cenotes, the deep, dark wells the priests of the old religion once threw young virgins into. *What a waste.*

Benny watched Ramón's face glisten—with sweat, not tears. Ramón would be worrying how to break the news to his mother back in Medellín. It would be interesting to see if the shock of Felipe's death killed the old *bruja*.

Ramón swung his head and looked at Lázaro, who stood with mouth open and rag hanging limp. Then he looked at the

brightwork. Ramón pointed, and said almost absently, "You missed a spot." He turned and headed for the house.
He didn't have to say *Heel*. Benny followed.

Ramón Díez took the steps two at a time but unhurriedly. He wanted at all times to convey stately efficiency.

Family honor called for him to change into something more suited to the occasion. One wore muted colors when identifying the body of one's brother. He riffled through the suits in the walk-in closet of his bedroom and picked the plain mauve.

The mirror satisfied him. After he pocketed key case, wallet, silk handkerchief, breath fresheners, coded list of phone numbers, and all the change he had, he looked again and assured himself there were no unsightly bulges.

It occurred to him that he might have on him less change than he needed. He did not intend to use his phone card for the call he would make if Felipe were truly dead. So when he stepped into the back of the Rolls he told Benny, "Give me all your change."

Benny dug deep and Ramón picked out all the silver, some two bucks in dimes and quarters. A dozen or so pennies remained in the cup of Benny's waiting hand.

Ramón struck them from Benny's palm. "Pennies are useless."

And Benny showed more sense than to throw good time after bad money; he did not retrieve them.

Ramón found two Metro Dade homicide detectives waiting for him at the morgue. Detective Sergeant Carol Shanley, a tall black woman, and Detective Sergeant Jack Vogelsang, a chunky white man. Ramón filed their names and faces in his head.

The attendant, whose name and face Ramón did not bother to acquire, pulled out a drawer. Ramón stared down at the body. The kid looked more relaxed in death than he ever had in life. The only marks on him, aside from the coroner's workmanlike stitching, were two puncture wounds in the chest.

"That is the body of my brother, Felipe Díez."

The attendant covered the body and rolled the drawer shut, and the detectives led Ramón into a small office.

Vogelsang asked Ramón whether he knew who might have had it in for Felipe, and Shanley asked him what he knew about Felipe's relationship with Marita García, but Ramón asked them sharper questions than they asked him and told them less than they told him.

He let them know he wouldn't be satisfied till Felipe's killer paid for the crime.

They said they wouldn't be satisfied, either. They said they would spend every waking hour on the case. They said they had put in a long day today and they would be at it again first thing tomorrow, even though tomorrow would be a Sunday. They said they would do their best to nail Felipe's killer.

But the way they said it, it sounded as though they were saying they *always* did their best. And that wasn't good enough for Ramón.

Halfway home, Ramón had Benny pull up at a roadside pay phone. Benny stayed at the wheel while Ramón placed the call.

Ramón direct-dialed the international access code, the country code, the city code, and the local number. There would be no record linking the call to him. An operator came on and told him how much to put in the slot.

The answering service of Dr. Carlos Rubéo in Bello, Colombia, asked how it might help him.

"Tell him Señor Narciso has an emergency." He gave the number of the pay phone and had the woman repeat it. He hung up and waited.

And waited.

A top-down convertible pulled up behind the Rolls, and a man built like a linebacker got out and breathed down Ramón's neck.

"If you're not using the phone, Mac, how about moving out of the way?"

Ramón paid him no mind.

The man lifted a hand to tap Ramón on the shoulder, but a hand tapped *his* shoulder. He turned to find Benny behind him.

Benny told him, "You don't want to wait."

The man said, "Damn straight I don't want to wait."

Then Benny gave his flowered shirt a hitch and the man saw the gun holstered at Benny's waist and the man said, "No, I don't want to wait, so I'll find another phone up the line." And he hurried away.

The phone rang and Dr. Rubéo gushed breathless apologies.

Ramón cut in. "Doctor, doctor. You know I'm a reasonable man. I don't expect you to keep the phone to your ear around the clock ready to take my call." Though that was just what he did expect.

Dr. Rubéo said he had never known a more reasonable man. "But then, any son of Doña Beatriz's—"

"How is she doing?"

Dr. Rubéo sounded cagily reassuring. "Coming along. Holding her own. You have to remember that only three weeks have passed since she broke her hip. Old bones take long to knit. And because of her advanced osteoporosis, she will be safer in a wheelchair from now on. Meanwhile, your mother is in no pain. She is getting painkillers and antibiotics intravenously." He grew cheerful. "Her mind is as sharp as ever. Doña Beatriz has many years to live."

Ramón's heart seized up. His eyes darkened in thought.

"Are you there, Señor . . . Narcíso?"

"Yes, yes. Hold on. I'm thinking."

"Of course."

Ramón shrank from having to break the news to his mother. *Many years to live.* Many years of taking her grief out on him: Why hadn't he looked out better for her youngest and dearest? *Why, Ramón? Because you were jealous? Because you wanted to break your mother's heart? Why, why, why?*

He had two choices. He could tell Rubéo to break it to her now or he could try to keep Felipe's death from her as long as she lived.

No, he really had no choice. He could not bring himself to break it to her and he could not keep it from her for long. She read the papers and watched TV; he had the power to keep papers and TV from carrying word of Felipe's death. But word of mouth was another thing. The grapevine would blunt even the machete of Ramón Díez. Returning couriers, travelers, diplomats, journalists would whisper to friends who would whisper to friends . . . Nurses and interns would talk about it in the halls or even at her bedside if they thought she was asleep. He smiled a smile of pride. She could feign sleep and inattention with the best and catch a whisper at twenty paces.

"Doctor . . ."

"I'm here."

"One minute." They waited while a plane flew over "All right. Listen well. She has suffered enough. I authorize you to pull the plug on her."

"You authorize me to do *what*? Do I hear you right?"

"I will say it again, slowly, clearly. I authorize you to put her to sleep. I'm sure you have ways of making it seem natural."

"Doña Beatriz is not a lower animal and I am not a veterinarian."

"Either she goes to sleep or you do. There'll be a death in Bello in the next few days—hers or yours. . . . Did you hear that?"

"I did."

"Good, Doctor."

Ramón hung up. He put on his dark glasses to hide the tears in his eyes from Benny.

They were tears of anger. Now he had *two* deaths to avenge. Blood would flow. If he had to kill and kill to get the man who had done this to him, let blood drown the earth in a cleansing flood greater than Noah's.

CHAPTER 6

It was a hit. Mal turned the set on the minute he walked into his co-op apartment and he watched the ball go. A grounder the right fielder or the center fielder should've nailed. But they didn't, and the runner on third scored the tying run and the batter reached second. The fielders would have their excuses. "Thought *you* had it." "Ball took a wicked hop." "Lost it in the light." Bottom line, a hit.

He unslung his flight bag and tossed it onto the daybed. The answering machine stood unblinking. He looked around. Nobody had been in here to disturb the dust. He slid the side of his shoe across the floor along the edge of the wall, all around the room, and at the end he had a handful of felted dust to throw into the toilet bowl. See? Didn't need any nosy cleaning lady to come in, like his mom, who would bring home along with the leavings and the takings all she had seen and heard. After, he washed his hands good, because in an old newsmagazine he had seen blowups of the invisible things on the floor that live on your dandruff. Manna from heaven.

Idea was to keep housekeeping to a minimum. No pets. No plants. Away too much of the time to keep things growing. Even if he had had the time, the things would wilt. As Uncle Phil liked to put it, a gangrene thumb.

The smell of fried bacon rose to his window from the apartment below. Somebody else who did not stick to the rules of what was for breakfast and what was for supper. Mal toasted frozen waffles, and when they popped up he peeled back the foil on a stick of unsalted margarine and rubbed it on straight from the stick. He could almost hear his mom's "Oh, Mal," but a guy living alone didn't have to worry about table manners. He had eaten on the plane and wasn't all that hungry—it had been the bacon smell—but he finished the two waffles and washed them down with coffee.

Station break. Time for the six o'clock news. He switched to a news channel, but the death of Felipe Díez in Florida did not cross the desks of the news readers in California.

Mal was cynical about what he saw or did not see in print or heard or did not hear over the air. Uncle Phil had worked as a reporter and made quite a byline for himself till he got canned when they caught him taking payoffs for not printing stories. That was before Mal knew him, before Uncle Phil staggered carefully into the lives of Mal and Mal's mother. But it sounded in character. You could not always trust Uncle Phil. "Peccadillo? That's a cross between a peccary and an armadillo." "C'mon, Uncle Phil; I don't believe that." "Can't kid *you*. All right, Pecadillo is a street in London." In the end, he would give you the correct answer, but first he had to have his laugh.

Mal rinsed the plate, the cup, the fork, and the spoon, and put them in the drying rack. He flossed and brushed his teeth. He looked in the cabinet mirror and backed away for a fuller view. He sucked in his stomach. No beer belly there. He kept in shape without straining fanatically. Taking the stairs instead of elevatoring, for the heart; putting his socks on standing up, for balance; walking instead of taxiing, for stamina. A walk right now. He looked at his wrist watch, not that the time mattered.

Mal's internal clock had begun to fall back into California rhythm the second the plane touched down. Mal did not have the feeling of going back to his own life. Between hits, he had the feeling of being between hits. Not that he lived to kill. How he put it to himself the rare times he looked into himself, he lived to live, and killing was his way of making a living. That did not have to make sense, it merely had to work. Like life.

Like life till death. That did not mean he did not get a bang out of pulling the trigger or dealing the deathblow or shoving the blade home; but much of that rush came from putting his own life on the line each time. Leave it at that.

He walked the ten blocks to his mail drop, a storefront operation. He ducked the drip from the air conditioner over the door and went in. He had a key to the door because he paid for twenty-four-hour access, but the woman who ran the place was still here and the door was unlocked.

The bank of private mailboxes was on the left wall. Straight ahead, a counter behind which a slim middle-aged woman sat ready to dispense the other services: faxing, copying, packaging, U.P.S. pickup and delivery, mailing, gift wrapping, cigarettes, stationery, balloons, gift items, candy.

The woman looked up.

He gave her a nod. She spoke before he could turn to locate his box.

"Good to see you, Mr. Pace. I have a few packages for you I signed for."

He brightened. The clothes he had bought in Nassau. He hadn't expected them this soon.

She unlocked a cabinet and brought three packages to the counter.

He patted them. "Good."

She spoke hesitantly. "My son collects stamps."

He looked at the packages. They bore metered postage. He frowned. "He saves this kind?"

"Oh, no, I don't mean these. I noticed some nice stamps on the envelope in your box. Can I have those?"

Mal looked at her. She noticed too much. Time for him to change to another drop under another name. "Sure."

He turned to fit his key into the lock of Box 423. Actually, his mail came to the mail drop's street address, *Suite* 423. He opened the box and took out the envelope he had mailed aboard the *Queen Mab*. He tapped the contents to one end and ripped open the other end, careful to tear the highest-denomination stamp. He pulled out Woolf's letters and pocketed them. He glanced at the envelope before handing it to the woman. "Gosh," he said, "I'm afraid I ruined a stamp."

He took his packages and said good night. It was really good-bye.

When he got home, he stopped at the half-landing below his floor. The stairway was a frame of steel sections holding stone treads. One holiday weekend early in his occupancy here when everybody, including the super, was away, Mal had used a small blowtorch to cut an opening in one of the right triangles where the steel frame hugged the wall in the underside of this half-landing. Nobody ever thought to look up at the underside of stairs; everybody was too busy looking down at his own feet. He had hollowed out the cement, welded a concealed hinge to the steel cutout, fitted the piece back in place, and then hid the alteration with some fresh paint. Here he had cached a loaded .22 automatic and five thousand bucks. And, just a few hours ago, Felipe's signet ring.

He set the packages down and listened. No one else was in the halls or on the stairs. He pried the little door open. The gun, the money, and the ring were there. He added Woolf's letters and resealed the cache.

First thing he did inside his apartment, he unwrapped his new clothes and held them up one by one to look at them before he put them away. They were surely what he had paid for, but he found himself vaguely dissatisfied. It was always that way. Somehow, once he got things home from the store they lost sheen. Here, the sea change from the Caribbean to the Pacific, maybe a difference in the quality of light and air, cast a shadow over his choices. They were of good material and he had got them at good prices and he would get good wear out of them, but right now, as he put them away, he felt kind of cheated.

The TV did nothing to brighten his mood. He shut it off and replayed old TV in his mind—for some reason, a basketball game from a few seasons back.

The referee handed Coach Lou Carnasecca a technical foul when Lou cursed him out for failing to call traveling on the other team, and handed him another, thirteen seconds later, when Lou picked up a loose ball near his bench and bowled it at the ref. The other team sank all four shots, costing Lou's team the game. Uncle Phil liked to say, "Sports is the last place to look for sportsmanship."

Mal knew what it was. It was the Miami hit. Felipe never stood a chance. The other team never stood a chance—till Lou's petulance factored itself in. In Mal's case, personal cat-and-mouse pleasure had wasted precious seconds, and if there had been a referee—a cop nearby—Mal could have easily lost the game.

He never thought about a hit afterward, except when it hit him how he might have pulled it off more cleanly. But even after he figured out what bothered him about this one, he found himself coming back to it—and it a freebie, at that. What mouthpieces called *pro bono*.

It was the broad, of course. He thought he had made the hit for himself, but by now he had begun to believe he had done it for her. He had walked into her life and walked right out. He would never see her again. Just as well. She wasn't his type.

CHAPTER 7

"Pardon me, have you any gray poop?"

Assistant D.A. Byron Oziel couldn't help himself. When Ramón Díez's Rolls pulled up alongside Oziel's Porsche at the red light and they lowered their windows to talk, it put Byron right into a TV-spot-for-Grey-Poupon virtual reality. The words popped out without benefit of cue card.

As soon as he heard himself and before Ramón could express puzzlement, Oziel fell all over himself regrouping.

After all, Ramón Díez's money-laundering institution, Banco de los Inocentes, Miami's fourth-largest bank, held the mortgage on the Oziels' house. Oziel had a sideline, a business registered under his wife's maiden name. They would buy a house, move into it, fix it up, then sell it at a big profit. They kept upgrading each time. This last time, though, they had overextended themselves: The housing market turned sour and they couldn't sell the place for the two million they had counted on and they still had to make big interest payments.

Another powerful reason to stay on Díez's good side: the D.A. had decided against running for reelection and Oziel had his eye on the job. To campaign effectively would mean dipping into deep pockets. Díez, as the drug lords' moneyman, had a bottomless pocket. Frivolity would not do.

"I mean, you must've seen that commercial . . ." Hell was

an eternity in which he tried to explain his explanation. Saved by the light change.

When they rendezvoused at the next red light, Díez looked across unsmilingly. "What's the latest blue poop?"

Oziel hoped his smile didn't look as nervous as it felt. "We've distributed the police sketches nationwide. But so far they've drawn a blank."

"Anything else?"

"We're giving this our all, but we must be realistic. If this was a simple bump-and-rob, we may never catch the criminal."

"Maybe you ought to try it from another angle."

"Pardon?"

"Go after the García woman. It was a hit and the bitch was in on it."

"Well, we're far from making that case."

Ramón narrowed his eyes. "I'll help you make that case."

Byron didn't like the sound of that but didn't say so. "How?"

"You have the sketches?"

Byron knocked his meditation tape to the floor digging the two sketches out of the glove compartment. "Here's the man Marita García says she saw stab Felipe on the causeway, and here's the man the restaurant workers say had some kind of a run-in with Felipe at the restaurant."

"Hand them to my chauffeur."

The front window lowered, and a man with a vacant expression on a crowded face and a massive gold cross mangered in chest hair took the photocopies.

"Look at them, Benny."

The chauffeur studied the sketches.

Ramón spoke to Byron. "Take a good look at my chauffeur."

Byron studied the chauffeur. The man did not grow on him. "Yes?"

"He's your eyewitness."

Seemed news to the chauffeur, but the chauffeur said nothing. A microsecond after the light turned green, cars behind them blared horns. But the Rolls and the Porsche stayed put while Ramón held Byron with a long hard look and said, "His name is Benny Sánchez. He'll get in touch with you."

When Benny came into the house after garaging the Rolls, he found Ramón on the phone. He started to backpedal out of the room, but Ramón gestured that it didn't matter if Benny overheard, so he continued on through toward the kitchen.

What he caught in passing puzzled him. Ramón *knew* the lines had taps, yet spoke as though it didn't matter if the Feds overheard.

Benny dragged his feet and all but flapped his ears to sweep in all he could. The boss asked about the weather in Brooklyn. Ramón told the guy—*called* him Guy, in fact—about Felipe's death and asked him to help make the hit man, get a name from the street. Ramón said he thought that Miguel Luqué had put the hit out and used a girl named Marita García to set Felipe up.

At the sound of the name Miguel Luqué, Benny could barely keep himself from jerking around and staring at Ramón. He felt a cold emptiness in his belly.

Miguel Luqué headed the rival drug cartel. As an Omega Siete veteran of the Bay of Pigs, Miguel Luqué had much clout in the Cuban community. Benny hoped Felipe's death would not mean open warfare between Ramón and Miguel. For the first time since Felipe's death, Benny actually mourned.

He stepped into the kitchen. Raquél made him forget Miguel Luqué. He stole up behind Raquél. His hand groped for her ass, then thought better of it, and reached over her shoulder.

She slapped his hand away from the lid of the pot. "Out of my kitchen."

"Now wait a minute, Raquél. I—"

She turned around with her hands on her hips. She was too busy for his nonsense, and didn't he remember last time she went to Don Ramón about him?

Benny said this was *for* Don Ramón.

She sighed and asked what he wanted from her life.

He told her.

She sighed again but lowered the flame under the pot, wiped her hands on her apron, took the police sketches, mixed them behind her broad back, and flashed one.

Ramón had told him which man had iced Felipe. Now the burden shifted to Benny to remember. "That's not the man. Again. *That's* the man. Again."

Detective Sergeant Jack Vogelsang whistled his impatience through his nose. "I don't know what more you want. You got an eyewitness handed you on a platter."

Detective Sergeant Carol Shanley gave a nod as good as a shake. "Oziel's platter. Two hundred percent 'artistic object. Precious metal pigments may be toxic. Do not use for eating.'"

"Sheesh. I don't know what the hell you're talking."

"I'm talking I don't buy Benny Sánchez's story for one minute."

"I'll admit the creep is a creep, but that don't necessarily make his story inadmissable evidence. Let the defense lawyer take him apart on the stand. It ain't our job to prejudge."

Hell it wasn't. To sift wheat from chaff was the essence of their job. She stared, at first unseeingly, at the sun-faded framed quotation on the wall opposite her desk. Then it came into focus, mirroring her thoughts.

> *What was the crime? Who did it?*
> *When was it done, and where?*
> *How done, and with what motive?*
> *Who in the deed did share?*
> —Unknown jurist in ancient Rome

She had worked up extra lines but lacked the guts to tack them on.

> *Who follows the truth where it may lead?*
> *Who enforces the law, to square the deed?*
> –Unknown rapper in futuristic Miami

She swiveled to face Vogelsang. "Let me tick off what ticks me off. Little finger, Benny comes forward two days late. Ring finger, Benny's on the causeway and sees his boss's brother's car off to the side of the road obviously in some kind of trouble and he doesn't try to help. Middle finger, Benny sees the García woman in Felipe's car and he doesn't see Felipe and he doesn't even call out to the García woman to find out what happened to Felipe. Index finger, Benny sees a guy hop into a junk heap parked behind Felipe's Caddy and work it back into traffic, and Benny figures either the two had collided or the guy was a good Samaritan, but *again,* Benny isn't curious enough to find out from the García woman which. Thumb, goes right to my nose."

Vogelsang's mouth twitched in a proto-smile. "I go now? Pinkie or ear finger, Benny was afraid to tell his boss after he learned Felipe was dead—then he was afraid *not* to tell his boss. Gold finger—in the *old* days they called it that, or the medical finger, because they thought a nerve ran straight to the heart; that's why it's the ring finger, and they stirred stuff with it because they thought it would warn the heart if there was poison; some people still believe it's bad luck to rub salve in or scratch an itch with any finger but it—Benny was jammed between the car ahead and the car behind and didn't want to risk scratching the Rolls by swinging out of traffic. The finger, when Benny didn't see Felipe in the Caddy but saw the García woman, he thought Felipe had loaned her the Caddy and she was the one with car trouble, or Felipe had already got a lift and left her to wait. Index finger, Benny thought the guy in the junk heap had stopped to help Felipe and was now going on his way, so the problem, whatever the problem was, was over. Thumb . . ." He put the thumb to his nose and waggled the other fingers. "You can't get around one thing— Benny picked out the right sketch. Explain that."

Shanley made a face. "I can't. But it still stinks."

Her face suddenly burned. Their commander stood in the doorway with another man, Caucasian, shrewdly maximized brown hair, gray eyes, thin nose, cleft chin, thirty-five, six-two, medium build. Shanley hoped they had not seen her and Vogelsang thumb noses at each other. She sprang to her feet. Vogelsang looked around and scrambled to his.

Their commander glanced back and forth. "Agent O'Keefe, meet Detective Sergeants Carol Shanley and Jack Vogelsang. Sergeants, this is Agent Eamon O'Keefe. He's with the D.E.A. It seems his agency is interested in the Felipe Díez case. I'll leave him with you and let him tell you." He nodded around and left.

O'Keefe's one chipmunk cheek had Shanley guessing. Abscessed tooth? Wad of tobacco? Then the bulge shifted and she caught a whiff of spearmint.

O'Keefe shook Vogelsang's hand, pointed to his cheek, and said, "Trying to quit smoking."

Vogelsang nodded. "I've been there."

O'Keefe offered Vogelsang a stick, then offered one to Shanley as an afterthought. Finding no takers, he built up the wad in his mouth with a fresh stick.

"So what can you tell me about the Felipe Díez killing?" O'Keefe asked, settling into a chair.

Shanley and Vogelsang traded glances. Shanley eyed O'Keefe levelly. "You first."

"It's no big secret Ramón Díez fronts for the Medellín cartel. So it won't jolt you out of your socks that we monitor the doings of the whole Díez bunch. When this Marita García took up with Felipe, we did a real background check on her.

At first we thought Miguel Luqué might've planted her. He's dying to have somebody on the inside."

Shanley and Vogelsang traded glances again.

O'Keefe grinned. "You thought of that, huh? Well, let me tell you: Luqué has nothing to do with her being there. García didn't worm herself in; Ramón is the early bird got her in his beak. I learned from Immigration who Maríta García really is. She's Guadeloupe Martínez, and her father is Geraldo Martínez. Geraldo Martínez runs a Medellín newspaper. Her whole family has a price on its head because the father dared to print about the cartel. So he sent the girl to the U.S. to attend college under an alias. But the Díezes found out, and our information is, Ramón would've had her knocked off, but Felipe fell for her and Ramón *gave* her to him." O'Keefe leaned back. "Now you."

Shanley told him what they knew and showed him the sketches. He studied the one they said was the probable perp. He told them he would try to get a make on the guy.

He grinned as he pushed away from the desk and stood up. "See how nice it is when we all work together?"

Shanley nodded, stone-faced. O'Keefe had known that Felipe was using and abusing Maríta. Yet he had not tipped off the police. Probably figured her worth more to him dead than alive if he could pin her death on Felipe. That was how nicely they worked together.

He waved so long. "I'll stay in touch."

"Okay," she said.

"That's me," he said, and strode from the room.

O'Keefe had a hidden agenda. Shanley knew that right off. He had been too damned interested in clearing Miguel Luqué of blame for Felipe's death. She was about to say as much to Vogelsang when it suddenly hit her that O'Keefe hadn't been chewing gum when he left. She couldn't remember seeing him get rid of his wad.

Vogelsang was saying something about, Now they could at least eliminate the rival-cartel theory.

Shanley mumbled encouragingly to keep him talking.

She crumpled a perfectly good sheet of typewriter paper and dropped it into the wastebasket. The wad of gum was not there. She drew a Kleenex from a box in a drawer and idly dusted the desk. She worked around the edge of the desktop, and when she reached near where O'Keefe had been sitting she found it. The wad was stuck to the underside of the desktop. She pressed lightly and felt a core of hardness. A bug.

She pulled her hand away, left the wad in place, balled up the tissue, and tossed it into the wastebasket.

Vogelsang had fallen silent. He seemed to be waiting for some reaction from her.

She eyed him innocently. "What did you make of O'Keefe?"

"That asshole? Typical D.E.A. goon. Why?"

"I'm trying to think what movie star he reminds me of."

"One of them Tinja Ninja turtles?"

"Nick Nolte, that's who."

"Women. No wonder the force keeps sliding downhill."

Guido Palmieri reached Miguel Luqué over a secure line, identified himself as Guy, gave him the gist of Ramón Díez's call, and then offered his thoughts.

"I been thinking why our friend runs the laundromat mouthed off about you so out in the open. He ain't all that sure you done his brother, but he figures some people might think you did and it's gonna look bad if he don't make no move to get back at you. So he gives two birds on the telephone wire the hotfoot with one call. Me he feels he can lean on to help him because I send him some of my dry cleaning, and the heat listening in he feels he can bring into the hunt for who done it."

"That part doesn't worry me. I'm confident that the heat knows I had nothing to do with the tragic event."

"Tragic event, yeah. Well, it's nice you have a wire in, keeps you from worrying. But that still leaves you looking back over your shoulder for our laundromat friend. It's him you got to feel confident knows you had nothing to do with the tragic event. Now, if you don't mind, I make a suggestion to stop this from escalating into a war that innocent bystanders like my people could get hurt?"

"I appreciate your candor. I welcome your suggestion."

"Thank you. My suggestion, you give him somebody close to you."

A long silence, then, "A goodwill gesture?"

"You got it."

Another long silence, then, "As long as our laundromat friend understands it's not an atonement, because I have nothing to atone for, and as long as he understands he now owes me one and at some time I may choose to collect."

"I'll make sure he understands. Been real nice talking to you."

"Same here."

Mindful of Agent O'Keefe's bug, Detective Sergeant Carol Shanley took care to discuss business with Detective Sergeant Jack Vogelsang only outside their office. She was always saying "Let's talk about that on our way over to see whosis" or "Won't it wait? I'm typing my report."

When O'Keefe phoned to say he'd like to come right over, Vogelsang covered the mouthpiece and said, "Shit. It's that asshole O'Keefe. Just when we're ready to break for lunch. Should I tell him sorry, we're on our way out?" Shanley shook her head and said in a full, clear voice, "He may have a lead on the shooting of Luqué's man. Maybe he can tell us if this ties in with the Díez killing. And I'd just like to see him, anyway. He's my idea of a good-looking man. The lines of his jaw when he chews gum."

"Kee-rist, are you sickening." Vogelsang took his hand away from the mouthpiece. "Sure, come right over."

Shanley had a good time watching Vogelsang's face when O'Keefe cold-shouldered him and shook her hand warmly.

All the while he stayed, O'Keefe ignored Vogelsang and leaned forward in his chair to speak to Shanley and to show her the lines of his jaw.

"First off, this Paco Morales that just got knocked off was Miguel Luqué's top lieutenant."

"That much we know," Vogelsang said, unheard.

"Is it tied to the Díez killing?" Shanley asked.

"It is and it isn't."

"That clears things up," Vogelsang said, still unheard.

"Luqué wanted to prove to Ramón Díez that he had nothing to do with killing Felipe, that he wasn't starting a war. So Luqué had his own man killed as a show of good faith. Morales was getting too big for himself anyway, but still. I can't prove any of this, of course, but I have it from a good source, somebody I have on the inside."

Shanley thanked O'Keefe, who left without a glance at Vogelsang.

Vogelsang stared after him, then turned with a frown of wonder. "Did you sense it?"

"Sense what?"

"For some reason, he has it in for me."

Shanley shook her head. "You've been working too hard. You're imagining things."

Vogelsang stood brooding, then shook himself. "I'm not imagining my stomach. See you after lunch."

They seldom ate together. They saw enough of each other on the job and had other people to catch up with on their free time. Besides, Vogelsang liked to eat Italian and Shanley liked to eat Chinese.

Shanley watched Vogelsang leave. It had not been worth discussing with him—especially here—her doubts about O'Keefe.

The street had it that *Díez* ordered the hit on Paco Morales. Why hadn't O'Keefe bolstered *that* theory instead of laying it on Luqué? Be better for Luqué than having Homicide focus the burning glass on him, no matter that Homicide could never even singe him. But maybe Luqué had a bigger stake in appeasing Díez and avoiding war. Luqué could take any amount of Homicide heat if he could cool it with Díez.

Shanley had the feeling it would all come down on Maríta García.

She pushed the feeling away from her and pulled two vinyl exam gloves from a dispenser box in a desk drawer, put them on, and felt for O'Keefe's wad.

It had dried hard and she twisted it off. She used a letter opener to pry the bug loose. She tore off a small strip of double-stick tape, removed one side's backing, and stuck that side to the bug. The bug went into a small evidence bag and then into a pocket; the gum and the gloves went into the wastebasket.

She strolled the block and a half to the Chinese restaurant. Any other time, she would have grabbed a better seat, but today she sat next to the kitchen door.

She gave her order. Then, working at lap level, she removed the other backing from the double-stick tape and stuck the bug under the table.

Now, every time the kitchen door swung, O'Keefe would catch the swell of Cantonese chatter.

Even had Ramón Díez wished to attend the funeral of Miguel Luqué's sacrificial lamb Paco Morales, he had a double funeral of his own to attend.

For, as her doctor certified, Doña Beatriz had died of heart failure upon learning of Felipe's death.

And now two open bronze caskets stood side by side at the funeral home and would ride in tandem to the cathedral and then to the cemetery.

A big draw, a crush. Press and TV lenshounds crowded the entrance. Government-agency photographers were more laid back, filming people the media didn't give a second glance.

Ramón held himself with dignity and controlled grief. His wife, Elvira, was in high-fashion mourning, black lace over her blond hair.

In spite of all the bombings and shootings back in Colombia, a few people high up in Justicia there remained able and willing to collar him for questioning. So he had found it more convenient to fly his mother's body here for burial with Felipe's than to go home to Colombia himself. But that went with the territory and was not what angered Ramón today.

Doña Pilar, Ramón's aunt, had accompanied her sister's body, and the loudness of her sorrow at times drowned out the priest. But that was not what angered Ramón. Nor was it his aunt's refrain, while the casket stood open: "She looks mad at me." Annoyance at such stupidity flashed in Ramón's eyes, but he shook his head and put an arm around her trembling shoulders and murmured something soothing; though when he gazed at the prettified but still fierce face of his mother he understood what his aunt meant and he gave a slight shiver of his own.

No, what *really* enraged him was the insult offered by Customs and the D.E.A.

They had met the plane with a dog that sniffed the coffin as if they seriously thought Ramón stupid enough to smuggle drugs in this way at this time.

Late that night, a car drew up near the house where the drug-sniffing dog lived with her handler. Chained inside the cyclone fence, the dog bristled as a stranger approached her territory and tossed a Big Mac to her. The dog cut short her bark, sniffed the meat, wolfed it down, and died in agony.

* * *

As the arresting officer, Detective Sergeant Carol Shanley was present at the arraignment of Guadeloupe Martínez, a.k.a. Marita García, for the murder of Felipe Díez.

Shanley thought that Assistant D.A. Byron Oziel carried himself like People's Exhibit A. He had a way of patting the rug on his pate—Byron the Brain. She thought that Oziel, under pressure from Ramón Díez, had a butcher's thumb on the scales of justice. She had not been in the grand-jury room for Benny Sánchez's testimony, but she thought that only Oziel's handling could have led the grand jurors to believe Benny. She thought that Marita—she still thought of Guadeloupe Martínez as Marita García—had helped Oziel convince the grand jury to indict her by sticking to her account. Good cop Shanley and bad cop Vogelsang had taken Marita through her story again and again, and Shanley had come to believe that while Marita had not helped set Felipe up, she *was* covering for the killer. Shanley thought that that was not enough to charge her with homicide. But nobody, not the prosecuting attorney, not the defense attorney, not the judge, asked Shanley what she thought. What she thought didn't matter.

Assistant D.A. Byron Oziel asked for high bail on the grounds of the seriousness of the crime, the defendant's having entered the country under an assumed name, the likelihood of flight, and the potential difficulty and cost of extradition.

The defense attorney, Peggy Passanante, argued that her client had no previous record and had no intention of fleeing.

The judge set the trial date and ordered the defendant held on one million dollars bail.

Despite all that, Shanley thought, if Marita had not been so photogenic—even with shadows under the eyes—she would not have hit the front pages or made national news.

Certainly, Miami had no shortage of bloodletting.

CHAPTER 8

Mal saw her picture before he saw his own. He grabbed the paper from the newsstand and started to read.

"Hey, this ain't the public lie-berry."

He dug out the coins and slapped them into the guy's hand so that the quarter bounced out and dropped to the sidewalk. He walked away, maintaining his preoccupation and leaving the guy to chase the quarter.

They had touched up the outline of her face to make it stand out from background confusion, but he thought the shot didn't do her justice. *Guadeloupe Martínez, to go on trial in slaying of playboy linked to drug cartel.*

So that was her name. *Guadeloupe Martínez.* Guadeloupe. Mal tried it on his tongue, listening to it over the sound of traffic, and had to smile.

No, he couldn't see himself saying, "Guadeloupe, get me a beer" or "Guadeloupe, let's go to bed."

Lupe, he could see. Like Lupe Velez, the Mexican spitfire who married Tarzan—well, the swimmer who *played* Tarzan—had a nowhere affair with a limey who thought he had too much class for her, so she had her hairdresser and her makeup man doll her up and she filled her room with flowers and she arranged herself on her bed and swallowed a lethal number of pills. Couldn't get any number than that. Lupe.

When you learn the names of things, you get both nearer to and farther from the things themselves. It's the uncertainty principle. Or at least the name of the uncertainty principle. So, my lad, if you want to get a passing grade, learn the name of your teacher. Correct spelling is a plus when you forge her name. That came straight out of a lecture by Uncle Phil.

What do you know? A college girl here in the States to escape the drug cartel that had it in for her father. Some escape; she had run right into their hands. The piece didn't say that, but that's what it was.

Then he saw himself below the fold. He was one of two police sketches.

At first he thought the bitch had given him away after all. Then the captions told him the *other* one represented Lupe's description of the killer. Looked nothing at all like Mal.

He felt proud of her. With her own life at stake, she had given a false description of him and stuck to it. If she were a guy, she'd be a stand-up guy.

He faulted the liker likeness, which must have come from the people at the restaurant, for the clothing details that showed rather than for the facial details. The collar rode too high and the jacket lapel was too wide. The features came fairly close but that didn't worry him. He knew he had an ordinary-looking face. If the picture had lacked connection with Lupe's story, he wouldn't have given it a second glance.

To play safe, he would grow a mustache and wear plain-lensed glasses.

He went back up above the fold. The piece said that Lupe's father wanted to fly to her side but that Immigration had called him a leftist and the State Department had refused him a visa. So she stood all alone in a strange land.

Mal crumpled the newspaper and threw it, remaining pages unread, into the first trash receptacle he came to.

The cops and the D.A. were crazy or crooked. Said they had a witness saw Lupe stab Felipe Díez. What witness? Lupe had nothing to do with icing Felipe. Shit, Lupe was lucky Mal hadn't iced her *too*.

It was a frame.

What was he getting so het up about? He cooled down.

He doubted that Lupe had the street smarts to know or the shyster to tell her how to beat the system: *On trial, blame Satan. In prison, discover God.*

What the hell, even if it was a frame, with her looks and a battered-woman defense she had a better-than-even chance if her lawyer knew how to play to the jury.

If not, tough shit. *He* was out of it.

Seated facing the tube in the back room of his social club, Guido Palmieri watched the quarterback throw a Hail Mary pass. Incomplete. Last play of the game, lost Guido a bundle in what he had been unable to lay off.

Guido let Fatso and Tax Man, who had nothing riding on the game, groan for him. Guido saved his breath, which was getting shorter as he got thicker, but switched channels savagely—who needed to wait for the replay or listen to the rehash? If he could switch the quarterback into an alternate universe, same pressure of the thumb, he would do it with pleasure.

The channel he switched to had one of them news bimbos smiling the news. Overbite just right for sound bites. Guido was going to switch again, but the bimbo gave way to a clip that held him.

It showed another bimbo, worth a once-over, then he heard the name Felipe Díez and it hit him this was the bimbo in the icing Ramón Díez had called him about. So Guido hung in there and a police sketch came on of the hit man he knew as Harry Pace.

He noted differences, sure, eyes narrower, nose longer, ears wider out, but not enough to throw Guido off. Not when Harry was in Miami at the right time, just coming off the Al Woolf hit. Not when hardly nobody but a Harry Pace had the balls to take on a brother of Ramón Díez's.

Guido felt the impulse to laugh, tickled to know what others could not even guess. But laughing would set off his wheezing, the fucking emphysema. Then his face suffused and he found himself gasping for breath after all.

The anger was for Miguel Luqué, not for Harry Pace.

Only Luqué would have had the balls to hire Harry to do Felipe. And then the prick had lied to him—to Guido Palmieri.

Had second thoughts about starting a war. Thought Guido's call was Guido's way of warning him that Guido sided with Díez. Backed down. Ate shit.

Righteous indignation fueled Guido. Sense of power swelled him. So when the anchor bimbo smiled the next news item, Guido was primed to take it big, though another time he would've just made a face and let it pass.

What he watched that set him off now, the mayor and the police commissioner of Rochedale, up in Westchester County, handed a good citizen an award for tipping the cops to a man wanted for a lot of liquor-store stickups. What got Guido, the good citizen's fucking big smile.

Boy, how Guido wished the remote control could switch the squealer into another dimension! Blow him to bloody bits! Wipe off that smile!

Guido suddenly sat taller. Shit, he *had* a remote could do that—and he didn't mean the Nintendo shit that where they placed it he had a piece of the action.

He had a remote in the person of a hit man. All Guido had to do was say, "I want the shitheel whacked."

Power imposed its own limitations on those who wielded it. Guido had learned to weigh his words, to keep the safety on his tongue. In the early days of his accession to donhood, he and a pair of his soldiers were stalled in traffic alongside Prospect Park, in his dondom. A street mime was performing and Guido said, "Get *him*," meaning "Get a load of that wacky bastard." One soldier said, "What, now?" and Guido said, "When else?" and the soldier drew his piece and pumped lead into the mime. The wheelman got them the hell away by swinging out into the opposite lane and running the light.

So now, as he watched this good citizen proudly accept the award for ratting on a racket dude, Guido pressed his lips tight and thought hard. And when he switched the smiling bimbo off and pushed to his feet—Fatso and Tax Man knew better than to help him—and headed for his secure phone, Guido knew that "Get him" was exactly what he meant when he would say, "Get him."

And because he had been reminded of Harry Pace and because he figured it could pay him to stay on the *canetta* of a guy everybody was looking for, he called Harry Pace.

CHAPTER 9

Mal didn't want to read about Guadeloupe Martínez or see about Guadeloupe Martínez. He wanted to put the whole thing behind him, forget it. Yet he didn't want to hide from it, feel afraid to face it. So the way Mal handled it, he didn't seek out news of Guadeloupe Martínez's case but he didn't shut his eyes and cover his ears to it. If her image flashed into his awareness like a pulsar, he could live with that; if a dark hole swallowed it up forever, he could live with *that*.

The new job gave him a reprieve. All he needed was the who and the where, and Guido told him those. He didn't ask Guido the why.

Up before 5:00 A.M. to catch the first flight east out of LAX, by the time he boarded he felt the need to conserve his energy. He felt the lift of takeoff, hung on a button of his jacket an Intercontinental Hotels DO NOT DISTURB sign he had picked up on a business trip to Finland, and shut his eyes. Even those who did not understand EI SAA HÄIRITÄ/VAR GOD STÖR EJ/DO NOT DISTURB/BITTE NICHT STÖREN got the idea and let him doze.

Uncle Phil told Mal bedtime stories. Uncle Phil said he heard them from a wood pigeon—they were dove tales. But they had no doves in them. They featured Rabbet and Mortise, who lived in the wood and could move only with the grain. They were players *in* a board game was what they were. They could make it into the real world through knotholes, but they lost if they fell for fake ones, which were *not*holes. Uncle Phil drew real-looking *nots* on the scraps of lumber they played their lives out in. An unlikely pair, they stuck together through warp and rot in search of the Holy Tenon. After each joint adventure they debriefed themselves and learned lessons from their deeds. *They chewed the fat till the cat got their tongue, then they fewed the chat.* And that meant it was time Mal fell asleep and let Uncle Phil get it on with Mal's mother. Uncle Phil was Rabbet.

Mal awoke for the meal. The old dame in the aisle seat was already into hers, and she pointedly ignored him. When he finished, he stood up to go to the john. She gave him a dirty look and took her time letting him out. He toted his carryon to the john and did his business and changed into thermal underwear. It would be cold in New York and he *hated* cold. Then he went back to his place and the old dame in the aisle seat threw him another dirty look and took her time letting him back in. He gave her a warm smile as he settled himself in his seat. That melted her and she opened her mouth to speak, but he rehung the sign on a button and sank again into a doze. When the stews readied the passengers for landing, he awoke again for good.

When they came out under the clouds, the world out the window was white. The New York metropolitan area enjoyed its first heavy snowfall of the season.

As they landed and taxied to the terminal building, he felt the tempo pick up.

Whenever he hit—landed in—New York and moved among the people, he heard Uncle Phil's voice say, "The human race is a string of beads. If we never cut the cord, all of us, the living and the dead, would still be linked from Eve on. Of course, be kind of hard for the living to move around."

As soon as Mal came out of the arrivals area—and he was among the first because he had no baggage to retrieve—he spotted the fat guy holding the marker-lettered-cardboard-from-a-new-shirt sign that said PEACE INDUSTRIES. A number of people, dressed more or less formally as chauffeurs, held up signs to claim passengers. The fat guy was just a fat guy holding a sign.

Mal checked to see that nobody took special interest in the fat guy. Then Mal walked up to him and said, "Harry Pace." He pronounced Pace "Potch-ay," way the pope did.

The fat guy looked him over, hid whatever he thought, handed him a customer's copy of a car-rental agreement and a set of car keys, and told him where the car was parked. Then the fat guy folded and refolded the sign, pocketed it, and walked away.

Mal looked outside and unzipped his carryon wide enough and long enough to pull out a pair of gloves. He put the gloves on and flexed them. Like a piano player, he couldn't let his fingers get stiff.

The car fitted Uncle Phil's generic term for small cars: Toyauto. But then, Uncle Phil had needed headroom and legroom. Mal checked that the car was gassed up and that the heater worked. The glove compartment held an envelope and nothing else.

In the envelope he found news photos of Alexander "Sandy" Levandusky, a phone-directory tear sheet with Levandusky's address and phone number highlighted, a street map of the Bronx, a street map of lower Westchester, a Metro-North train schedule for Rochedale with a Rochedale–to–New York time highlighted and a New York–to–Rochedale time highlighted, and a menu flier of a Bronx pizzeria.

Okay. Get heeled, case it, do it, get clear.

He looked at a digital display hanging outside a bank branch. 4:12. He reset his watch to match it. The time gave way to the temperature. 30°. That he could not reset, but the heater compensated. He took the Van Wyck Expressway and then the Whitestone Expressway to the Bronx. He pulled over long enough to study the Bronx street map and get a fix on the pizzeria. Snowplows had been through, but you had to watch out for icy patches.

As he waited at a red light he saw a guy, a civilian, standing at a Police/Fire call box. The guy wore an expectant smile and Mal followed his gaze.

Up the block, on the far corner on the other side of the street, two kids stood on a snowbank winging snowballs at passing cars.

When Mal drew near the kids he slowed the car, lowered the window, and yelled, "Better beat it. The cops are coming." He jerked his thumb back toward the guy at the call box.

He got no thanks, and a snowball hit his rear window as he pulled away, but the kids were beating it and he grinned.

The sidewalk at the pizzeria looked mushy from stuff that had been spread to melt the snow and ice. Mal dug into his carryon for a pair of plastic bags. He always tore a few extra bags off the roll when he shopped for fruits and vegetables. They had lots of uses. He pulled these two bags over his Western boots, tucked them in, and got out of the car.

The oven steamed up the place snugly. A middle-aged couple sat sharing a big one. Their eyes stayed narrowed in pleasure and their jaws missed no stroke, though Mal let in a chill: casing as he entered.

Mal breathed the smells in while he moved toward the dough tosser behind the counter.

The guy dusted floury hands and smiled at him for his order.

Mal leaned over the counter. "I'm supposed to pick up a cold hero with twenty-two slices."

The smile lost definition momentarily. "Yessir, coming right up."

The man went into the back and returned with a plain white cardboard box, no store imprint.

Mal asked what he owed. The guy said it was paid for. Mal

started to go, but the smells were too much. He ordered a slice of pizza and a large Coke. Then he sat at a table with his back to the couple and ate. The taste didn't quite live up to the smell, but the pizza maker seemed so antsy for Mal to go that Mal had another slice. When it came time to pay, the guy said it was on the house.

First thing Mal did after he climbed back into the Toyauto, he checked out the piece. A factory-fresh .22, never been fired since they test-fired it at the factory. Good feel. Smooth action. Two full clips. He shoved one into place. Silencer. He screwed it on. Nice balance, even with the silencer.

Mal got back on I 95 and followed it to the Rochedale off-ramp. He found the main stem and parked long enough to study the lower Westchester street map. Levandusky lived on Bonniecroft Circle. Mal got a fix on Bonniecroft Circle and determined the nearest Thruway entrance.

Bonniecroft Circle turned out to be one of a tangle of winding streets in an upscale part of town. A recent development of frame houses, brick-veneered or stuccoed, just too fucking cute and quaint, token small trees and bushes stuck in to replace bulldozed monarchs. These people paid the right taxes and voted the right way, so their streets had first call on the snowplows, but you could get lost fast in all the poorly signposted intertwined streets.

The Levandusky house hunkered on a small lot. Mal cruised by. Snowman stood in the front yard. Garage door half-raised showed clutter that left no room for a car, showed too a snow thrower used to clear the driveway and walk. No car in the driveway. Mal checked his watch, then looked at the Metro-North train schedule for Rochedale. Levandusky commuted to the city, left his car at the Rochedale Metro-North station to catch the 7:24 express that reached Grand Central at 8:01, came back on the 5:33 express, arriving at 6:02. Maybe the station would be a good place. Had an hour to size it up.

Mal drove to the station and ruled out a hit there. Too many cars jockeying in and out of the cramped station plaza. Too many chances you could get locked in, spoiling the getaway.

On his way back to Bonniecroft Circle, he saw ahead on one side of the road a sweat-suited woman jogger jigging in place while waiting for the light to change so that she could cross the road.

That's right, lady, he thought, echoing Uncle Phil, look both ways before crossing even a one-way street. *Especially* before crossing a one-way street.

She looked his way as he drew near. Her breath fogged her face so you could read any features you wanted into it. She was bareheaded save for a sweatband and she was dark-haired and slim. His scalp tightened.

For a flash he saw Lupe.

His stomach knotted up. Of course, when he slowed in passing for a really good look, which seemed to make her nervous enough to back up few steps and glance where to run if she had to, she was nothing like.

He stepped on the gas and watched in the rearview mirror as she streaked across and out of sight.

By now it was coming on dark. Streetlights were conspicuous by their fewness in this countrified end of town, so all faces were fuzzy, plus there was that breath fog. Could happen to anyone to see someone as someone else under the best of conditions. But it shook him a bit.

Meant Lupe was on his mind.

Bad time to have anything on his mind but the hit. The Levandusky hit. Keep his mind on that.

He eyed his watch. Levandusky's train from Grand Central almost due. Trains seemed to be running on time despite the weather. Take Levandusky five minutes to get off the train and into his car and out of the station plaza, another ten minutes to make it all the way up Meridian Avenue to Bonniecroft Circle. Mal was five minutes away from Bonniecroft Circle. Head there now, have ten minutes to get into position.

He reached Bonniecroft Circle, drove its length, and came around again to reenter it. Only hitch, a woman and a kid, but they were on a lot at the other end from Levandusky's house. A small hill from digging the foundation for a new house—weather or finance halting construction—had snow cover, and the toddler sledded up and down a slope that seemed to seem a mountain to him or her. At least the woman, an earmuffed blonde, chunky, didn't remind Mal of Lupe.

Then why did not reminding him remind him?

Shit. Focus on the hit.

On the second go-round he parked at the invisible curb just past the Levandusky driveway. He left the engine running and took the .22 out. He checked the gun and its load, then let it rest on his lap and waited.

Levandusky drove a Volvo. It turned into the drive.

Mal was out and over to the driver's side before Levandusky had unbuckled the safety harness.

Levandusky saw him only after opening the door and leaning to get out.

Mal held the .22 out of sight along his thigh and gave Levandusky a big smile. "Hi, Sandy."

Levandusky looked up at him with an answering smile, then lines of puzzlement etched in. "Do I know you?"

"Just making sure."

Mal swung the .22 up and pumped the first shot into Levandusky's forehead. Mal took a step back, because sometimes a kind of internal backlash whipped the body forward. But this shot blew Levandusky backward, onto the seat, head lolling to one side. Dead. But just making sure again, Mal leaned in and fired the second shot behind the ear. Couldn't be deader.

As he drew himself back out, he heard the crunch of feet

on packed snow. He looked over the car roof. The woman was pulling the sled by a doubled rope, the kid sitting on the sled and waving its arms to urge her on.

He hoped they were neighbors of Levandusky's, making for a house farther along the street. He hoped they were not all that familiar with Levandusky and would pass on by with no more than a smile and a nod. He could not close the car door because Levandusky's feet stuck out, so he stood by the open door as if he were the driver and blocked the view. But the woman with the kid did not pass on by. Shit. The snowman should've tipped him. This was their fucking house.

The woman had to smell wrongness. Stranger standing at the open door of their car, husband not visible behind the wheel.

She dropped the reins of the sled. She cut across the yard. In her hurry, she skidded on an icy patch and bumped against the snowman. She recovered and headed for Mal. "Is something wrong? Where's Sandy?"

Mal stepped in front of her. "I think he had a heart attack." He put a hand on her shoulder to keep her from coming around. "Better go in the house and call an ambulance."

But she slipped from his grip and pushed past. "I want to see my—" She saw her husband.

Before she could scream anything, Mal brought the gun down hard on the back of her head. She was out before she hit the ground.

Mal turned and strode toward his car. He passed the kid on the sled. The kid was not looking at him. The kid was looking at the fallen snowman and crying.

CHAPTER
10

Bobo Newsom knew something about himself. Why he quit pitching: "I was throwing the ball as hard as ever, but the ball wasn't going as fast." Maybe Mal ought to hang it up too.

Then do what? Shit, no. Wasn't his reaction time, that was quick as ever. Not reaction but distraction.

Lupe.

Unresolved chord. *Shave and a haircut, two . . .*

It had kept him from concentrating on the Levandusky hit. It had kept him from considering the possibility that the woman and the kid on the sled belonged to the Levandusky household.

All the way home, while ditching the .22 and accessories in a Bronx sewer, while parking the rental car at the air terminal, while seeming to doze behind the DO NOT DISTURB sign, Mal and the matter gnawed at each other.

Lupe.

He had to get her out of his mind. To do that, he had to get her out of her fix.

Once home, he gave it deep thought. He had it almost worked out when a call from Guido Palmieri almost sidetracked him.

"You done swell, Harry."

"Thanks."

"No problems?"

"No problems." Fucking easy to start Guido worrying about him; fucking hard to stop Guido worrying about him.

" 'At's what I like to hear. Say, why I called, I just been watching this here Judge Wapner on the television. What a *testadura*! He listens to this poor widow woman tell how her neighbor's power mower throws a rock through her window screen, through the glass, till it hits her wall. First, the neighbor says he'll pay damages; then he stiffs her. Now, even though the rock can't come from no place else, this Wapner, this *judge*, tells her she ain't met the burden of proof. What I like to see, I like to see a rock go through *his* window. *Capisce?*"

Mal didn't *capisce*. He specialized in hits. "You're talking about a rock and a window?"

"A rock rock and a window window."

Mal choked off the impulse to say a couple of things: that Guido had become quite the television critic and that Mal didn't do rocks.

"I get the picture, Mr. P. It would give him a good scare—"

"Yeah, yeah."

"—but unless a note was wrapped around the rock to remind him about the case and tell him he really fucked it up, he wouldn't connect it with a bum decision taped months ago and he wouldn't be ashamed of himself he came down with such a lousy ruling." Mal admired the way his mind worked, feeding him the right words as he spoke them. Like Uncle Phil said, Life consists of vamping till ready; you have to keep vamping because by the time you're ready your act is over. "Other hand, if a note was wrapped around the rock, they put the knock on the poor widow woman." Way Lupe got blamed.

A long pause, then, "Ah, forget it. But this other thing you did, you did real good. So long."

"So long."

* * *

Mal went to see a photographer he knew, Freddy Friday. Freddy's legit line was pornography. But Freddy made more on the side with forged I.D.

Freddy failed to make him through the peephole because of the mustache and the glasses. Mal took off the glasses and said it was Harry Pace. Freddy unshot the bolts and let Mal in with a big hello. New fax machine; Mal saw, before Freddy edged between, a Mexican-government blank form that had come in.

Next night, Mal returned to pick up two new sets of I.D.— driver's license and Social Security card—in the names of Philip Oom and Philip Zio. Cost him two grand cash and worth it.

Morning after that, Mal garbaged all the food he had on hand in his apartment that might spoil.

He repacked his carryon. He did not plan to travel by air; he simply found the carryon handiest for his away-from-home needs whatever way he went.

Mal did not plan to travel by air because however lax airport security might be, he did not want to risk boarding in L.A. heeled, and he did want to reach Miami heeled. Shop around for a piece in Miami and it could reach Ramón Díez's ear that a guy like the guy in the police sketch—take away his mustache and glasses—was heeling up.

A zippered pocket of the carryon held, along with his various I.D.s, the prescription the ship's doctor had given him for the motion-sickness preventive Transderm Scōp.

He rehung his best tropical suit in a Travalet bag and carefully folded and zipped the bag to its toting dimensions. He put on his Rolex and set it to the second.

Mal did not change the message on his answering machine. But he checked to see that it functioned. To *hear* that it functioned. He lifted the little plastic flap that gave access to the buttons that controlled greetings and autodialing. He pressed the Check Greeting button and heard, "Peace Industries. All our lines are busy right now. Please leave your name and phone number and one of our operatives will get back to you as soon as possible. Thank you." He didn't advertise. It was all word of side of mouth, but it kept him busy enough. It always surprised him that that voice was his voice; it seemed deep enough, but he would have liked it more resonant, more like Uncle Phil's.

On his way out of the building, he paused at the stash under the stairs to heel himself piecewise and geltwise and to pocket Felipe Díez's signet ring.

He walked to the nearest car-rental agency, and Philip Oom drove away in a Lincoln.

Mal averaged 550 miles a day. Interstate 10 all the way across, then I 95 and U.S. 1 down. Driving alertly but taking it easy, breaking no laws or speed limits, stopping often to stretch and rest, eating regularly and sensibly, drawing no attention. He did no night or even dusk driving. Whenever the hands on his watch, reset for local time, touched 5:00 P.M., he started looking for a half-decent-looking motel and pulled into the first such place to come along.

Hard to do, with the sameness of the miles wearing down his senses as the road eroded the rubber, but he held his energy level, kept his edge.

He did not get the motion-sickness prescription filled till the trip had almost ended, when he stayed the night in Jacksonville. But then, the Transderm Scōp was not for him.

He cruised through Miami and checked into a motel on the Tamiami Trail.

The phone directories in the office had no listing for Ramón Díez in Key Biscayne, but the news accounts had said that Ramón Díez was chairman of the board of Banco de los Inocentes, and the directories did have listings for the bank's headquarters and branches.

Next morning, Philip Oom checked out of the motel. After a light breakfast, Mal turned in the Lincoln with California plates at the local office of the car-rental agency and paid up. He walked to another car-rental agency, and Philip Zio drove away in a Cadillac with Florida plates.

He located a uniform store and bought a chauffeur's black cap and black suit.

The salesman commented on the fact that Mel could wear a 38 regular right off the rack, that Mal needed no alterations.

Mal corrected him. "You mean the suit needs no alterations."

The man looked surprised, then chuckled. Mal could see him store it for retelling to his customers—or maybe his fellow tailors, if tailors got together to cut up. *The* customer, *get it, needed no alterations to fit the suit.*

Philip Zio checked into a motel on the Dixie Highway.

Mal tossed his bag onto the bed and hung up the uniform, already on its own hanger in a plastic bag the salesman had given him, in the closet. He unzipped the Travalet and hung it, too, in the closet, letting the tropical suit hang loose for gravity to iron.

Iron made him think of magnetism, and it hit him that magnetism might be only concentrated gravity. Uncle Phil once told him he had a good mind it was a shame wasting. Uncle Phil had been drunk at the time, but Mal knew anyway of himself that he could outthink most of the people he met. *What the hell. A lot of things different, next time around.*

Sure. Next time around he would case physics. Be a second Einstein. No—the first Mallory Foy.

This time around, at this point, he had to case the Ramón Díez operation.

* * *

When he went out in the morning, he left in his chauffeur's uniform, though he did not put on the hat and jacket till he had passed through the motel's gate, in case the desk clerk's beady eyes joined the beaded curtains at the window.

It took Mal three days of staking out the pink-glass-and-green-aluminum Banco de los Inocentes headquarters building to spot Ramón. Mal knew him at once from the news photos, which showed him to be an older version of Felipe. In the flesh, he sized up smaller than Felipe but weighed up shrewder.

At 3:00 P.M., Ramón strode briskly out of the building. He passed so close that Mal felt tempted to gun him down right there and then. Blow out the brains—the smarts and the will—behind the search for Felipe's killer.

But that wouldn't help Lupe.

Mal had been parking the Caddy in one of the reserved spaces. Bank headquarters took up the ground floor and a number of other floors, but the high-rise building housed other businesses as well. If anyone asked, Mal was waiting for his boss, CEO of one of the other companies. Nobody asked. Because he made it plain it was nobody's business.

At first the other chauffeurs cast curious glances his way, but he stuck a newspaper in front of his face to show he had no interest in joining their schmoozing society, so they ignored him.

Today, soon as Ramón came out, the Rolls's chauffeur broke from the group and opened the car's back door. Both car and man were new to Mal. Guy looked like a bear. Tightly clustered eyes, nose, and mouth. Gravitational pull of the nose?

Heavy gold cross swung across his hairy chest as he bent to close the door after Ramón climbed in. Religious-slash-superstitious. Mal stored that away. Useful, if this was the Bernardo Sánchez, Ramón Díez's chauffeur, that the news accounts said witnessed Felipe's killing.

Mal let the Rolls get a half block into traffic before he pulled out of his slot and followed.

The Rolls headed straight for the causeway and rolled across it, past the spot where Felipe had died, and through a neighborhood of the rich and famous.

Mal held back when he saw the Rolls slow, when he knew the chauffeur had taken his foot off the gas pedal but before the brake flashed red. The Rolls's chauffeur didn't bother with turn signals. Didn't see the Caddy far behind him or didn't care. The Rolls turned in at a gate flanked by masonry posts.

When Mal cruised by, the gate had already closed behind the Rolls—apparently opened and closed automatically by remote control; Mal saw no gatekeeper. Saw a television eye. Moved along.

Moved along a chain link fence with green plastic strips woven through for privacy and a crown of razor ribbon to enforce that privacy.

At the property line, another chain link fence, less paranoid, without woven screening or razor ribbon, took over for the width of the neighboring estate. Mal pulled up at this neighbor's gate.

A padlocked chain kept this gate closed. Mal got out of the Caddy for a closer look. Oil drippings on the cement turn-in near the gate seemed undiluted by rain and unfaded by sun, so a car had been there not long ago. But the lawn inside the fence badly needed mowing and the mansion at the end of the long driveway had the blind look of desertion.

Just within the gate, a wooden post stood planted on one side of the driveway. It had the gallowslike arm of a real estate agent's sign, but no sign hung from the two hooks screwed under the arm. If he had not been looking for the sign, he would not have seen it almost buried in the grass at the foot of the post. But it *would* have to be blank side up. Tantalus's Law, Uncle Phil called it.

Mal looked up and down the road. No cars in sight, but what did you want to bet one wouldn't come along just as he climbed over the gate? But the view also took in the occasional flanking tree. He strolled to the nearest one, tore off a long, straight branch, and strolled back stripping off the leaves and the twigs.

He poked it through the cross-hatching of the gate. Now if anyone came along and asked him what he was doing, he could say he was fishing. The truth. He was fishing for the name of the real estate agent.

The pole reached the sign all right and dug under it easily enough, but flipping it over was no cinch. The chain link openings gave him little play for leverage. Just when he thought he had the sign on the point of turning over, his end of the pole would hit fence wire and the sign would slip back down unflipped. After many "Shit!"s he got the bastard.

Could just make out the lettering. He drew the pole out and flung it far over the fence into the grass. He brushed off his hands, then took out pen and pad and copied the name, address, and phone number.

He drove back to his motel on the Dixie Highway and changed into his tropical suit. He looked himself over in the mirror and thought he looked like money. Maybe not big money; but then, big money didn't always look like big money—especially in these days of scruffy rock stars and pimply drug dealers.

Anyway, Denise Koloski seemed to think him worth a bright smile when he walked in. She had a storefront office in a shopping center. She was alone in there, sitting at a computer setup and lifting her eyeglasses off and squinting at the screen.

She swiveled around to greet him with that bright smile on

her talk-muscled face. "I think I need bifocals. I try to stay two feet away from the monitor because of the radiation or the magnetic field or whatever. Scary what they keep finding out about the things we use." She got up and thrust out her hand for shaking and her bosom for admiring. "Denise Kay. That's easier than Koloski. Nobody knows the area better and nobody has finer listings. How can I help you?"

He said his name was Philip Zio. If he had said it was Philip Oom, would she have said she couldn't help him with that? She seemed the type, a great kidder. Her face didn't exactly fall but her smile lost much of its candlepower when he told her the property he was interested in.

"I'm surprised they didn't take the for-sale sign down like they said they would."

"You mean it's already sold?"

"Not prezackly. The owner's holding it off the market because there's litigation. Long story." She gestured to a TV-VCR hookup and a rack of videocassettes on a shelf and started toward them. When she walked, what had looked like a dress turned out to be pants. She reached for a cassette. "Let me show you some fantastic properties. Beachfront estates, condos with private marinas or private golf courses. Whatever your game is, name it and claim it. All with the same ballpark figure."

"I don't want Fenway, I want Wrigley."

She blinked. "You mean your mind's set on that one?"

"Prezackly."

She made a cute face. "I never thought I'd try to *unsell* a prospect. But there's a first for everything, so here goes. Woman who owns that estate can't stand bugs. She bought it a year and a half ago and moved in—and right away she was ready to move out. Saw her first palmetto bug. That's nice for American roach."

Mal nodded. He had squashed his share of them.

"So-o-o, she had exterminators tent-fumigate the house and spray and dust the grounds. She had them, while they were at it, control for German roaches, millipedes, ants, fleas, termites, ticks, silverfish, spiders, moths, earwigs, rats, mice, possums, chinch bugs, armyworms, sod webworms, waterbugs, scorpions, wasps, bees, mole crickets, and white grubs. I may have left out a few."

"I get the idea."

"Anyway, she pestered them to do a thorough job. And they did. *Over*did. They chemicaled the place to where it became what is technically known as a sick house. A case of overkill. The saturation of fumes made it uninhabitable, at least for her, and she moved to a hotel. Last time I saw her, couple of months ago, she still looked a sorry sight. Inflamed sinuses, stomach and kidney trouble, emphysema, muscle soreness. She put the place up for sale, listed it with me, and sued the exterminators. They claim their chemicals are harmless to humans and they say she should blame her allergic reactions on outgassing from her new furnishings—the carpeting and foam stuffing and vinyl and paint. So she's holding on to it just the way it is to preserve her evidence. That's what I meant by saying it's in litigation. If you ask me, it won't go to court. The exterminators aren't covered for this big of a liability, and they'll go into bankruptcy before they pay what she wants for physical suffering and mental anguish. Give her another few months and she'll settle for hotel expenses and medical bills. Meanwhile, it's off the market. There. Have I unsold you?"

He shook his head.

She shook hers, but smiled. Dollar signs whirred behind her eyes. "To convince you, I'll do what I shouldn't do. I'll take you out there and show you. If you still want the property after that, I think I can sell her on selling it. If you make a firm offer,

I'm sure she'll settle with the exterminators and be happy to get the place off her hands."

She looked at the wall clock and then opened an appointment book. "Ten A.M. tomorrow suit you?"

He nodded. "I'll be here."

CHAPTER 11

"Bright and early," Denise Kay said when he walked in.

Mal held up flashlight and binoculars. "I was brighter earlier. Picked these up at a sporting-goods store."

She stared at him.

"Flashlight to see around inside," he explained, "in case the electricity is off, what's in dark corners; binoculars to see around outside, what kind of view."

"You don't leave much to chance."

Triple play, Uncle Phil used to say. Tinker forever with chance. Past to present to future. Everybody out.

Mal watched Denise get her keys from a locked file. Had on another of those split skirts. Something Japanese about it. Maybe the flower pattern. All she needed was knitting needles through her hair and a fan in her hand.

They left her office. He waited while she secured it, then they got into her car, an open Corvette, and she drove them to Key Biscayne.

Along the way she pointed to this property and that property she said she had sold. She said nothing when they passed Ramón Díez's.

"Here we are."

"I'll unlock it." He held his hand out for the padlock key.

"Thanks."

He took the key and got out of the car, and on the way to

the gate he hid with his body that he was making an impression in clay of the key. Just in case.

The little box holding the clay impression slid into his pocket and the key slid into the padlock and turned. The bow jumped up, and he lifted it out of the links of the length of chain that fastened the gate to the gatepost and rehung the padlock on one link and swung the gate wide. He got back into the car and gave Denise the key and she drove in, right to the front door of the mansion. A passing cloud subdued the lawn.

They got out. He followed her to the door and watched her unlock it.

She did not at once turn the knob. "I really should have had the place aired out for a few days before showing it. I'll go in with you, but I can't stay long or I'll get a headache and start choking. You can explore if you want to. Take your time—though I don't think you'll want to take too much." Still smiling, she eyed him sharply. "Most of the furnishings are in storage. What's left has been inventoried."

He smiled back. *She* didn't leave much to chance, either. He had seen her look out the window around the gilt letters of MIAMIGO REALTY when he left her office yesterday afternoon, and he felt sure she had made a note of his license-plate number. But Philip Zio would disappear and the license plate prove a dead end. Only if she got too nosy would he have to snuff her.

Before opening the door, she took a deep breath and held it.

He smelled why. The place stank of fumigant.

She covered her nose and mouth with a tissue and led the way. Spacious rooms. Solid construction. Exotic woods. Picture windows. She pointed out these selling points in a voice more and more muffled. Then, with a strangled cry that he interpreted as "Gotta get outa here," she ran for the outdoors.

Mal had the place to himself. But the place was getting to him too. He held his breath till he found the nearest john.

Rushed in and raised the window and let out the old air and topped himself up with the new.

He held his breath again, turned the faucet, found that the water ran, tore off a long strip of toilet paper, one of the things not in storage or probably even inventoried, soaked it, and held it over his nose and mouth. Uncle Phil had been in chemical warfare during WWII and said that an instructor had told him to piss on a handkerchief if he needed a gas mask in a hurry. If there hadn't been paper and water here, Mal would have done just that.

He slung the binoculars around his neck and clipped the flashlight to his belt so that he could hold the mask in place and still have one hand free. He returned to the living room, unlocked the glass doors leading to the terrace, slid them open, and stepped out. Took a good fresh breath of Atlantic air.

He lifted the binoculars to his eyes and glassed sea to the horizon. A breakwater divided the top half from the bottom half. Halves only from this point of view. Far half reached to Africa. Inside and outside the breakwater, a scattering of sailboats and powerboats sliced the surface. But he wasn't here for the scenery. He scanned the grounds. Patio, blades of grass stabbing up between the stones. Waterless pool. Netless tennis court. Boatless dock.

Denise *had* invited him to explore.

He stepped back inside and slid the doors shut but did not lock them. He saw wires of an alarm system, but Denise hadn't punched the control box he had spotted at the front door. The system was off. Guess they figured the fumigants burglar-proofed the place.

Explore. Light switch at the head of the basement stairs flicked futilely. Flashlight showed him damp empty space. Rest of the house let in plenty of light through windows bare of curtains and drapes. Probably saturated with fumes, subsequently laundered and stored. Room above the living room looked like it must be the mistress bedroom—all pink and mirrored. In the bedroom next to it, windows overlooked the Díez property.

Staying out of sight himself, Mal got close-ups of it—from house and pool to dock and boat. *Medallion.* He smiled. He spotted a guy on patrol with an attack dog and he spotted a woman he took to be Mrs. Ramón splashing in the pool.

That had to be enough for now. He couldn't keep Denise waiting too long.

He flushed away his gas mask and didn't bother holding his breath, and by the time he left the house he was choking and tearing.

Denise Kay massaged her temples with her forefingers and opened her eyes. She raised an eyebrow.

Mal shook his head sadly. Lost Eden. Love Canal. Chernobyl.

She relocked the front door and they got into her car. When she stopped outside the gate, Mal sprang to shut it and rewrap and repadlock the chain.

If he had not had the clay impression of the key, he would've faked the action. He did fake having trouble getting the bow to engage so that she would listen for and hear the satisfying click.

On the drive back she pointed out other fantastic buys, but her heart seemed not in it once he made clear it was that one or nothing—and that one was out. When they parted in front of her office, she said if he changed his mind about what he was in the market for, he knew where she was.

He said he *did* know where she was.

Mal spotted a hardware store in a shopping center a couple of doors down from Denise's office, but he didn't think it would be smart to buy key blanks and a set of files there.

* * *

He bought these things at a hardware store in a shopping center miles away. He did a lot of shopping at that other shopping center.

Noticed looking out around gilt letters of MIAMI on the window of one shop that they spelled IMAIM.

On the last trip back to his car with a full shopping bag, he bought the latest *Miami Herald* from a coin machine. He sat in the car and skimmed through the paper, ignoring the glares of a guy driving around and around waiting for him to give up the slot.

Only one small mention of Lupe; again the judge had denied reduction of bail pending trial. Trial scheduled to begin next week.

Mal folded the paper but did not leave right away. Saw another car head into the lot, driver looking for a slot, so Mal waited till the first guy had gone by again. Guy gave him the hottest glare yet. Then Mal pulled out and the newcomer grabbed the slot. On his way to the exit, Mal caught the first guy's eye and shrugged. Hey, pal, Tantalus's Law.

In his motel room, he cut a piece of cardboard to fit the clay mold, then he used this template to file a key blank to shape. He held his handiwork up to the light. Far as he was concerned, the key to Key Biscayne.

Then he put it in his breast pocket, buttoned the flap, and stretched out and rested up for the night ahead. Dreamed, something about his mother and Uncle Phil, but he never tried to remember his dreams when he woke up.

Mal drove slowly past the lit-up perimeter of the Díez estate to the darkness of its neighbor, turned in at the gate, killed the lights.

He had the files handy, ready to refine the key by moonlight or flashlight—but the key sprang the bow first try.

Off with the chain. He swung the gate open and drove the car in far enough to clear the gate's arc. He swung the gate shut and reached through to rewrap and repadlock the chain.

He felt tempted as before to leave the bow disengaged. Faster getaway. But he remembered Murphy Slaw.

According to Uncle Phil, that stood for potato salad, guaranteed to turn bad if you thought cool weather would let you get away with not refrigerating it.

Murphy Slaw would guarantee a neighborhood security patrol conscientious enough to try all locks on its rounds if you thought you could get away with not securing the bow. Mal shoved the bow home. *Click.* Fastest getaway now, if it came to that, rev up the engine and bull through the gate, hell with damage to the car.

He got into the car and eased it all the way down the drive and right into the open and empty four-car garage. He switched off the purr and listened through the rustle of trees and the smoke-detector-dying-battery chirp of cicadas. He clipped his flashlight to his belt on the right and clipped his holstered gun to his belt on the left and checked the sheath knife strapped to his left ankle. He got out of the car, out of the garage, and walked lightly around past outside stairs—chauffeur's quarters above the garage—and down the path intended for kitchen deliveries.

Listening, listening, looking, looking, he stole past the kitchen and around back to the sliding doors on the patio.

He crouched at the door he had left unlocked, drew his gun, looked, listened. He put his left hand to the door pull and gave a sudden hard shove, at the same time launching himself through the opening—to the right, to keep from silhouetting himself against stars and moonlight. He crouched again, listening.

No one home. He holstered his gun and straightened without feeling the least bit foolish. Foolish was going in any other way.

His eyes and nose and throat began reminding him *why* no one was home. He went back to the car and strapped on the oxygen tank with its breathing mask. Then he carried in his first load of shopping bags.

Way moonlight streamed in through the naked windows, he didn't need the flashlight beam to show him upstairs and to the bedroom overlooking the Díez estate.

He paused at the window for a look out. Blue flicker of TV in the cook's or maid's room. No other sign of life in the house. Down at the other end, the *Medallion* was not at its dock. In between, the dog and its handler strolled into sight and paused under a light to yawn and scratch.

Mal made a face. If everybody else was on a cruise and he had to stick around here waiting for them to come back, he was going to do a lot of stretching out and resting up. Be hard to keep himself keyed up. Be doing a lot of yawning and scratching himself.

Right now, though, he felt hyper. Not used to breathing pure oxygen. Didn't want to get hooked on it and didn't want to waste it. He set the shopping bags on the floor and opened a couple of windows for cross-ventilation. Nice sea breeze. Tried doing without the mask for a few minutes. Did all right. Be able to unstrap the tank after he brought up all his supplies. Picked up the shopping bags—full of granola bars, raisins, shelled nuts, canned tuna, fruit juices, peanut butter, crackers, bread, bottled water, plastic plates and cups and cutlery, paper napkins, and trash bags because he didn't want to leave anything behind if he could help it—and carried them to the closet.

Soon as he set the first one down in the far corner of the closet, a floorboard tipped up a few inches.

He froze.

Then he carefully lowered the other shopping bag to the floor outside the closet, and with that hand he took hold of the risen edge of the closet floorboard. Then he lifted the first shopping bag back out of the closet and swung it out of the way.

He was grinning, wondering just what he had stumbled on. The lady of the house's hidden strongbox? Under the circumstances, probably no jewelry in it at the moment, but it was always nice to know the location of loot. Gave him information worth trading.

He raised the floorboard all the way. Something, but not a strongbox. It took raising the board next to it to show him fully what he had found.

A tape recorder. Power pack, headphones, mike still in its plastic bag.

Plugged-in pickup led him to a phone wire that ran down out of the closet. No need to follow it to the basement; from there it would make a buried run out to the street.

By now he knew it had nothing to do with the lady of the house. It was here for the same reason he was here: Ramón Díez. This place right next door made the perfect observation post. He returned to the bedroom closet and looked down at the tape recorder.

Question was, whose?

Rival drug cartel's? He had heard the name Miguel Luqué. A hit he had made a few years back he had guessed, without really caring, was a subcontract, and Luqué was the hidden prime contractor. Luqué and Díez had no love for each other and both played for keeps. Mal grinned. Be funny if Luqué worried that Ramón thought Felipe was a Luqué hit. Could be good reason for Luqué to listen in on Ramón, aside from what he might pick up in the way of industrial espionage.

D.E.A.'s? Wouldn't put it past their goons to fix it with exterminators to overcontrol pests and so force the lady out. That way, need no court order to eavesdrop, word of which could get back to Ramón.

Those were the two likeliest players.

Outside chance the lady of the house was a high-class hooker or madam and had been planning to tape clients and that the overcontrol of pests had been an honest mistake that drove her out of business.

One way to prove this had nothing to do with the lady and everything to do with Ramón: Mal knelt to read the number on the counter. 423. Just as he reached to press Rewind, a ruby light flashed on. The voice-activated machine was recording another call. Mal fitted the headphones on.

A voice, faint. Mal turned up the gain. A man's voice, deep and gravelly.

". . . out on the boat. Won't be back till tomorrow afternoon."

"I see. Well, I'll try again then." A man's voice, very cultured.

"Yeah."

"Will you tell him Mr. Ames called, about the benefit tomorrow evening for Hispanic artists, and that Mr. Ames will call again?"

"Yeah."

"Thank you."

Click. The ruby light winked out.

Mal started again to press Rewind, but again the ruby light flashed on.

Outgoing, this time. Mal heard the gravelly voice make it, if you could call it that, with a Marilyn Monrovian voice stationed at a 900 sex number. Apparently Ramón didn't audit his phone bills; and while the cat was away . . .

The woman, if it was a woman and not a program, called herself "Scarlett—with two *T*'s." Tease was right. The guy called himself Bernard.

Mal rubbed his palms together. Now he could put a face to the name. The dog handler was out on patrol, so that left this the bearlike guy Mal had seen through his binoculars.

Bernardo Sánchez, the witness against Lupe named once in a while in the news accounts Mal had come across. The guy he wanted.

He pressed Stop and pulled the tape cassette out.

A two-hour tape, one hour each side. Luqué's or the D.E.A.'s operative would pick it up and replace it every other day at least. About one-third recorded, so Luqué's or the D.E.A.'s operative had been here yesterday or day before—the oil drippings at the gate—and would be back tomorrow or day after.

Or—who knew?—a minute from now.

First thing Mal needed to do, after reinserting the cassette, was carry his shopping bags back down to his car. Erase signs of himself, hope whoever came to trade new tape for old did not notice the car in the garage. Meanwhile, stay on the lookout and keep your ears open. Watch both road and dock for anyone.

He meant *anyone,* leery of a mind-set that left him open to surprise if it turned out to be a broad or a black or a senior citizen or a kid or any mix thereof. Couldn't let surprise freeze his finger. Equal-opportunity destroyer.

Carried the full shopping bags back down, tossed them into the trunk, rummaged through the other full shopping bags he had been about to carry up. He had purchased a selection of condiments and spices at the supermarket. He opened those containers now and poured the contents into a paper bag, closed it, held the fold securely, and shook. He now had a one-pound mixture of ground black pepper, red pepper flakes, hot paprika, and dry mustard.

Out on the patio again, he wet a finger and tested the wind. Blowing right. He moved to the property line, opened the bag, walked slowly along the plastic-strip-weave razor-ribbon-topped chain link fence, and sowed the wind blowing over onto Díez land. He folded the empty bag small, pocketed it, withdrew as far as the sliding doors, took out a silent whistle, and blew it.

He heard a loud bark. He blew again, harder. A louder bark, then running feet, heavy snuffling, painful yowling.

The yowling accompanied him into the house and up to the bedroom overlooking the Díez property. The window showed him the dog rolling in agony and pawing its nose, while the handler stood helpless.

Then the handler left the dog and went into the house.

Mal watched the tape recorder in the closet. The ruby light was still on. Then it winked out. After a minute, it flashed on again. Mal put on the earphones.

A woman's voice. ". . . Pat-a-Pet Animal Hospital, Dr. Thorsen."

"Doc, it's Mr. Díez's dog. You gotta come right over." A man's voice, high with anxiety.

"I'm here all alone, so I can't make a house call. But if you bring the dog in, I'll see him right away."

"We ain't supposed to leave."

"Sorry. You'll have to bring him in."

"Just listen, will you, for Chrissake?" The man must've held the phone out the window; the dog's whining and whimpering came through loud and clear.

The vet said she was certainly sorry, but she *was* alone at the hospital and *couldn't* make a house call, even for Mr. Díez's dog. If Mr. Díez's dog needed treatment, Mr. Díez's dog would have to come to the hospital.

"Okay, okay. I'll bring him in. But this is Mr. Ramón Díez's dog and if he dies because you didn't come, you're going to be *certainly* certainly sorry."

Click. The ruby light winked out.

Mal took the headphones off and sat back on his heels thinking. He had meant the spice bouquet to put the dog out of action. Turned out better than that, taking the dog handler out as well. Instead of going in the back way, from the sea, knocking off the dog handler, then kidnapping Sánchez, he could go straight to the front.

He went downstairs, out the front door, took one step up the drive toward the gate, stopped, and veered toward the garage.

Sánchez, as a witness in the case against Lupe, must've seen the police sketch of his face.

He took two Band-Aids from the kit in the glove compartment and stuck one on his right cheek and the other across his nose. These and the mustache and the eyeglasses should give Sánchez enough to look at that he wouldn't see the face behind them.

Mal headed again toward the road. He reached the gate in time to hear a car roar out of the Díez estate. He unlocked and opened his gate and strolled down to the one next door.

He pressed the button on the intercom speaker affixed to the post.

"Yeah?" The gravelly voice, with a big smile in it. "Forget something, Hernando?"

"This isn't Hernando. Hernando's on his way with the dog to see Dr. Thorsen at Pat-a-Pet Animal Hospital."

"Hey, how the fuck you know that?"

"That's what I want to see you about, Bernardo. Come to the gate."

"How the fuck you know my name? Who the fuck are you?"

"Jack Edison. Days, I work for Southern Bell. Nights, I kind of moonlight for myself. And while I was moonlighting just now I came across something next door that should interest your boss."

"He ain't here."

"I know. Ramón won't be back till tomorrow afternoon."

"How the fuck you know that?"

"I could say Mr. Ames told me, but the truth is *you* told me."

"Fucking liar. You I never talked to before."

"You can talk to me now. Come to the gate."

"Bet your ass I'll come to the gate." *Click.*

Mal waited. His black turtleneck sweater overhung his gun; he touched his waist to feel the butt. He could take Sánchez right away without any trouble. That would eliminate the witness against Lupe. But the trial might still go on with Sánchez's pretrial statement entered as evidence. The case would be much weaker, but it would still be a case. Better to do this one right, clear Lupe once and for all.

He heard footsteps and turned his right side toward the gate.

A windowlike section of gate opened and Mal saw the top half of Sánchez.

Sánchez had hiked up his flowered shirt to let this Jack Edison see *his* gun. Mal saw that, and a heavy gold cross on a bed of curly black chest hair, then Sánchez switched on a light that bathed and blinded Mal.

Mal made himself stand still.

"What the fuck happened to your face?"

"Nothing."

"No? Then why the fuck you got the bandages?"

"Disguise."

Sánchez digested that. "Oh." Then, "What the fuck is that under your sweater?"

"Flashlight."

"Very slow, lift your sweater."

Mal looked away in boredom and daintily bared the flashlight clipped to his belt. "Okay? Sheesh, if I'd known I'd be dealing with a hardhead and getting this kind of reception, I wouldn't've bothered." He let the sweater drape over the flashlight again, faced Sánchez, and put up a hand to shade his eyes. "Look, I got something to show you next door I figure is worth something to your boss. You interested or not?" He turned as if to go.

"You're fucking crazy. Next door's empty."

"That's what you think." Mal took a step away.

"Hey, wait. What's next door?"

"For one thing, a tape recorder. Somebody's been tuning in on you guys."

"That's no news."

"Fine. Sorry I wasted your time and mine." Mal took another step away.

"Hey, wait. Just where is this tape recorder?"

"Where you'll never find it unless I show you. You coming?"

"I ain't supposed to leave."

"Hernando wasn't supposed to leave either, but he left. You chicken?" Mal walked away.

"I'll show you who's chicken." The gate opened.

Mal heard footsteps behind him. They crunched after him down the road and followed him through the gate next door and up the drive to the front entrance.

"Where's your car?"

"In the garage."

"You got nerve."

"Thanks." Mal had left the front door unlocked; he opened it and walked in.

Sánchez followed him into the house.

Mal flashlighted the way.

The beam picked up the emptiness. Sánchez said, "Fucking place is stripped. What the fuck you expect to find here?"

"Serendipity."

"Huh?"

"You never know. I found an expensive tape recorder."

"That I got to see."

"And you will. Up these stairs."

Mal took one last breath of the fresh air coming in through the front door and held it while he led Sánchez upstairs.

Sánchez began to wheeze and choke behind him. "What . . . fuck . . . stink?"

Mal shrugged. He led Sánchez along the hall and into the bedroom.

Sánchez made for the open window and stood sucking the night in.

Mal gave him a minute, then spotlighted the tape recorder buried in the closet floor.

"Shit. You wasn't kidding." Sánchez took his hand off his gun butt and leaned in for a better look. He jerked upright and whirled to face Mal. "You heard the tape?"

Mal nodded. "You want a listen?"

"Yeah. Make sure it's us they been tapping."

"Be my guest. Just let me rewind the tape enough you get an idea."

He knelt to punch Rewind, then Play, with his right hand. His left hand he kept near the butt of his hidden gun in case Sánchez got *that* idea. Then he picked up the earphones and straightened. He handed Sánchez the earphones.

Sánchez put them on. Mal saw by flashlight beam a dark flush creep up Sánchez's neck and suffuse his face. Listening to himself and Scarlett. His eyes, then his face, slid away from Mal.

Now. Mal drew his gun, reversed it, gripped the barrel and swung the butt at the back of Sánchez's head. Hit the right spot with the right force at the right time. Cloudsthewits, Uncle Phil would say. Uncle Phil was high on Clausewitz and Machiavelli.

Mal drew Sánchez's gun from its holster. A Smith & Wesson Model No. 41 .22 long-rifle automatic pistol with 7 3/8-inch barrel and ten-round magazine. He shook his head. Pure Freud, that long of a barrel. He stashed the gun on the closet shelf for the time being. He felt Sánchez's carotid. Flutter, flutter. Alive but out for a while.

From the same shelf, Mal took what he had already stashed, a kit that held paper tissues, package of Transderm Scōp patches, vinyl exam gloves, roll of gauze bandage, dispenser roll of surgical tape.

The gauze was to keep from bruising the skin or leaving traces of stickum. Mal bound Sánchez's wrists together with plenty of gauze and held the gauze in place with several turns of tape. He bound Sánchez's ankles together the same way, right over the pant legs.

He wiped the skin behind Sánchez's ears vigorously with paper tissues to remove the oiliness. He put on the vinyl exam gloves and opened the package of Transderm Scōp. He took out a disc and unwrapped it, removed the peel strip, and stuck the metallic, adhesive side to the dry skin behind the left ear. He pressed hard on the tan side that showed to make the thing stick good.

Sense of balance depends on nerve fibers deep inside the ear. Travel motion keeps these nerve fibers busy. Too much motion overworks the nerve fibers, leading to dizziness, nausea, and vomiting. Way the package said Transderm Scōp worked, scopolamine on the disc osmosed through the skin and into the bloodstream, then swam through the bloodstream to the nerve fibers deep in the ear.

He stuck a second disc next to the first one. Then he stuck two more discs behind the right ear for good measure. Should be enough scopolamine oozing through to make the side effects the main effect.

Sánchez's breathing loudened and quickened. Stuff already going to work. Add to that some Chinese-restaurant syndrome . . .

Mal began to gather things to clear away. When he came to the nearly depleted roll of gauze, he had a sudden thought and shot a look at the gold cross on Sánchez's chest.

He pulled straight the tag end of the gauze. Just enough. He wound it around the neck of his black turtleneck sweater and knotted it behind. A clerical collar. To blurred vision, at least.

Now to help Sánchez come to, ready for last rites. Taking the things he no longer needed, he went down for some bottles of spring water and a dispenser container of monosodium glutamate. He opened a bottle, poured MSG into it, and shook well. All that burning and sweating and palpitating, should be a foretaste of hell.

CHAPTER 12

"Water, my son? I know your mouth must be very dry."
Dry? A fucking desert.
Water dribbled in. Benny almost choked, trying to say, *More, more.*

More came anyway. Ah. The fucking priest was a good guy, though he looked so fuzzy he almost wasn't there. Benny felt like crying thankfully, but he could not raise the tears.

Still, why the fuck couldn't he grab the fucking bottle himself? Why the fuck were his fucking hands and legs tied? He tried to shake his bound hands and to kick with his bound legs. His belt looped through his bound hands and immobilized them, and his bound legs hung from a doorknob. Body curved as in a hammock, head and shoulders on the floor and feet in the air. No wonder he felt mind pressure, blood rushing to his head. What the fuck?

"Those are called Poseys, my son. The nurse tells me they're to keep you from throwing your arms and legs around in delirium and hurting yourself."

Something was hurting him. He felt dizzy and itchy and hot and his belly held a rat scratching and biting to get out and his heart hammered like a pneumatic drill. Where was the fucking nurse when you needed her?

Wait a fucking minute. What fucking kind of hospital treated you like this?

Where the fuck was he? It seemed to him someone had led him down a dark road and into a dark house. Then what? A flash of darkness. And now here he hung, his belly chewing itself up and his heart pounding itself to pieces, his mind ashriek with the rat and the drill.

And now here came the fucking voice of the fucking priest cutting through from the outside.

Asking him something he didn't give a shit about. About Felipe's death, for Chrissake.

"Confess, my son, what story did Ramón lay on you to tell? You don't want to die with a lie on your soul."

Benny croaked, "Die?"

"Yes, my son. We all must die. And we must all be prepared to meet our Maker at any moment. Your time is soon, I'm afraid."

No. No. No. "What happened?"

"Only the autopsy will say for sure, my son, but the doctors think, and the tests confirm, that you suffered a massive stroke, and that when you fell and hit your head you sustained a severe concussion."

So the darkness of the room was not just the darkness of the room but the gathering darkness of his mind, and the far, fuzzy light was not just a night-light or the moon through a window but the light of retreating life. Shit.

The voice of the priest kept at him. "But we're wasting time talking about why and when your time is up. Come, my son, clear your conscience. What lie did Ramón lay on you about Lupe?"

He pulled his mind back a bit from darkness, pushed it a fraction toward the light. He tried to bring the priest's face into focus, but it stayed in shadow. All he could make out was white collar and gold cross—and they were so blurry he had to take them on faith. "Lupe?"

"Guadeloupe Martínez, a.k.a. Marita García."

"Oh, *her*. You mean what happened that day."

"Yes, my son. You must tell me. The power of truth is working within you."

If he was going to die, let him die in peace, swiftly and silently. He shook his head. The hardness under it gave him a fucking dutch rub. Where was the fucking nurse with a fucking soft pillow? Talking was the last thing he felt like doing. But *something* was working within him and he could not hold back his words.

"Well, I'm supposed to say I'm driving back to the house with some stuff Elvira—Mrs. Díez—sends me to pick up. So I'm on the causeway and I spot Felipe's car stopped on the shoulder with a junk heap stopped behind it. I slow down to see what the fuck is going on. I don't see Felipe, but I see Marita on the front seat of the Caddy and she's talking to a guy I figure belongs to the junk heap. I get a good look at him and the cops show me some pictures later and I pick out the guy. But right now while this is going on and I'm creeping along I see this guy hop into the junk heap and squeeze back into traffic. So I figure he stops to see if he can help, lady in trouble, and when Marita tells him Felipe walked or got a lift to a garage, the guy finds he isn't needed and he takes off. So I figure I can't help, either, better keep going because Elvira's waiting for the stuff. That's the story."

"But that isn't the truth, is it, my son?"

"No, Father."

"You don't want to die with a lie on your lips, do you, my son?"

"No, Father."

"Now, here is the truth, my son. And when you get it off your chest, your suffering will end and you will die in peace. After the guy hopped back into the junk heap—it was an old, beat-up Chevy, wasn't it?"

"How did you know?"

"I know all, my son. When the guy hopped back in and took off, you did not keep moving yourself. You pulled in behind Felipe's Caddy to find out what the fuck was going on. Can you see yourself doing that?"

"I can *see* that, but—"

The priest overrode him. "Your mind is confused."

That was true.

"Don't fight the truth, my son. Let it prevail. Trust me. You pull in behind the Caddy. Looks to you like Lupe—I mean Marita—looks to you like Marita is out cold. Felipe put her in her place again. That's right, she's out cold. You can forget about her talking to the guy. She never said a word to him, never saw him. Okay, my son. You get out and go around to the passenger side—and *now* you spot Felipe. He's sitting on the ground, leaning against the Caddy's rear door. He looks like he's just coming out of getting knocked down in a fight. Can you see all that?"

"Yeah, but—"

"Just look and listen, my son. Felipe's in a daze, but he's far from finished. He feels his jaw and looks at you. He thinks *you* landed the blow knocked him down. He climbs to his feet and comes at you. You don't want to mix it with him, but he's too apeshit to listen to you. He doesn't want to hear some other guy bumped his car and coldcocked him. He's after your ass. There's a screwdriver on the ground. You pick it up. You hate to use it, but he's in a 'roid rage and you don't see how else to stop him. After you stab him to death, you lift his signet ring and his wallet to make it look like this other poor bastard pulled a bump-and-rob. Then you take off. You see all that, my son?"

He saw all that, and himself in it. It played under the priest's voice-over like a film. So it was real enough. But he didn't remember it happening a first time. Was truth not the cold hard thing they said but melting and shifty as a dream?

The voice insisted. "You see all that, my son?"

"I see it, but I don't remember it."

"Easy to explain, my son. You hated Felipe, didn't you?"

"Everybody hated Felipe. Spoiled rotten sumbitch."

"You wanted him dead, didn't you?"

"Sure like to see that big-shot smile wiped off his face for good."

"But if you stopped his clock, you're scared what Ramón does when he finds out. Right, my son?"

"Sure don't want Ramón thinks I do his brother."

"So you repressed it, pushed it way back in your mind."

Like to push lots of things way back. The rat, the drill, the priest's voice. No strength, though. Everything—the world and himself—melting and shifty as truth.

He groaned.

"More water, my son?"

He nodded. Where was that nurse with the pillow?

Water dribbled into his mouth. Cool. Cool. Helped some against all the burning stuff backing up into his throat from his belly.

"Now, my son, for the good of your soul, tell me, in your own words, how you saw Felipe's car stopped on the causeway and how you pulled up behind it, and how you saw Marita out cold on the front seat and Felipe sitting on the ground and how Felipe came at you in a 'roid rage and how you picked up a screwdriver and stabbed him in self-defense. See it and tell it."

Benny saw it all again and told what he saw.

"Now, my son, I am ready to hear your confession."

"I just told it."

"That was rehearsal. This is for the record." What seemed a hand shape held what seemed a mike shape to his mouth. "Go."

He repeated it.

The hand shape holding the mike shape withdrew.

"Okay, my son."

Hands lifted his legs off the doorknob and shoved the door away and lowered his feet to the floor. Hands grabbed him under the armpits and swung him around to sit leaning against a wall.

A hand shape made the sign of the cross before his face. Then a hand shape stuck the barrel of a gun shape in his mouth.

Cold, hard.

"Take, eat."

CHAPTER 13

At once Mal stepped back from the body and to the window. But loud as the shot had seemed in here, it had not set the Díez place astir. No lights switched on, no voices raised in question. He watched and listened a good minute, then returned to the body.

He unbound Sánchez's hands and started on the feet.

In the corner of his eye, the machine's ruby light flashed.

Had someone in the house heard the shot after all? Calling for the cops or security to look into it?

He cupped an earphone to an ear.

An incoming call. Hernando, in Spanish, asking for Benny.

A woman's voice answered. She didn't know where Benny was. She had expected him to take the call, but the phone had rung and rung till she had to go pick it up herself. She didn't know where Benny was and didn't care where Benny was.

Hernando said to tell Benny that the dog would have to stay overnight at the animal hospital but that Hernando was on his way back home.

The woman said maybe it would be better if Hernando stayed at the animal hospital and let the dog find its way home, but if she saw Benny she would let him know.

They kept going at each other, but Mal put the headphone down and finished untying Sánchez's feet.

He hung the gold cross back on Sánchez's chest and forced

Felipe's signet ring onto Sánchez's ring finger, signet on the palm side. He rolled the pads of Sánchez's fingers over the cross and over the mike. Would've disturbed the body too much, would've left signs of tampering with it after the fact, if he stretched it to leave fingerprints on the tape recorder and the uplifted floorboards, so he merely smeared those salient points with his gloved fingers. He had used Sánchez's own gun, and now fitted it in Sánchez's gun hand hard enough and long enough to take nice clean prints.

Then he released the hand and the gun fell. He let the gun lay where it landed.

He patted and rubbed the backs of his gloved hands against the backs of Sánchez's naked hands to transfer blowback particles that would prove Sánchez had shot himself.

The confession would back that up. He had planned to have Sánchez write the confession and sign it, but taping it was much easier and infinitely surer.

Could've turned out Sánchez was illiterate. Where would he have been then?

Murphy Slaw. Have to be ready when things cross you up by going right.

Now he cleaned up. Into a trash bag with everything that did not belong to the suicide scene.

He looked around one last time before going. Not for luck, but lucky he did.

His flashlight beam speared a shiny, small, hexagonal object on the floor. He picked the thing up. The clear plastic backing he had peeled off one of the Transderm Scōp patches.

He eyed it, shook his head, and hurled the thing into the mouth of the trash bag. He went back to the body and took hold of a lock of Sánchez's hair to pull the head farther down for a better view of the back-of-the-ear regions. But the flesh the hair grew out of had torn loose from the skull, so Mal's tug only lifted a flap of scalp.

With a tight smile, he let go of the lock and handled the

head by the ears. Messy back there. But the patches were still in place. He peeled them off and tossed them into the trash bag.

One *last* last look, then he got the hell out of there.

First pay phone he hit, he called Metro Dade headquarters. In his best imitation Hispanic accent he asked for the detective in charge of the Felipe Díez homicide.

"That's Sergeant Shanley. But she's off duty."

"You call her, then. Right away. Give her this message: 'Benny Sánchez say to tell you meet him right away at the empty house next one past Ramón Díez house. Benny say he have a tape recording with important information. Benny say don't tell nobody—especially don't tell Díez or none of Díez people. Benny say hurry.' You got that?"

"I got that. Who do I tell her called?"

"Friend of Benny Sánchez. You don't give her message right now, she gonna be very mad with you." He hung up and got back into his car and drove on. He set himself to look for a Dumpster he could get rid of the trash bag in on his way to the airport.

Last things in had been the gauze clerical collar and the vinyl gloves. Uncle Phil had the last word about last things. "That's when you shake the dust off your sole."

Finished. They had to let Lupe go now.

He had broken the chain.

Shaking the sand of Miami. He was almost sorry. Not about Miami. About not getting to see Lupe again. But considering all he had got himself into after seeing her just the one time, it was probably just as well.

Detective Sergeant Carol Shanley waited till forensics had gone, then she flicked the light switch. Nothing.

Her partner, Jack Vogelsang, frowned. "I told you. I got the real estate agent on an outside line, and she told me the owner stopped paying for electricity." He looked around the bedroom. With the windows wide open to let in fresh air, it wasn't too bad in here now. And with the early sun streaming in, it was plenty bright in here. "It's plenty bright in here. You don't need the lights."

Shanley flicked the switch again. "I know. I heard you the first time. I'm just thinking."

Vogelsang sighed and waited.

She didn't keep him waiting long. "I'm asking myself how Sanchez saw his way around in the dark. Because the M.E. guesses Sanchez died six hours ago, and six hours ago it was dark."

Vogelsang thought. He remembered a full moon last night. Nothing romantic about it; he had noticed it was a full moon and had wondered fleetingly if it would bring out the head cases. "Not all that dark. Full moon last night."

"Even so." She flicked the switch a couple more times, then gave it up with a shrug.

A cop came in. He spoke to Shanley. "Guy won't give his name or show I.D. is outside the gate. He asked who was in charge and said to give you this." He handed Shanley a folded slip of paper.

She unfolded it and Vogelsang read it over her shoulder. The slip of paper had the letters *OK* on it.

Shanley and Vogelsang traded looks.

She turned to the cop. "Caucasian, wispy brown hair, gray eyes, thin nose, cleft chin, thirty-five, six-two, medium build?"

The cop nodded. "That's the guy."

"Let him in."

The cop left.

Vogelsang frowned. "Wonder what *he* wants."

Shanley smiled. "We'll find out soon enough."

"Do we let him listen to the tape?"

She patted her pocket. "It's already bagged as evidence. It stays bagged."

"We don't let him listen to the tape. Do we even tell him about the tape?"

"Let's see if he knows there's a tape."

Vogelsang narrowed his eyes. "Think the tape recorder's his?"

"Wouldn't surprise me. But he won't claim it. This smells like an illegal tap."

"Whole house smells. But I know what you mean. So far, we know the tap isn't Metro Dade's or the D.A.'s. Does smell like the Feds. Can't wait to hear what Mr. D.E.A. has to say."

The sun washed gold over everything, but Shanley thought O'Keefe's face looked pale, as though he saw a ghost instead of a chalk outline.

By unspoken consensus, Shanley and Vogelsang greeted him outside the bedroom, blocking him from more than a crane's-eye view of it. He could see the spattered wall dead ahead, but if he wanted to see the closet he had to stretch his neck. Where the body had been should have held his gaze. So why—unless he knew that the closet was there and that the closet held something of interest—did he stretch his neck for a look at the closet floor?

"Who got it?"

Shanley did the fielding. "What's your interest?"

"Heard something went down right next door to our old friend Ramón Díez."

"You keep *that* close tabs on Díez?"

O'Keefe spread his hands. He smiled, trying to turn on the charm he didn't have. "What can you tell me now I won't find out soon anyway from other sources?"

"Like the media?"

O'Keefe frowned and his mouth tightened.

Shanley dropped the needling. "*Who* was Benny Sánchez."

She raised an eyebrow.

O'Keefe nodded.

"Somebody tapped the Díez place from here."

O'Keefe did a creditable job of looking surprised. "Oh?"

"How it looks, Benny got onto it and came for a look-see." She shook her head. "Sloppy operation if a stupid like Benny Sánchez got onto it."

O'Keefe flushed slightly.

"How we see it, Benny came over last night and listened to the tape."

He leaned at her. "Tape?"

"We sent it on to the lab for duplicating." She looked him straight in the eye. "We played it once already and didn't hear anything that sounded all that incriminating. But we'll go over it and over it, because Benny must've heard something that panicked him. Or maybe he just had a guilty conscience. Or maybe he was afraid Ramón suspected him of killing Felipe and would slice him to bits."

"Benny killed Felipe? I thought it was that girl from Colombia I told you about and some guy they're still looking for."

"On the tape, Benny says he did it in self-defense. But that's no argument Ramón would listen to. Benny knew that and added his confession to the tape and then ate his own gun. He sounded high, like he was on something. We'll have to wait for the coroner's report to know for sure. He sounded high, but he told a believable story."

"Believable enough to get the Martínez woman off?"

"I'm not the D.A. But if I were, I'd feel my case died with the key witness."

"Well, well, well." O'Keefe turned away. "Thanks," he said absently.

"Anytime."

Assistant District Attorney Byron Oziel disliked meeting in a parking garage. An echo chamber, not only of sound and silence but of light and shadow. Gave you the uncanny eye-corner presentiment of hidden watchers, one of them—in an out-of-body way and in a materialized-conscience sense—yourself.

Ramón Díez seemed at home. He poured margaritas into chilled glasses with a steady hand, though his whole body appeared charged with barely contained fury.

They sat, faking relaxation, on the backseat of Díez's limo. Díez's new chauffeur stood outside the car, partly to steer other cars toward other parking spaces but mostly to not hear.

Díez and Oziel lifted their drinks in salute, and their mouths took sips while their eyes took measure.

At half-margarita time, Díez gave Oziel the nod.

The combination of meeting place and meeting partner made it hard for Oziel to explain calmly and reasonably why his office planned to drop the case against Marita García, a.k.a. Guadeloupe Martínez.

"The situation is such that we have to rethink the situation."

Díez burned a look at him. "Without fizz. Tell it to me straight."

Oziel's eyes shuttered in a prayerful blink. "Benny's confession changes everything. It clears the woman."

Díez put down his glass. "Benny's confession is laughable." Díez formed finger quotes around "confession." "I *know* Benny couldn't've killed Felipe. It was this other guy. And there *has* to be some tie between this other guy and the woman for the guy to kill for her again."

"Kill? But—"

"Benny's suicide is laughable." Díez formed finger quotes around "suicide." "Great job of staging. Fooled you and your people. Doesn't fool me."

"All the evidence points—"

Veins throbbed in Díez's temples. "Screw all the evidence." He drew a deep breath and brought his voice under control.

"For the sake of argument, let's say you're right and I'm wrong. I want the guy, and the way to get the guy is through the girl. So I want the girl to stand trial. This new so-called evidence"—he abandoned finger quotes—"is in the way. Get it out of the way."

"How?"

"Will the judge listen to reason?"

"Green reason?" Oziel thought, then gave a half nod. "But there has to be a balancing color of legal reason." He gave a half shake. "And I don't see a legal reason."

Díez stared at him. "You're the lawyer and you don't see? *Madre de Dios*, an illegal wiretap."

"But it wasn't ours. And because the wiretap wasn't ours, we can use its fruits."

Díez looked briefly to heaven. " 'Can use' doesn't mean 'have to use.' "

"In this case it does." Oziel raised a dike-plugging finger. "Let me tell you why. We can't just lose it. Too many people know. Copies have been made. Transcripts have been made. Copies of the copies and copies of the transcripts are probably being leaked right now to the media. Make book on it, the public is going to know all about Benny's confession. If I try to suppress it, the public outcry will make the state and maybe the federal government investigate. Can you imagine the circus? I couldn't run for dogcatcher. I couldn't even run for dog."

Díez looked at him.

Oziel tried not to show fear, tried to keep his voice from quavering. "I'd like to help. I *want* to help. But . . ."

Díez looked through him and gave a small wave of dismissal.

Oziel climbed out.

The chauffeur stepped back to the car, closed the door, and got behind the wheel. The car purred away.

Oziel breathed the exhaust fumes gratefully.

*   *   *

Ramón Díez drew from the inside pocket of his jacket the much-folded-and-unfolded police sketch.

He studied it again. This face was the face of the guy had the run-in with Felipe at the restaurant, stole the chef's car to follow and bump Felipe's car, stabbed Felipe with a *screwdriver,* for God's sake, came back, and made Benny "confess" and commit "suicide."

This one guy doing all this to *him.*

Ramón held the sketch in one hand and with the other hand started to pour himself another margarita. He stopped himself. Nothing, not even this guy, especially not this guy, was going to drive him to drink. Only thing he wanted to get drunk on was this guy's blood.

Where was this face hiding?

Someone out there knew this face.

Reach that someone.

Ramón pressed a button and spoke in Spanish to the chauffeur, an eager young man too fresh from Colombia to be spoiled worse than useless. In time, though, he, too, would turn lazy and weak and stupid like Benny and Hernando.

"Mateo, stop at the copy shop on Southwest Seventeenth Avenue."

Fifty thousand circulars for express shipment to contacts in key cities around the country. No, make that one hundred thousand. If that did not work, one million. Whatever it took to find this face.

Freddy Friday quickened his step as the bar up the street came nearer. But a hassle seemed in the making at the doorway, so he slowed his step.

What it looked like, a runt handing out circulars stood kind of half blocking the entrance, and the bouncer came out to suggest that he not do so. What it looked like next, the bouncer loomed over the runt but the runt not only stood his ground but called something up to the bouncer's ear that made the bouncer back off and go in and leave the runt half blocking the entrance.

Freddy was sort of curious about what the runt might've said, but not interested enough to forget what awaited him at the bar. So Freddy gave the runt the once-over—found nothing special there, nothing awe-inspiring—and passed up the circular.

He had no interest in saving whales or in buying schlock goods at giveaway prices or in having Mme Abrams (1 flite up) read tarot cards and identify his friends and enemies by name without asking him a single word. He had all the interest in the world in grabbing a quick one and then a number of slow ones. So—though he caught a glimpse of a big question mark, a row of dollar signs, and a sketched face—he brushed by the character at the entrance who proffered the circular about whatever.

Freddy knew that recent psychological research debunked the efficacy of subliminal advertising. But *something* made him turn on his heel and go back for a real look at the drawing on the circular.

Harry Pace.

Freddy knew the face even before the circular made it from the runt's hand to his. And fifty thousand dollars reward for coming up with the face's name and whereabouts. But he made himself put off reading the details till he had the quick one under his belt. Could be a catch in the fine print, and he needed fortitude against letdown.

He brought the circular and a slow one into a vacant booth and sat down and read. And forgot to sip.

Fifty grand for putting a name to the face.

Imagine, he had almost passed up something that would change his whole life.

If he were the first one to come up with a positive identification.

The circular gave a phone number. Area code 305. Florida. He patted his pocket. Felt like enough change.

The slow one became a quick one and he legged it to a wall phone.

He dialed the number. Got a busy signal. Shit, people on the make all over the country phoning in phony leads. And here he had the real lead and couldn't get through.

He hung up, had another quick one, hurried back to the phone, tried again. Still busy. He looked around desperately.

The runt was still handing out circulars.

Freddy legged it to the entrance.

The runt started to hand him a circular, then eyed him hard. "I already got you."

Freddy smiled. "You don't have to hand out any more to anybody. I know the guy you're looking for."

The runt eyed him even harder. "You do? You absolutely sure?"

Freddy nodded. "I can provide actual photographs of the guy. More up-to-date and lifelike than this piece of crap." He gave the sketch on the circular the back of his hand.

"Sounds great. So what's your problem?"

"I rang the number but I can't get through. Do you have another number or know how else I can reach the party wants Harry—" Freddy clapped a hand over the barn door. "Oops, almost gave away fifty grand."

The runt smiled, just with his mouth. "You don't want to do that. Charity begins at home. But it's all right. I'm like an agent for the sponsor. You know how when you enter a contest, the rules say nobody working for the sponsor or the ad agency is eligible for the prize? Well, since I'm connected, I'm not in the running for the fifty grand. You can count on me to get you through to the sponsor at no cost to you. That sound righteous enough?"

It did. The runt stuffed the remaining circulars into a pocket, and he and Freddy walked around the corner to the runt's car, where Freddy gave directions and the two drove to Freddy's studio apartment.

The runt took in all the framed poses and the photographic and lighting equipment this side of the dividing curtain.

Freddy rummaged through his files, getting that hollow feeling. The photos weren't where he thought they were. Then he backtracked his wobbly fingers a bit and there they were. He handed them to the runt. "See, I always print up a couple extra. You never know."

The runt spoke absently, studying the photos and comparing them to the sketch on the circular. "That's right. You never know." His mouth formed a smile and he seemed to try to get his eyes into the act. "Now, you said Harry. Harry who?"

"Harry Pace. That's his real name. I don't mean that's his *real* name; it's the one he goes by as long as I know him. But the names on the driver's licenses and the passports and et cetera are different. I have to think." Freddy squeezed his eyes shut. "Let's see. Yeah, Philip Oom and Philip Zio."

"Mind writing them down for me?"

"Sure." Freddy turned away to find paper and pencil.

"Know where he lives, where he hangs out?"

Freddy found a scrap of paper and a stub of pencil. The paper would not have met the 3″ × 5″ requirement of a contest entry, but he nonetheless printed the names in neat block letters. "He don't hang out, but he lives here in L.A. somewhere."

"Well, that narrows it down." The runt pocketed the slip.

The pictures had already disappeared and Freddy grew anxious. "About the fifty grand."

Now the runt gave a whole-faced smile. "Oh, don't worry about the fifty grand. I'll spend it wisely."

Before Freddy could work that out, a butterfly knife flew at his throat.

* * *

Mal slept at a different motel in the area every night. This time, he meant to stay handy to Miami till he knew for sure Lupe would be getting off.

Sánchez's suicide and confession had made the news, and the media agreed that the prosecution had no choice but to drop all charges against her and yet for some reason was dragging its feet.

To Mal, the reason was clear.

Ramón Díez.

But even Díez could shackle Justice's ankles only so long.

Mal stood waiting outside the courthouse the morning Lupe walked out.

She looked dazed by more than the photo flashes and the reporter shouts. Dazed by freedom.

She was dazed and Mal did nothing to draw attention to himself, so he did not see how it could be, but it seemed to him that for a fraction of a second her eyes picked him out of the crowd and that their eyes met. Then they were both lost in the swarm and she went her way and he went his.

Their eyes had met. Good enough. As Uncle Phil said, "Contact is contact. Can be heartfelt or belly-button lint, as long as we each know the other is there."

The courier delivered proofs of the new circular that showed how the bastard really looked now, and stood by.

Ramón Díez gripped the circular fiercely. The paper suddenly ripped at the top, near his right thumb and forefinger. Ramón recovered his composure and repaired the tear with cellophane tape.

He picked up the circular and held it almost tenderly. He was staring at the face when he heard the bitch's name. His finger arrowed the sound upward on his remote control and his head jerked around to face the television screen.

The damned cause of it all came down the courthouse

steps. Ramón had to will himself not to snatch his gun out of the desk drawer and blast the tube.

The news footage told him less than he already knew about the Martínez bitch's release and more than he wanted to hear about her reactions to her ordeal as mouthed by her lawyer to the flailing mikes.

Then, as the camera swung around to follow the bitch down into the car taking her away, Ramón saw a face in the sweep past the onlookers.

He flashed his gaze back to the circular. Same face. He whipped again to the screen. Gone.

Ramón found himself on his feet, his hand on the gun in the desk drawer.

He was aware of the courier, frozen, gaping. Ramon withdrew his hand, empty. The gun was not for the meaningless gesture of popping an image on the tube or for a fruitless dash to the courthouse after a man long gone from there by now. Ramón smiled pleasantly at the courier and reseated himself slowly.

The anchorwoman held center screen now, displaying her teeth over another sound bite.

Ramón pressed the mute button on the remote control to shut her up while he thought. Now, way her mouth worked, she looked like a fish—do her justice, a cartoon mermaid.

As soon as he had fixed upon what to do, he arrowed the volume to its loudest and beckoned the courier close. Closer.

"Tell Julio to print two hundred thousand of these circulars by tonight. Job it out to any number of shops if he must. The man may still be in this area, so the priority is to saturate Dade County fast. One hundred thousand circulars go for local coverage: hotels, motels, apartment complexes, restaurants, shopping centers, the works. Every last one to be delivered by dawn. Catch anyone making sewer service, it's their head. Ship the other hundred thousand express for national distribution.

Drop everything else; put everyone on this. Now let me hear you repeat what I told you."

The courier whispered it all back, stumbling only once, over the word *saturar*.

Denise Kay of Miamigo Realty didn't believe in phoning ahead. Best to catch people off-guard, keep them off-balance. "Hope I didn't catch you at a bad time?" Then, stepping on her own rhetoric, "Happened to be in the neighborhood and thought I'd take a chance on finding you in." That was her approach, and it almost always worked.

Besides, in this case, phoning ahead seemed the least prudent thing to do. The development in the Felipe Díez murder case having to do with a wiretap on Ramón Díez's phone made talking on the phone with Ramón Díez about *anything* a dumb move.

She showed the man at the gate her copy of the circular. "It's about this." She handed him her card. "Tell Mr. Díez I've seen the man and have his license number."

The man looked her over, then turned and walked in no particular hurry to the house. He came back walking much faster.

He opened the gate. "Drive up to the front door and wait for me."

Didn't take him long. Long enough, though, for her to have second thoughts. Maybe she should have kept out of it. Too late now. Story of her life.

He climbed the stairs and turned and looked down at her and nodded. "Leave your bag in the car."

She made to put it on the seat, then stopped herself. If he wanted to play hardball... She stowed it in the glove compartment, took the keys out of the ignition, locked the glove-compartment door, and pocketed the keys. She eyed the man levelly, got out, and mounted the steps.

He didn't open the front door at once. "Have to pat you down."

Her mouth tightened. But she had come this far and there seemed no turning back. She was on his turf. No sense fighting a fight she would lose. "If that's what you get off on."

He eyed her coldly. "Mr. Díez's orders."

"For all his guests?" She knew that Díez's guests had included the governor.

His mouth tightened.

She stood stiffly for his efficient pat-down.

He opened the door and gestured her in, then closed the door, walked around her, and led her down a hall and into an office.

All the way her mind was clicking, making note of selling points. The place should go for five million easy, even in today's crappy market.

Ramón Díez stood up behind his big desk, a beat or two late for a born gentleman, and came around to take her hand. He held it, rather than shook it, almost as though taking her pulse, then let go.

He looked more imposing in person. Not his size; he fell far short of a heroic build. His bearing. The cant of his head. More especially, the look in his eyes; the look of world ownership.

"Please sit down, Ms."—he glanced at her business card in his left hand—"Kay."

He saw her seated, then, with what seemed a flicker of disappointment that her split skirt ended the exposure, he retook his own chair. He flicked a finger at her card. "Your firm's name, how do you pronounce it?"

MIAMIGO appeared twice, substance and shadow. Forerunner had MI in green and AMIGO in red, doppelgänger had MIAMI in red and GO in green.

She gave him her warmest smile. "In present company, '*Mi amigo*,' of course."

He smiled back. "Of course. And I imagine that when you're with civic boosters you pronounce it 'Miami go.'"

"Exactly."

He put the card down on his desk and rested his clasped hands atop it. "*Bueno, amiga,* what are you here to tell me about the man I am interested in?"

She took a breath. "First you have to understand that I had no way of knowing he was interested in you. He presented himself to me as interested in the property next door."

Díez leaned forward. "You showed him the place?"

"I tried to talk him out of it—because of the owner's troubles with it you may have heard of?"

He nodded, and broke up the mating of his hands to wave her on.

"I was honest with him about that, but he had to see—or smell—for himself. So I took him there and let him in. And when he came out, he was totally unsold. So, as he didn't care about my other listings, that ended it." She spread her hands apologetically. "Honestly, the last thing I dreamt I was doing was giving somebody the chance to wiretap you."

Díez smiled. "You think that's what he did?"

She stared at him. "But the papers and the television said somebody bugged you, and I assumed—"

"Oh, he bugged me all right." Díez's sudden change of expression scared her. Then Díez smiled at her again. "What name did he use?"

"One of the ones on the circular. Philip Zio."

"You mentioned a license-plate number."

She quickly fumbled a slip of paper from her pocket. She reached it across and he took it.

He pressed a button that produced the man who had let her in. He handed the slip to the man. "Trace this license plate."

The man left the room.

Diez leaned back in his chair. "Tell me about Philip Zio."

She eyed him helplessly. "Honestly, I've told you all I know."

"You haven't told me your impressions of the man. I don't want to seem sexist, but women do have a better eye for detail than men. Close your eyes and think back. What mannerisms do you see? What facial or other physical characteristics?"

She did as he asked but could come up with only one thing. "Every so often he would scratch the whiskers on his cheek."

Diez looked disappointed in her again. "It was a new beard. Probably itched." Then he smiled. "But that's better than nothing and more than I had before." He frowned suddenly. "Have you told any of this to the police?"

"No."

"Good."

"You mean I shouldn't?"

"I mean if they had known what you've told me but had neglected to pass it on to me, it would have annoyed me. I don't care now if you tell them or not." He smiled. "Strike that. Tell them—but don't tell them you've already told me. Be interesting to see if they pass it on to me." He slid back his chair to get up. "When we find this man, you will share in the reward. Meanwhile, I am indebted to you."

She emboldened herself. "Then promise me if you ever put this property up for sale, you'll give me first crack at brokering it."

He looked solemn. "I promise." Then he smiled wickedly. "An empty promise. I do not foresee selling."

"Oh. Well, then." She stood up and stuck out her hand.

He took her pulse again, but this time he held on while he withdrew into thought. He pulled himself back to her. "I'm not selling—but I am buying. To protect my flank. Name me an attractive price on the place next door and I'll take it off your hands." He smiled at the glow on her face. "See? Honesty pays."

Motor Vehicles said the car belonged to a car-rental agency. The car-rental agency said a Philip Zio had rented the car but that Philip Zio had already turned the car in. No Philip Zio lived at the address the car renter had given.

Detective Sergeants Carol Shanley and Jack Vogelsang sat down on their dead ends.

They drank coffee and argued the merits of cardboard flavoring against plastic flavoring. The argument ended with the coffee, unresolved.

And undissolved. Shanley gazed into her cup at lees of sugar. "Do we tell Ramón what he already knows?"

"Think the Kay woman went to him first?"

Shanley plucked the circular from the open file folder on her desk and shook it at Vogelsang. "Wouldn't you if you were Kay and the dollar signs jumped out at you?"

"Did he tell *us* he was distributing these things?"

"Habit of not telling all he distributes."

"Hope he don't get in the habit of taking the law in his own hands."

"Too late to hope that. The guy—Pace, Oom, Zio, whatever—is doomed. Only chance I see of keeping him out of Ramón's hands is if these scare the guy into *our* hands. And even then, Ramón will reach him."

"Maybe we should thank Ramón, doing our job for us. Put him in for an honorary badge."

"You sound bitter."

"That's the coffee talking."

"Ah, hell, we tell Ramón what he already knows. At least he'll know we're still on the case."

"Cardboard sucks." Most reinvigorating part of coffeeing was crumpling the container and hurling it at the wastebasket, hit or miss.

"Recycles better than plastic."

"Everything recycles better than plastic. Including people."

What Don Guido Palmieri thought when he received the updated circular from Ramón Díez boiled down to: *Harry Pace was useful to us, always been straight with us. Do we owe him that we call him and warn him? We owe him shit. We owe ourselves what we can get out of this. We need Díez way more than we need Pace. If we don't tell Díez we can finger the guy, and Díez finds out we can finger the guy but won't tell Díez we can finger the guy, we're on Díez's shit list. We finger the guy for Díez, Díez owes us one and we stay on Díez's most-favored list. The guy is a goner anyways, so let his going do us some good. Bottom line, the guy is as expendable as any of his slugs. Why am I even thinking? I got no choice. I tell Díez I can deliver him Harry Pace.*

An hour before boarding time, Mal got set to decide the fate of his gun. Depended what his answering machine had to say.

He threaded through the throng on the concourse of Miami International Airport to a pay phone.

If he retrieved no message, he would ditch the gun in a men's-room wastebasket and take the flight home.

If he had a message giving him a job in the area, he would keep the gun and be a no-show and do the job.

If he learned he had a job outside the area, he would, if it was a rush job, ditch the gun and take this flight or an appropriate flight and get another gun at the other end and do the job.

If it was outside the area but he had an easy deadline and a reasonable destination, he would be a no-show and keep the gun and take a bus or a train or a rented car and do the job.

He dialed home. He had set the unit's ring-select switch to Toll Saver so that it would answer on the first ring if there were messages or on the fourth ring if there were no messages. He heard the first ring, and then his greeting played. He waited for the first beep tone after his greeting. He pressed his answering machine's remote code, the number 3. He held pressure on the 3 button till he heard a low tone.

The machine played a message.

He recognized the voice. Guido Palmieri. "Say, Harry, I got something might interest you. Call a friend of mine and mention the name Richards. Take down this number." The number began with area code 702. Nevada, which meant Las Vegas.

A low-high tone let him know the messages had ended. Then came a series of beeps.

He wanted the number to remain in the machine's memory so that he would still have it if it faded from his, so he pressed the 3 button again, for a full second. When he released the button, the beep tones changed to a lower pitch, indicating that the machine had accepted his command and saved his messages. He clicked off.

Now he dialed the number Guido had given him.

An Irish tenor answered. "So what do you want?"

Mal smiled. *Tough* guy. "I got this message asking me to call you and mention the name Richards. So what do *you* want?"

The Irish tenor sang a different tune. *Nice* guy. "Preciate the quick response. The name Harry?"

"Check."

"You calling from a pay phone?"

"Check."

"Give me the number, then hang up but stay put. I'll call you back in five minutes."

Five minutes passed. Mal seated the shoulder strap of his flight bag more comfortably and walked away from the phone. He was still in earshot when it rang; he walked back, in no hurry. He let it ring a full minute before he answered.

The Irish tenor sounded off-key with relieved anxiety. "Geez, I thought I heard the number wrong, or misdialed."

"You said five minutes."

"Geez. So it took me a fucking minute longer than I figured to get to a pay phone. You touchy or something?"

"Something."

"Geez. I hope you're half as good as you think you are."

"I hope so too. What's the deal?"

"There's this Ajay Richards guy, pit boss at a casino. Got caught skimming—for himself. Not by the gaming commission; they're sewed up. By the people with the points. These people would like their money back, but Ajay pissed it all away. Only way they can recover, and at the same time teach him a lesson, is if he croaks in an accident. They got life insurance on him and double indemnity will just about pay them off. The casino owns a twin Cessna they use for things like junkets for high rollers. Tonight it's taking Ajay to what he thinks is a meeting with the casino's chief owner at the owner's ranch near Tucson, Arizona, to talk over the situation. Now, if something happens to the plane, it's a nineteen and seventy-eight model and they been thinking about getting a nineties plane, they collect insurance on that too."

"So I'm also supposed to be aboard that plane tonight?"

"You got it."

"What about the pilot?"

"What about him?"

"He know anything about the plane crash?"

"All he knows is he's flying two passengers to the ranch."

"Why me?"

"Why you? Why you think we're talking? To make it happen."

"Why me? Why not a clock guy, a plastics guy?"

"You wouldn't leave those kinds of traces."

Made sense, but Mal still felt a nagging need to stall. "Does it have to be tonight?"

"Has to. The guy's shaky enough to run for witness protection if we don't handle him fast."

Mal made a face. "Even if I can catch a Vegas flight gets me there in time tonight, I can't board packing."

"Lemme think." Humming evinced thought. Or an Irish lullaby.

Mal used the time to think, too. His way would leave other kinds of traces. Thing was to make the traces fit the way you wanted them to fit, tell the story you wanted the law-enforcement people and the insurance people to believe—or at least to have no choice but to accept.

Best way for it to go down, knock Richards cold before they landed and shoot the pilot after they landed. Make it seem Richards tried to force the pilot to change course and the pilot tried to fight back. Then taxi the plane at a rock outcropping or a tree and jump out. Have to be a fucking stuntman.

If there was no rock outcropping or no tree or if the crash into a rock or a tree didn't finish Richards off naturally, loosen a fuel line and light a match and touch the leak off, leave it for charred teeth to identify the two.

The Irish tenor came back from dreamland. "No problem. The Cessna Chancellor has a potty under one of the rear seats. You'll find a piece inside the potty."

"No problem unless Richards runs to the potty first."

Whole setup stank. A piece he would not have had the time to check out, a staged plane crash he would not have had the chance to rehearse, a getaway over terrain he would not have had the opportunity to reconnoiter. He smiled tightly. Look at it as a challenge.

Have to take place on the casino owner's ranch for Mal to walk away from the crash sure of no outside witnesses. "What's the nearest town? How far is the ranch from a highway? Who'll be around to witness the crash and alibi the owner?"

The Irish tenor answered these and Mal's follow-up questions fully, but when Mal hung up it was with an empty feeling.

Ramón Díez took a call from a Mr. P.
"Weather's fine in Arizona."
Díez and three unbankerlike men with attaché cases that did not have to pass through a metal detector because they left from a private field flew in a Banco de los Inocentes executive jet to Tucson.

Weather in Arizona *was* fine. Díez breathed it in.

CHAPTER 14

For losers who couldn't wait to lose, who had to sow coins as soon as they got off the plane, McCarran International terminal had slots that returned less than casino slots, the perfect deal.

On the downside, the terminal had clocks and windows; losers couldn't absent themselves from time and space, lose themselves entirely, as they could in reality check–proof casinos.

Mal, one of the first off and, with his carryon, one of the first through, did not slow as he passed the plungers. Uncle Phil would've had something to say about them, some highbrow allusion to Circean swine. Mal followed slung signs and arrows that guided him next door, to Hughes, where the Irish tenor had told him he would find the Punto Gordo Hotel's corporate plane.

His plane had beat sunset. Day lingered, but the outside lights were already on, adding to the glow. Mal had almost too much light to find his way by.

A man with a flight jacket that bore a wings patch and a Punto Gordo patch lounged beside a Cessna Chancellor that bore the Punto Gordo logo. All the *o*'s were gold coins. The pilot could have used a shave. Mal at once thought of maintenance and looked to see if there were fresh oil spots on the tarmac under the plane. He noticed some. He made a face. But what the hell, there was a loosened fuel line in the plane's immediate future anyway, and the plane's fate would not surprise people who knew the pilot.

The pilot spotted Mal and straightened up. Mal's imagination, or did he catch the light of recognition in the pilot's eyes?

Mal looked him over closely and frowned. He felt sure he had never seen the pilot before.

The pilot glanced at his wrist watch as Mal approached; he eyed Mal sourly. "You the party for the flight to the ranch?"

Mal nodded. The party pooper. "Harry Pace." He pronounced "Pace" to rhyme with "chase."

The pilot shrugged. "I don't need a name. You're not being listed as aboard." He gestured Mal toward the open door. "Get right in. Mr. Richards is already aboard."

Mal swung his carryon in ahead of him and nodded at the big man who sat in a passenger seat. The man held a coffee cup to his lips and nodded without taking it away.

A smoke alarm went off in Mal's mind. If he had registered the man's presence anywhere but here, his mind's nose would have been warning him it smelled cop. In this setting, Mal judged Ajay Richards to be a retired or fired cop who had found himself a soft spot on the other side and then fucked up here as he had fucked up there.

Mal dropped his bag next to another on a seat in back and stuck out his hand and gave the man a friendly smile. "Harry Pace."

The man took a last swallow and set the cup down. He put his left hand to his throat, and with an apologetic smile mouthed, "Laryngitis."

Uncle Phil would've come right back, "Please to meet you, Mr. Laryngitis." Mal said, "Too bad."

Richards had a twitch at the outer corner of his right eye. Understandable nervousness in a man who faced the ordeal of explaining the unexplainable to an unresponsive ear at the other end of this flight. But when he squeezed Mal's hand hard, the effect was not that of a man shaking hands convulsively because of inner tension but that of a man testing his strength against another's.

But Mal had to put off thinking about that.

The pilot had installed himself and was warming the engines and getting clearance for a flight to the Tucson area. He called back to them to secure themselves, and the plane rolled to the flight line. It took off smoothly into growing darkness. The plane had a pressurized cabin. Stereo, oven, refrigerator, coffee warmer, and service bar walled off the pilot's compartment from the rear of the cabin.

The pilot, flying without a copilot, rode in the left-hand seat to reach electrical and engine controls mounted on a subpanel along the left-hand wall.

Mal unbuckled. He got up to pour himself a cup of coffee. Not to refresh himself; to study Richards.

Before taking care of himself, he offered Richards a refill. Richards gestured thanks but no thanks.

All the while Mal poured and sweetened and lightened and stirred and sipped, he gave Richards a hooded once-over.

Richards looked preoccupied but just as automatically measuring. The cop in him, Mal guessed.

Mal wondered how a guy with laryngitis could hope to talk himself out of a fix. Maybe Richards was wondering the same thing; Mal saw sweat crescents spread under the armpits of Richards's light jacket.

Then Mal saw something else; tailoring designed to hide the fact told him Richards was heeled.

Inside himself, Mal jumped to attention. He would have to make his move ahead of plan.

Richards must *know* he couldn't talk himself out of this fix—not even if he had a silver tongue instead of laryngitis. Yet, without any sign that anyone was strong-arming him, he had boarded a plane taking him to a bad end. Why?

Heeled for a shoot-out he had to know he had no hope of

winning? Thinking, then, at least to go out in a blaze of glory? Glory, shit.

In his shoes, Mal would be nerving himself to force the pilot to change course and fly him across the border.

Had to be that. Once on the ground in Mexico, all set to vanish, Richards would have the good sense to knock off the pilot and Mal.

Mal held the cup to his lips and looked over it at Richards. Breath deepening, face hardening, guy psyching himself up to hijack the plane.

Break that building rhythm, gain a minute to get the stashed gun to beat him to the draw with.

Mal aimed his voice at the pilot. "Hey, pilot, you ever been to this ranch?"

Shook Richards out of his psyching-up. Took the pilot by surprise, too.

"What?" Then the pilot regrouped. "Yeah, I been there a time or two."

"What's it like?"

"What can I tell you? It's a ranch."

Mal turned to Richards. "You ever been there?"

Richards shook his head.

Mal said pleasantly, "Well, I won't get my ears bent this flight."

But Mal had got the pilot going. "What the hell, I guess it won't matter what I tell you. 'Ranch' is the wrong word. Bare spot between mountains. Ghost-town territory. But like they say: Location, location, location. Handy to the border, you know what I mean."

"Vague idea."

"Funny how it changed hands. Guy name of Jack Sutro owned it, a real degenerate gambler. Got in way over his head. Put the ranch up as a marker. Busted flush. Bad loser, but he finally signed it over, then blew his brains out."

Jack Sutro. Mal remembered the name. "Funny is right. There's a lesson there somewhere."

Richards wore a frown, but it went in the pilot's direction. If Richards had looked ready to make his move, Mal would have flung the hot coffee at his eyes and pulled his jacket collar back down over his arms and taken his gun. But the man had slid back from the edge of his seat.

Mal finished the coffee, put the cup down, and patted his groin. "Think I'll make a pit stop."

Richards looked up in vague inquiry, then gave an absent grin.

Mal stepped around to the rear pair of seats and found the one with the potty. You could curtain it off. He yanked the curtain in place and lifted the seat, releasing a heady chemical smell into the air from a solution in the potty, and saw a plastic bag taped to the lid's underside.

As soon as he pulled the bag free he knew Guido Palmieri had set him up.

What the bag held had the wrong shape and felt too light.

He heard Richards—if that was the hit man's name—stir behind him.

By now the man would have the drop on him. But the man would be feeling fucking sure of himself and not eager to fire shots in a pressurized cabin. So Mal took his time reacting to the shock.

He withdrew the thing from the plastic bag. It was wrapped in silver foil and had the shape of a bunny.

The curtain pulled away from around him.

"Why don't you unwrap it? You could use a rabbit's foot about now." The man had faked the laryngitis to mute the Irish tenor.

Mal did not stiffen or turn. Slowly he unwrapped a chocolate bunny. He balled the foil and let it plop into the potty. He bit off a bunny leg and chomped deliberately while his mind raced. He pictured the holster bulge; the guy was right-handed.

Slowly he reached the mutilated bunny back over his shoulder. "Good chocolate. Want a piece?"

"Shit, no." The man swatted it out of Mal's hand.

Mal ducked and pulled the potty up and out and swung around and sloshed the chemical solution into Richards's face.

The bunny had diverted Richards just long enough. The shot Richards got off before Mal knocked his gun hand aside went wild. It tore through the foam and plastic of a seat back and had its death rattle on the floor.

"Hey!" came from the pilot.

Mal followed through, slamming the potty down over Richards's head. It made a helmet that covered eyes, nose, and mouth.

Richards swore hollowly and chokingly inside it. Richards needed both hands to work at lifting it off, and that freed Mal to concentrate on twisting the .22 out of Richards's gun hand. The man had let himself go but was still damned strong.

Mal pulled downward and worked at wresting the gun away. As long as Richards held on to the gun, the helmet would stay in place.

The handling of the plane changed. Mal sensed mechanical control. On automatic.

Mal turned his head to see the pilot start around from his compartment. Mal caught his eyes and shook his head.

The pilot looked at the gun, still in Richards's grip, and took a step toward the struggle.

Mal shook his head again.

The pilot hesitated, took a half step toward them.

Mal tried his damnedest but could not force the gun around to point at the pilot. He made his voice forceful. "Fly lower and depressurize before a shot tears the skin." He didn't know if explosive depressurization would come from a .22 shot.

But the pilot backed up and took his seat again. The plane returned to its human feel and the floor took on a slant.

Richards let go of the gun suddenly and Mal fell with it, rolling downhill. Richards quickly doffed the potty and looked around to bean Mal with it.

But his hair and brow dripped chemicals into his eyes, and he struck out at a seat he must have taken for a crouching man.

Mal took braced aim at Richards's right knee. "Drop the potty and sit down or I'll kneecap you."

Richards turned in a crouch of his own and tried to focus on Mal. Behind the bleary eyes the mind was sharp. He set the potty down and straightened slowly. He put his hands up and a smile on. "Hey, Harry, let's both cool it. I was supposed to deliver you alive, so there's no call for deadly force."

The pilot piped up. "Hell yes, let's all lighten up. All's I know, Im flying one listed and one unlisted passenger to a landing strip thirty miles south of Tucson. But if you got different ideas, hey. I'm leveling off now at two thousand. You want me to continue my heading?"

Mal thought a few seconds' worth. "For now."

"That's being smart." Richards shone his wet face in Mal's direction, but a bit off. "I'm going to be smart, too, and sit in my seat." He squeezed tears out and smiled reproachfully. "Geez, my eyes."

He felt his way back to his seat.

Mal's mouth twisted. Guy's sight was coming back but he was miming blindness. Real as his laryngitis. Mal eased past to the seats holding their flight bags. He kept an eye on Richards while unzipping Richards's bag.

Richards cocked an ear but did not turn around.

Mal had tape in his own bag, but Richards might have something better. Mal's free hand felt around inside. It came out with two sets of handcuffs. And a swiftly pocketed bonus of two spare clips for the .22.

Mal saw Richards stiffen at the rattle of the handcuffs, then lean forward in his seat and ease a hand down toward an ankle.

"Freeze."

Richards froze. "Just scratching."

"I know that itch. I feel it right now in my trigger finger on this .22 aimed at your spine. I'm going to hand you a pair of bracelets and I want you to snap them on. But listen first to how I want you to snap them on. I want you to cuff your right wrist to your left ankle."

"Man, how am I going to do that?"

"You rather I conk you and do it myself?"

"Ah, shit, give me the fucking cuffs."

Mal handed Richards one set and watched the cuffs go on, an awkward business for Richards, and listened to them snap into place. Then he lifted Richards's right trouser leg and impounded the holdout .22.

Stuck this into his waistband, covered Richards with the first while he one-handedly snapped the other set of cuffs into place. Locked one cuff onto the left wrist, pulled the hand down, locked the other cuff onto the right ankle. Stuck the first .22 in his waistband to balance the second.

He and Richards had flattened the chocolate bunny. Mal scuffed the remains aside and sat beside Richards. He beamed down at Richards. Uncle Phil always said politeness and cheerfulness were the best offense; nothing could seem more offensive to the other guy. "Now we can talk in comfort."

If looks could kill.

"Start with name, rank, and serial number."

Richards tightened his mouth.

Mal spoke softly. "What's your real handle and who do you work for?"

Richards stayed mute.

Mal kept to a near-whisper. "Relapse of laryngitis? Or

worrying about the audience?" He nodded in the pilot's direction. "Engines keep him from hearing the words. He'll think you're spilling your guts anyway."
If looks could cremate.
Mal murmured the words of "Danny Boy" as he went through Richards's pockets.
Richards stiffened at his touch; could be the guy was ticklish. But Richards didn't fight it more than maybe an involuntary squirm or two.
No wallet, no driver's license, no credit cards, no keys. Nearest thing to a credit card or a key was a piece of plastic Mal recognized as an entry card for an electronic lock; it had no logo other than a big U that cast shadows both ways. Could open up something interesting at the ranch, so Mal held on to it.
If looks could send him to deepest hell.
Money clip holding a grand in hundreds and twenties, and a folded circular.
He unfolded the circular and, on the nth time around of "the pipes, the pipes are play-ay-ing," just about the only words he knew, fell silent.
He caught a vicious smile on Richards's face.
The circular had two photos of Mal, with captions making him as Harry Pace in his old pose and as Philip Oom/Philip Zio in the forged-licenses pose.
Two had done a job on him, two snitches: Guido Palmieri and Freddy Friday.
But that could wait. Had to wait. This needed dealing with first.
At burst flush, as Uncle Phil would've worded it, he should fold. Forget overflying the ranch to dump Richards's body onto the reception committee. Order the pilot to change course. But head where?
Circular must've reached everyone Ramón Díez and Díez's connections such as Guido could think of. Circular must've

convinced Guido that Harry Pace was a goner anyway, so it was politic to sell him out—didn't make Guido any less of a snitch, but settle that later. Circular made Las Vegas too hot for him, L.A. too hot for him, Miami too hot for him, New York too hot for him.

Richards's smile had fattened. It wasted away fast as Mal glanced at him. Richard's gaze slid from Mal's eyes to Mal's fist.

Mal looked at the fist and saw he had crumpled the circular. He opened his hand and smoothed the circular and carefully refolded it and pocketed it, along with the money clip and the card. "Who's waiting for us?" No more whispering.

Richards's mouth tightened again.

Mal sighed. He got up and set himself, gripped Richards under the armpits, heaved him out of the seat to the floor, then rolled him to the door.

"Hard guy. Half a minute, I'm opening the door and shoving you out, see how hard you are. Betcha the ground's harder."

Richards looked anything but hard. Big-eyed, pale, boneless under the flesh. His words tripped over each other stampeding out. "Take it easy, Harry. You win. I got no reason to hold back. Might as well tell you anything you want to know. Sam's gonna want my ass anyway for fucking up."

"Sam Terminiello?"

"Check. He owns the ranch. He's there with his bodyguard and a show-girl friend. I was supposed to hand you over to Sam for a fellow from Miami."

"Will this fellow be there?"

"Don't know. It was all fixed up in a hurry, and it wasn't sure the fellow could be there in time to meet us. Whatever, some of his guys were coming to pick you up."

Mal returned to his seat to think.

"Hey, you gonna leave me here like this?"

"You rather go out the door?"

Richards shut up and let Mal think.

"Uh, excuse me, Mr. Pace." The pilot.

"What?"

"The landing strip on the ranch will be coming up pretty soon. Should I flick on my landing lights and put down? We have to put down somewhere."

Mal glanced out the window for a glimpse of the night. It was dark. "Yeah. Land on the landing strip. But not before I tell you to. I'd like you to circle the ranch so I get an idea of the layout."

Mal stood, stepped watchfully around Richards, and moved up to sit beside the pilot.

After one look at the two guns in Mal's belt, the pilot kept his eyes strictly on the instruments and the night ahead. "Right about now." The pilot flicked the landing lights on and off, then left them on.

Amber runway lights came on almost dead ahead.

Mal looked down. They expected him to arrive as Richards's prisoner. If, against expectations, he managed to take over in midflight, they would trust him, knowing the odds, to make the pilot head anywhere but here, get him far away fast. They would not expect this stones-in-the-head move.

Mal buckled up, rested hand on gun butt. "Remember, slow circle."

The pilot nodded.

"Hey, what about me?" Richards; Irish castrato.

Mal did not look around. "What about you?"

"Well, I'd kinda like to be buckled in."

"All of us have wish lists. I'd like to live a thousand years. Just brace yourself best you can. Our fly-boy will bring us in nice and easy." Mal looked at the pilot. "Right?"

The pilot watched his instruments and the points of light. "Right."

Mal ran a mind search. Forgetting anything? Just one, his carryon. But it would only get in the way, and it held nothing he couldn't replace and nothing that would lead to him. He could and should forget it.

"Circling." The pilot taking care the banking would not startle him.

Mal mapped in his brain what unfolded below. The landing strip. An executive jet, looked like, parked off the far end next to a shed, somebody under a work light refueling it from a cluster of drums, looking up and waving. Maybe quarter mile southeast, a long, low building picked itself out in window glow and outdoor lights; the ranch house. Then, what looked like corrals and stables against a background of vague hills. Then, as they continued the curve, a dim aura that stretched away.

Mal pointed. "What's that?"

"Interstate Nineteen. Running north and south, Tucson to Nogales on the border."

"Why not fly across the border? I know people in the Nogales on the Mex side." Richards, pitching eager to help but coming across worried. Troubled him Harry Pace would set foot in what they all knew was a trap. Figured Harry Pace envisioned a deal with Sam Terminiello, one that boded no great good for Richards.

Mal shook his head. Still casing, and the guy distracted him. "Shut up."

"If you count on using me and Haynes as hostages, human shields, forget it. Sam don't give a—"

Mal had unbuckled, come around to Richards, whipped out a .22, and hammered him silent. Mal resumed his seat and rebuckled.

"Which way's the nearest town?"

The pilot looked pale in the instrument glow. He pointed. "North a ways. Green Valley. Retirement community. Past their bedtime, but you can just make out the lights."

Mal nodded. "And the other way?"

"Mostly nothing. If you go off the highway on your right, you find your national forest and your ghost towns. If you go off on your left, you hit a lot more nothing and then an Indian reservation. We're coming up on the landing strip again. Do we land?"

Mal looked off at the ranch house. Action there. Tiny Nintendo figures.

Four silhouettes came out the door. One remained in the doorway, and three got into a toy four-wheel drive. Jeep Cherokee or its clone. It came to life. Its headlights beamed it toward the landing strip.

Three to one. Acceptable odds if he loaded the dice with surprise. Only the first throw, but one bet down at a time.

"We land."

The plane landed bumpily.

"It's the lousy surface. Heat and cold crack it up."

Mal patted the pilot's knee. "Long as *we* didn't crack up."

No complaint from Richards. Maybe Richards would never complain again.

Mal squeezed the pilot's knee, felt the tension. "Don't cut the engines." If it looked bad and Haynes didn't fall apart on him, they might still swing around and take right off.

The plane braked with a final lurch. Lousy surface, nervous pilot, or a combination.

Mal and the pilot sat waiting, maybe fifty feet from the executive jet and the guy in a flight jacket still pumping fuel. Way he looked at them suggested mild curiosity. The Jeep Cherokee pulled up twenty feet from the Cessna.

All three men climbed out. Three Uzis. All three wore them slung. A muscle beat in Mal's cheek. He committed himself.

Couldn't afford to worry about his back. Fast, before the three gunmen outside made sense of movement inside, Mal pistoled the pilot cold and sat him up straight.

Breathed deep, opened the door—stayed to one side as he did so. Took another deep breath, then moved into the opening, his hands out of sight behind him as if handcuffed so. Each hand held a .22.

The three men stood spread-footed in a row. His honor guard. They gave him the once-over.

"That the big hit man we been hearing so much about?"

"Can't be. Big hit man we been hearing so much about would never get suckered or come tame."

"Nah, it's some poor dumb shit got mistook for the big hit man."

The honor guard laughed.

He stumbled out of the plane as if someone had pushed him. He regained his balance and stopped ten feet from the men and jerked a resentful look back over his shoulder.

The three men laughed.

In another fraction of a second, they would wonder about Richards and the pilot and stop laughing.

Mal swung both .22s around front and pumped shots into surprised faces. Guy on the left managed to bring his Uzi to bear, but Mal gave him two more in the face before he could get a burst off. Four, five seconds the whole thing.

He whirled to line up the executive jet's pilot. The guy had seized up. Beautiful target. But Mal waved one hand calmingly and held his fire, gambling he could take the guy prisoner for a jet getaway after he finished here. However, the guy unlocked his muscles and made a break for it. Mal got one off, but, fucking .22, the shot just winged him, should've gone for a leg, and the guy ran around the shed and headed for the hills.

Mal swung back to the three. They lay crumpled, one still and two twitching. He gave each a finishing shot in the back of the head.

He looked over the Jeep Cherokee at the ranch house.

The figure in the doorway moved. Maybe the cough of the .22s had not carried, maybe the bulk of the Jeep Cherokee hid the fall of the three, but the figure had to have seen the pilot turn and run and realized *something* had happened. The figure turned to face inward with the slowness of numbing shock or uncertainty. Another, thicker figure joined it, and both looked Mal's way.

Too bad. With more time Mal could have set the plane to taxi toward the house, split attention, divide forces.

Maybe not so bad. This way, they could not be sure till he was nearly on them what was up and who the car was bringing to the house.

Mal grabbed the three Uzis, slung two over his shoulder, slid behind the wheel of the Jeep Cherokee, and rested the third in his lap. He released the brake, swung the vehicle around, and lowering the windows as he drove, headed for the ranch house.

By now the two in the doorway knew *something* had happened. They removed their silhouettes from the light, Mr. Thin vanishing into the framing darkness inside, Mr. Thick reaching as for a shoulder holster before merging with the framing darkness outside. The door closed.

Mal picked up speed.

He squinted ahead of the headlight beams. A shed roof, tiled, with posts of a gallery, ran the length of the ranch house.

A flash came from beside a post near the door.

The windshield starred. At a guess, a .45.

Mal swung the wheel left, then right.

Two more flashes. The Jeep took two more hits, in the metal.

Maybe two hundred yards. Mal kept his foot steady on the accelerator and told himself to hold on. He steered with his right hand, took the Uzi from his lap with his left, and held it out the window and swept fire—the full magazine—at the post the flashes had come from.

The post's midsection splintered apart, leaving a stump and a dangle. And probably a lot of torn flesh. No more flashes.

Fifty yards. The tile roof of the gallery sagged where the post no longer supported it. Mal veered the Jeep toward another post, opened the driver's door, and kicked himself out.

He hit the ground and rolled away. The Jeep's bumper snapped the post and the roof thundered down. Buried the Jeep, blocked the ranch house's front windows and door. Lots of broken tiles, big cloud of dust.

Mal pushed to his feet. He felt sore, especially where his Uzis and .22s had dug into his flesh, but didn't believe he had broken any bones.

He hobbled around to the back of the ranch house. Wide open kitchen door lit up a truck garden. Beyond the garden, a hill.

Forms scrambled away uphill through silver-edged scrub that stippled into night. Chicano chatter. The household staff; he hoped all of them.

He sent a burst into the air over them to encourage them.

Uzi ready, he edged toward the open door. A side stitch hit him just below the rib cage. He showed his teeth and moved on, reached the door, listened. Nothing. He swung inside. Nobody.

He stole to the kitchen's inner archway and listened. Nothing. He swung through. Somebody.

A small, gray-haired man sat in a big chair at a great natural-oak table, his back to Mal. Dining/living room. Archways left and right into halls, empty. The man faced a large window intently, though there would have been nothing to see even if it had been day because the fallen shed roof blocked everything. Just the grillwork window itself, dust still swirling in through overwrought iron scrolls and turning all the air milky in the light of milk-glass globes.

Mal had made no noise, far as he knew, but the man turned his head slowly. A cold cigar hung out of the left side of his mouth. It matched cold, wet eyes.

The eyes tracked Mal's face rather than the muzzle of the Uzi as Mal stepped around to the side.

The man was in shirtsleeves under a brocaded western

vest; a copper slide set with turquoise cinched a string tie. One bulge, in a vest pocket, but much too small to be even a derringer. "Sam Terminiello?"

The man did not answer.

"Ashamed of the name?"

The man spoke around the cigar. "Fuck you. I ain't ashamed of nothing. I'm Sam Terminiello. Mr. Terminiello to you."

"And I'm Mr. Pace." Mal pronounced it "Potch-ay." "I did some work for you a few years back."

"That so? I don't recall."

"Guy named Jack Sutro."

"I don't recall."

"I recall."

"You might be better off you remember to forget some things. Have a lot more room to think straight. Like you ain't doing yourself no good pointing that thing at me."

"That thing and a few more like it were pointing at me a few minutes ago."

"They wasn't my people."

"Your ranch, your guests."

Terminiello pulled the cigar out of his mouth and looked at it as though to see if he had chewed it soggy enough. He carefully laid it on the table. "All I know, they wanted to talk to you. Just talk. And look what you done." He gestured at the window. "This is the original adobe building. Goes back to the 1880s. I stabilized the walls and added a new roof. Now look what you done."

Mal glanced at the wall around the window. Falling roof had stressed the beams, had sent shock through the adobe wall. Sure a lot of cracks. "Yeah, I destabilized. Where's Ramón Díez?"

Terminiello poked a finger at the cigar on the table, giving it a nice spin that if you got close enough should be throwing a fine spray of spittle. "What makes you think he's here?"

"The people who weren't your people were his people."

"That don't have to mean he come here with them."

"I'm not going around and around with you. You don't give me a straight answer, no sense us talking."

Terminiello's eyes flickered. "Stay cool and connected. Last I heard, Díez ain't left Miami. His people was supposed to deliver you there. You wanna have it out with him, you gotta look in Miami." He lifted his left forearm to eye his gold wrist watch, then sent shining earnestness at Mal. "Tell you something else, because I done somebody enough of a favor—"

"Guido Palmieri?"

A slight shrug of one shoulder. "—and I don't need no more trouble here. I phoned the sheriff soon as you started shooting up the house. Forces of law and order on the way." A smile like a hairline fracture. "Cars and a pickup truck in the garage." He tilted his head to the left. He reached toward his vest pocket, then froze. "Going for the car keys."

Mal nodded but remained wary.

Terminiello slowly dipped thumb and forefinger into the vest pocket and came out with keys on a ring. He handed them to Mal. "You beat it right now, you got a head start on the sheriff."

Mal narrowed his eyes. "Sheriff's the last guy you'd call."

Terminiello looked honestly surprised. "I pay my taxes like any good citizen. What makes you think he's the last guy I call?"

"This." Mal didn't bother with the Uzi's selective fire for the one or two shots it would take. Quick and dirty. He tightened his finger on the trigger. "Say hello to Jack Sutro."

Terminiello's body jarred the cigar from the table.

The burst had an immediate echo: a woman's scream from a room down the left hallway.

Mal walked down the hall, shooting out locks and kicking in doors. Fastest and surest way to open doors and faze anyone inside. Three rooms empty: bathroom, steamy from a recent shower; two bedrooms.

Last, bedroom, woman on the floor, towels wrapping torso and hair. Not hit, cowering. Water-beaded and goosefleshed from the shower she had been enjoying when the world fell in on the ranch house. Open closet full of woman's things. More things on the bed, some still in a designer shopping bag, some spread out on the counterpane. Couple bottles on the dresser.

"Don't kill me."

Should've killed her already. Should waste her now. He gestured with the Uzi. "Up."

She got up, the body towel falling away. Young, rounded, tall brunette. Goose-bumped with terror.

"Where's Ramón Díez?"

"Who?"

He could see she had never heard the name; no actress. He gestured with the Uzi. "Into the closet."

Her eyes whitened, her head jerked away. Pleading look, trembling smile. "I'm scared of the dark. Got locked in a closet when I was two."

"You look like you survived that." He gestured closetward again with the Uzi. When she still hesitated, he pointed the Uzi at her belly button.

"Don't!" She whirled and plunged into the arms of the gowns and coats in the closet.

Mal kicked the door shut on her bare ass. He shouldered the brass bed around and up against the door, shoved a chair to fill the space between bed and wall. Take Wonder Woman to force the door open from the inside.

He started to go. Two bottles on the dresser caught his eye. He emptied the shopping bag on the bed, swept the bottles into the bag, and carried that with him.

Back through the central room where Terminiello lolled dead and into the other wing, to blast open three more bedrooms and another bathroom. All empty. Back through the central room for the kitchen way out, then around to the garage, an ex-stable.

He passed up a sleek sedan for the Ford Bronco; four-wheel drive for cross-country. He tried the keys Terminiello had given him, half-expecting Murphy Slaw, but one fitted the Bronco's ignition. When he turned it, though, the engine did not start. He nodded. Murphy Slaw. Then he saw the trouble. The driver had left the pickup in first gear. It would start only if it were in park or neutral. Okay. He tapped the fuel gage. Plenty of gas. Get going.

CHAPTER
15

Soon as the closet door slammed shut on her—on *them,* because she had company the scary man with all the guns didn't know about—Lauri Knowles teetered on the edge of giggling out of control.

Maybe this Latino big shot hiding behind her clothes—this slick-looking character that Sam had made a point of not introducing her to and that Sam had warned her to forget laying eyes on—thought he sensed a coming explosion of hysteria. She just suddenly found it funny was all, him hiding in here, but maybe he believed the lie about her being locked in a closet when she was two.

Because at once his clammy palm clamped itself over her mouth—same as it had cut her off when shots right inside the house, shots she recognized as shots, caused her to shriek.

What with the shower noise and her own singing—singing she pitched for Sam to hear in hopes he would holler in wonder "Hey, you can sing, too!" and drop everything to see about sticking her in a solo spot at the Punto Gordo; hey, that could make a nice act, Lauri Knowles clothed in rainbow-colors soap suds under, like, a waterfall or in maybe a bubble bath and the water sound covering her flat notes—what with all that, she had been only mildly puzzled by what sounded like fireworks.

Figured some Mexican fiesta she would try and remember to ask one of the servants about.

Then, when the roof out front caved in, she had been too scared to think anything but earthquake—and bumped into Slick running for cover, too. But now, after hearing all those shots and knowing they were shots and after seeing the man with all the guns, she felt, like, battle-hardened, a veteran, a—what the man with all the guns had called her—a survivor.

You got tired being scared; you got mad. You did not appreciate being muzzled and forced to feel scared all over again. If she had had on her stiletto heels, she would have spiked Slick's instep without thinking twice. Who did he think he was, roughing her up like this? Just wait, when she told Sam, Sam would—

But all that shooting. Did that mean Sam was—

Sweet Jesus.

Be thankful she *wasn't* wearing heels. Don't fight the hand over her mouth. Get in good with Slick.

Sam had only one bodyguard and Slick had, count 'em, three—though right now it didn't look like the whole lot of them had done a whole lot of good against the man with all the guns. Still, Slick could turn out to be the only game in town. She rubbed up against him, like, for luck.

Easy to feel excited. All that banging, and Slick running into her room and cutting off her shriek and hiding in her closet and begging her not to give him away, and then that man with all the guns busting in and nearly reaming her with that weapon.

Sweet Jesus.

She thought she felt Slick feel the excitement too. But he held them both still while the man with all the guns moved it sounded like furniture up against their closet door.

They waited, locked together, doing nothing but waiting.

Then the man with all the guns left. Slick still did not take his hand from her mouth. Only when she heard an engine start up somewhere did he relax himself and release her.

He shoved her aside and pushed at the door. It did not give. He put his shoulder to it and it gave some. "Come on, *puta,* help me open the door."

She wasn't sure what *puta* meant, though she sensed it wasn't nice, but she lent her weight and the door slowly forced the bed to crush the chair and let them squeeze out. He started to elbow her aside and get out first, then remembered his manners—or maybe the man with all the guns. He pressed the small of her back to push her through first. Then, when she was out and nothing happened, he followed.

She turned and looked at him.

Sweet Jesus.

He had pissed his pants. She felt giggles rise and covered her mouth and looked away.

Out of the corner of her eye she saw him glance down at himself, watched color flood his face.

She wanted to tell him, "Hey, honey, we all have accidents." But silence seemed better. Make believe it never happened, make him think of other things. Let her body talk for her of these other things. Move like she needed to stretch and twist after being shut up in a closet. If that didn't turn him on . . .

He reached back into the closet for her dressing gown.

Shit, a gentleman.

She made a face behind his back and turned to let him help her on with the robe. This faced her toward the dresser. She noticed that the two bottles were missing from the dresser top. The bottle of peroxide and the bottle of artificial suntan.

Looked like the man with all the guns meant to change his look. She raised her eyes to the mirror to tell Slick.

But instead of lifting the robe to her shoulders, he had pulled the belt out of the loops and let the robe fall to the floor and twisted the ends of the belt around his wrists and was in the act of swinging the belt over her head and yanking it around her neck.

Swee—

A dirt road ran from the ranch-house compound toward the distant highway. But Mal headed for the landing strip.

The executive jet's pilot had not come back; hose still connected drum to tank. Mal pulled up by the Cessna, but not so near that the Bronco would pick up the blood of the three Díez men and leave tread marks showing his direction.

Take two minutes. He parked so that the headlights washed over the three men and into the plane's cabin.

The three lay just as before. He climbed into the plane. Richards had no pulse. Haynes slumped in his seat and breathed shallowly. Mal sat him up again.

Mal pulled a .22 from his waistband and gave Haynes one between the eyes. He wiped his own prints off the gun and climbed out and rolled one of Díez's men's prints on it and planted it by the man's hand. He wiped his own prints off one of his Uzis and climbed back in and rolled Haynes's prints on it and dropped it just outside the plane door. He retrieved his carryon and got out of the plane. He used his other .22 to puncture the fuel tank. He watched the trickle, took the circular of himself from his pocket, touched the flame of his lighter to the circular, and tossed his burning likenesses into the pooling rivulet.

Shielding his face from the blaze, he trotted to the pickup. He hopped in and drove away from the landing strip and the ranch house, headlights probing the darkness.

Ramón had waited till the sound of the pickup faded. Then he left the bedroom, passed what had been Sam Terminiello, ventured out the kitchen door, crept around the house, and watched the pickup head for the landing strip. The *bastardo* seemed bent on flying away in the Cessna.

But the *bastardo* did not fly away. The *bastardo* looked busy around the Cessna. And then the Cessna went up in flames and the pickup drove away and diminished into darkness.

The fury in Ramón's blood hammered in his ears, drowning any roar from the flames. It felt good to feel fury. Fury washed away the shame of fear.

Ramón had not wanted Sam's cold eyes to see him run scared, so he had not fled out the back with the faithful retainers when he had the chance. Sam was as dead as the whore, so the fear would not have mattered. But Ramón knew his fear and hated its cause.

The *bastardo* Harry Pace owed him a thousand deaths.

Right now, though, Ramón had to think about disassociating himself from the carnage.

Sam had phoned the sheriff. If the sheriff's deputies came before Ramón got out of here, Ramón could lay it all on Harry Pace, the man who hit Felipe. Better, however, to keep from having to answer questions and explain ties. Especially with Sam no longer around to exert influence on the sheriff.

When the pickup's lights merged into the merest speck, Ramón jogged to the landing strip.

The three bodies and their shadows writhed in the Cessna's flames, and his fear grew again, conjuring up the pilot dead as well. He approached his executive jet at the refueling shed. He found the hose connected to the jet's fuel tank, but saw no body.

He got his wind back and shouted around at the night.

"Bill! Bill! Where are you?"

"Back here, Mr. Díez. I got hit." The voice came from behind the shed.

Ramón's heart nose-dived. "Is it serious?" A badly wounded pilot had no worth. "Can you fly?"

The pilot edged into view, his face crimson in the glow from the burning Cessna. He had hung his flight jacket from his shoulders like a cape and bound a torn-off shirtsleeve about his upper arm. "On one wing."

"Good."

"Yes, it's just a crease."

Ramón's sigh of relief turned into a gust of impatience. "We must leave at once."

"I didn't finish topping her off."

"Do we have enough fuel for Miami?"

The pilot creased his brow. "Just about."

"Then take the hose out and get her into the air."

"Yessir."

Took them only a few minutes to get airborne, but Ramón fumed an hour's worth.

Then he settled back in his seat as they rose toward the dawn. Next time, next time, the *bastardo* would not get away.

Bill put the plane on automatic and fingered the bullet hole in his leather jacket. "Bastard ruined my jacket."

Ramon nodded. "He has much to answer for."

Mal figured he had covered a mile when he saw that the executive jet's lights had come on. He watched it taxi onto the landing strip and roar aloft. He switched off the pickup's lights and braked and got out. He moved a dozen paces away from the pickup and planted his feet wide and faced the sky with an Uzi ready, just in case the pilot had a gun or grenades and, once in his own element, figured on a strafing or bombing run. But the jet kept right on going. And Mal saw why.

Down here on the ground, tiny flashing lights joined the blazing Cessna in the frame of his look back at the ranch. Forces of law and order speeding along the dirt road from the highway.

Two cars. One stopped at the ranch house, the other went on to the pillar of fire and smoke at the landing strip.

Spotlights made no sweep in his direction, so he did not think they had spotted him.

He got back into the pickup but kept it dark and held it to a painful crawl, climbing out and scouting ahead every hundred yards for rocks and gullies. Even after he put a hill between him and the ranch, he did not switch on his low beams for another half mile.

Mal put another hill behind him, then stopped for the night. Didn't know how to steer by the stars; didn't care to catch himself circling back to the ranch.

He felt too keyed up to drop off and anyway he wanted to get started on his head. Now was better than later. Racing with himself. Leaving the parking lights on, he stripped to the waist and poured half the bottle of peroxide onto his hair. He massaged it in, and a fizzy feeling crawled over his scalp as the peroxide went to work.

Then he got his travel kit out, clipped off his mustache and beard with manicure scissors, and slapped shaving foam on the stubble and shaved. He massaged hydrocortisone cream into his bruises.

He began to shiver; no matter how hot the days, the nights got cold out here. He took an undershirt and a sweater out of his carryon, and added them when he covered himself again. The layered look.

He yawned. He killed the lights and lay on his side, knees drawn up, on the seat. Not all that comfortable, but things on the ground stung or bit. Not all that warm either, but the heater wasted power better put to mileage.

Tail end of some animal sound woke him during the night. He sat up and listened. But it did not come again, so he could not tell what it had been. He changed sides and fell back to sleep and did not waken till first light struck through the windshield into the cab.

He rose and unkinked and looked in the mirror. His hair had lightened considerably but could stand more. He stripped to the waist again and poured the rest of the peroxide into his hair and rubbed well. He shivered again, but before changing into fresh shorts and getting fully dressed he slapped the show girl's liquid suntan over his face, neck, and hands. His stomach had started growling and he ate a granola bar from his carryon. Then it started talking lower down and he kicked a hole in the ground and relieved himself and kicked the dirt back over the hole.

Now for that mileage.

He had made a mess way back in Florida, and it still belonged to him to clean up after himself, filling and covering holes along the way.

Mal hit what might have been a cow trail or wagon track, a faint scar from the old days. It roughly, truly roughly, bore north, so he followed it. It should parallel the highway, Mal thought, and he kept hoping to glimpse that ribbon and find a way to swing over.

Five miles along, he spotted the highway. Twice he had to backtrack when he came near and met a steep drop or a sheer face. Third time looked barely doable, but he was through being balked. The pickup groaned some, but it bucked its way down and up onto the highway.

Traffic was light, and he swung right on. Headed north. Signs confirmed: Tucson thataway.

Not much to see along the way, but all he cared about was miles. Once, off the highway and on the left, he saw an Indian kid tending sheep.

So a little later on, when cars slowed and bunched up ahead, he thought *sheep* first thing. But oncoming traffic flowed freely, so the problem could not be a flock crossing the road.

Mal smelled roadblock.

He pulled over onto the shoulder. He got out and raised

the hood to make the works under it seem the reason for pulling over. Then he stepped farther out on the shoulder and got a good look up the line.

Pair of cops and their flashing patrol car, checking northbound traffic. The sheriff had not bought a shoot-out between the people on the ranch and the people on the plane. Maybe the show girl had described Mal and maybe the servants had drifted back and reported the pickup missing.

Messed up again. Should've knocked the show girl off. The Lupe syndrome. Ever since running into Lupe and getting involved . . .

Uncle Phil had a saying that hit the mark: "What saves us is we can't carry out all our good intentions." Wouldn't happen again.

He returned to the cab for the field glasses in his carryon and eyed the cops. Getting younger every year. The more untried, the likelier to use guns instead of brains, and to use them wilder. These guys, even if they jerked their pieces out and crouched behind their car as soon as they spotted the pickup moving up the line and made the plates, he could take them with his Uzis.

But he did not need the all-out manhunt that would follow. Two dead cops would generate heat the way seven dead racket guys on the ranch never would.

He put the hood down and got back into the cab and put the field glasses away. He left the carryon unzipped so that he could yank out his Uzis fast if the cops spotted him turning away from the roadblock and gave chase. He waited for a bubble in the traffic flow, then made a U-turn.

The cars he cut in front of shielded his move; the rearview mirror showed no sign of alarm or pursuit. He swung off on the first dirt road to come along, a couple miles down the highway. It had no sign to tell where it led; he would follow it as long as it went if it did not swing south, then he would turn north. Sooner or later he would have to hit Interstate 10, which he had taken on his drive from L.A. to Miami.

A mile into the wasteland, he saw his first habitation, a derelict bus down on its axles. Wind had sandblasted it in tree-ring stages to the primer; with the right equation, you could figure man-made materials' length of exposure to natural forces. Most of its windows had plywood or cardboard in place of glass.

An old Indian sat cross-legged on a blanket on the ground beside the steps. Another blanket shawled the Indian, and a third blanket hung as a door replacement. The Indian wore a red bandanna twisted into a headband over long, straight, silver locks. Dark sunglasses tracked the pickup. Mal could not tell the Indian's sex.

Mal let the pickup roll to a stop alongside the motorless home. Doubleparking in the desert. He looked for a stir inside the bus, for a face at one of the good windows. But the Indian seemed to be by his or her lonesome. Mal set the brake and climbed out, with just the .22 in his waistband under his loose jacket.

Each step raised a puff of gray dust, dust that took a death grip on Mal's shoes and pant bottoms. The dark glasses filled with sky as the Indian's head lifted at Mal's footfalls.

"Hi." It rasped out of Mal's dry throat.

A moment, then the pieces of sky lightened and darkened with the Indian's nod.

"I need water." Nothing. "You got water?" Still nothing. "*Agua.*" Mal poured his thumb into his mouth.

"Ah." A claw walked out of the blanket shawl and pointed around to the back of the bus.

There, a dipper sat in a bucket that rested on a wooden lid laid on an oil drum in the meager shade of a tin awning nailed and braced to the bus.

The oil drum held a few inches of water. Overdue for a refill. Could mean running into the replenisher.

Mal filled the dipper. In oaters, the white hats watered their mounts first—*out* of the white hats if they had to. Fuck that. He was a no-hat. He chugalugged the dipperful, then leaned forward and poured the second dipperful over his head and face. Now he saw to his pickup. Poured half a bucketful into the radiator. Sloshed the rest over the windshield to sluice away the bugs and the dust.

The Indian's face grew more wooden. The dark glasses fixed on Mal.

Mal switched the windshield wipers on for a minute. At least he had a cleaner smear to look through. He put the lid, the bucket, and the dipper back where he'd found them.

He peeled off one of Richards's hundred-dollar bills and walked over to the old Indian and stuck the bill out in front of the wooden face. "Thanks for the water."

The old Indian said nothing and made no move to take the bill. Maybe the offer of money was an insult. Old Indian owned nothing worth anything but blankets, prize possession a threadbare security blanket of pride. Mal could respect that. With a shrug he restored the bill to the wad. "Well, thanks. *Gracias.*"

The Indian nodded.

Sitting there like the fixed center of the world. Never been a day's walk from this spot. Some life.

Mal felt choked by the wide open spaces all around, weighed down by the limitless sky. Be good to get inside the air-cooled cab of the pickup and the hell away from here. But with the sun beating straight down on his head, and with no certainty that he had kept his bearing, he needed direction.

"Tucson which way?"

"Tucson?"

"Yes. *Sí.* Tucson."

The claw came out again and pointed in roughly the direction Mal had been heading.

"*Gracias.*"

The Indian nodded.

About to turn and go, Mal caught sight of himself in the dark glasses. Shit. The old Indian could describe the driver of the pickup as a blond white man with a deep tan.

Mal drew his .22 and chambered a round. "Sorry."

The old Indian stiffened. The claw slowly lifted to the sunglasses as though for a last naked look at the world and at the blond white man with the deep tan who would end the world for the old Indian. Then the claw stopped short and dropped to the lap and the Indian just sat waiting.

Mal made it a quick, clean kill.

The old Indian toppled sideways off the blanket. The sunglasses came unhooked and glaucous eyes stared the sun down.

Mal went cold all over. Why the fuck hadn't the old Indian gone ahead and shown him the blind eyes, eyes that had not registered a blond white man with a deep tan? Why hadn't the old Indian spoken up? Mal would have thought it safe to spare the old Indian.

Then Mal got it. The old Indian did not want pity, would not beg. Mal could respect that.

He climbed into his pickup and drove away. He felt a bit better about it, but he kept saying, "Shit shit shit shit shit," and hitting his fist on his knee.

A few miles on, he hit a road that had signs pointing the way to Tucson. He stopped outside Tucson in what looked like the right neighborhood and packed the Uzis and the .22 into his carryon and wiped all prints off the pickup before abandoning it to the strippers. He caught buses to the center of town. He shopped at a drugstore for peroxide and liquid suntan and located the Greyhound office and bought a one-way ticket to Las Vegas. He boarded the Greyhound bus and touched up his bleach and tan at comfort stops along the way.

CHAPTER 16

Guido Palmieri had a close call when coverage of the S-Bar-T Ranch Massacre flashed onto the tube. Guido liked to sit in a corner of the restaurant kitchen and watch the seven o'clock news on a black-and-white set while he ate; other people's woes lent savor; scenes of disaster sharpened his appetite. Guido started choking on a forkful of veal and the waiter gave him the Heimlich maneuver so enthusiastically that Guido had to reach back to the guy's balls to signal *Leggo* after the veal plug popped out.

After he got his wind back, Guido went down to the basement and slipped behind the boiler and through a concealed door into the basement next door. This put him inside a small room that held a desk and a chair and a phone. He could stay in the small room and use the phone or he could pass through other doors and other basements and come out on the side street at the other end of the block. By virtue of various corporate entities, Guido owned the block.

This time he used the phone. He sat down gingerly—*Fucking waiter prolly cracked some ribs*—opened a desk drawer, and took out a sheet of printout with a column of initials and a matching column of ten-digit numbers with commas in the right places and with an eleven-digit bottom line opposite the word TOTAL. Like a Chase Manhattan balance. His business should only be so good. If you went to the trouble of adding it all up, and got it right, you would find the bottom line correct. His personal accountant had a spreadsheet program, so no problem to make it come out correct whatever number you inserted or deleted. Guido ran his sauce-stained forefinger down the initials to F.T., which really stood for T.F., and along the green stripe to the matching number, which was also written in reverse order. He picked up the phone receiver and poked 1, then dialed the number backwards.

He started shouting as soon as the other phone answered, then realized he was talking on top of an answering-machine greeting, and with great difficulty held himself to a mutter till the go-ahead-and-leave-your-message beep. He didn't leave his name and number as the greeting asked, just said, "Get back to me and tell me the burned body in the handcuffs is Harry Pace. If you don't, I'll know it's you, you fucking fuck-up."

He slammed the receiver down, thought a minute, then ran his finger down the list to L.M. and across to the number and lifted the receiver again and dialed.

The phone answered on the tenth ring. Miguel Luqué didn't identify himself, but Guido recognized the voice and identified himself as "a friend in Brooklyn."

"I don't know if you seen it on the news about what happened in Arizona?"

"The Grand Canyon fell in?"

"No, that I didn't see. No, this is about Sam T. and a lot of people got knocked off on his ranch out there."

After a pause, "I haven't been watching the news, but I hear something bad happened to Sam T. and his cohorts."

"Yeah, Sam and his cahoots is wiped out. I just wanna pass on I hear it was a Ramón Díez operation went sour. Díez set something up and it backfired. I hate to say it, but I think the guy's falling apart, so if you're innarested you might wanna think about picking up the pieces."

Another thoughtful pause. "And you'd sweep them my way?"

"You're thinking like I'm thinking, why not?"

"I'll certainly be thinking."

"Ciao."

"*Hasta luego.*"

Guido hung up and sat thinking. Thinking and the wine of the half-finished meal made him doze off. The ringing of the phone shook him awake.

The voice of Ramón Díez. "Mr. P.? This is your friend in Miami."

"Ah. That's a sigh of relief. I thought you might be one of the bodies they didn't make yet out in Arizona."

"You heard about that?"

"I like to keep up with what goes on in the world."

"Then maybe you can tell me just what happened—and why?"

"Me? You're the guy that was right on the spot."

"What gave you that idea? I never left Miami."

"Then that makes two of us like to know just what went wrong."

"I have been thinking about that. One might hazard that somebody at your end tipped Harry Pace off. But I wouldn't like to think there was a cross. I'd be very . . . cross."

"Works both ways, friend. I wouldn't like to think I was set up to set Sam up. Sam has friends could look cross-eyed at me. So don't just look at it from your point of view. Why does it have to be my end? Why not Sam's end? Or your end?"

"You have a point."

"Well, when people start pointing fingers."

"Yes, that's not constructive. Let's think positively, show good faith."

"Like how?"

"If your people spot Harry Pace, I'd be grateful to know."

"I been trying to think positive, like that was Harry they found cremated in the plane cuffed. But if it ain't, and I hear from him or about him, I'll let you know right away."

"That would certainly lay doubts to rest."

"And Harry."

"And Harry. *Bueno,* Mr. P. I'll be waiting to hear from you."

"Fine, Mr. D. Say, you hear anything about the Grand Canyon fell in?"

"No. How can a hole fall in on itself? Oh, I see. You make a joke."

Guido blinked. "Haha. Yeah, I make a joke."

Mal thought he saw Lupe in the window he sat next to, but it turned out to be the faint reflection of the old woman in the seat across the aisle. She looked nothing like Lupe, so he figured it must've been a carryover from the dream he was dreaming when the bus jolted him awake with one of its abrupt brake hisses in stop-and-go city traffic. Not that he remembered the dream, only that it left him with a sense of loss. He had never possessed Lupe and could come up with *real* other losses in his life, so he couldn't even be sure he had been dreaming of Lupe. Then why did he feel so sure he had seen Lupe? Something Uncle Phil once said: "It's like an apparition of the Virgin Mary. You have to believe it to see it."

They were in Flagstaff, and the driver announced a comfort stop. Mal got out with a few others to touch up his hair and skin, and that's when he saw his first headlines. EIGHT SLAUGHTERED ON MOB RANCH!

Eight? That had a wrong ring. He tallied: the man he knew as Richards, the pilot Haynes, Díez's trio, Sam's one, Sam. Seven.

He had winged the jet pilot, not wasted him. Unless the pilot had bled to death afterward. He had stitched the air above the fleeing servants, not sprayed them. Unless one of them had somehow stopped a slug. He bought a paper.

Shit. Number eight was the Las Vegas show girl. Lauri Knowles, her name.

He felt a twinge. She had *said* she was afraid of getting locked in a closet. He read on, expecting to see that she had died of fright in the closet.

But according to the reporter's sources, Lauri Knowles had been strangled to death with the cord of her dressing gown in the middle of the room.

Mal stared unseeingly at the newsprint. Who had let her out and then strangled her?

One or more of the servants, if any snuck back and jumped at the chance to rape or loot? Unlikely, in their state of mind and in the time frame, shots still going off almost up to the deputies' lights and sirens. Then who?

Ramón.

In the closet.

The fucker had been there all along. Explained the show girl's uneagerness to enter the closet. Not what Uncle Phil, who had it, called Santa Claustrophobia, fear of tight places. She just did not know if she could squeeze in with Ramón already inside, feared that would give Ramón's presence away and trigger the Uzi. Poor bitch had that figured right.

Mal understood why Ramón would knock her off. To seal her lips. To erase her memory of him hiding. To take out on *someone* his rage at Harry Pace. All of the above. Bottom line, because she was there.

It took Mal from Flagstaff to Kingman to come down from the rage *he* felt. Look at all that happened because he made the mistake of not taking Ramón out way back in Miami when he had the chance, say at the entrance to Banco de los Inocentes. Look how he could have ended it all only a matter of hours ago back on the ranch with one burst into the closet if only he had had the sense to make sure of the closet.

Instead, Ramón had lived to skip on the jet and by now was orchestrating another attempt to get Harry Pace.

A scattered three of Mal's fellow passengers sat marching to different Walkmans and he fought down the urge to grab one for an update of the S-Bar-T Ranch Massacre story. At the Kingman stop, he bought the local paper.

Nothing new.

Cops still unable or unready to give names to the two charred corpses in the burnt Cessna, though records at Hughes Airport in Las Vegas listed the pilot as Daniel Haynes.

No mention of Ramón Díez. The servants had not drifted back—or had but no-savvied.

The left side of the front page headlined a juicy local sex scandal, but Mal refolded the paper and stuck it into the crack between seat and window and dozed off.

He snapped awake as the bus pulled into the Las Vegas bus terminal.

This time the vision reflected in his window was clearer because night had fallen and he did not mistake it for Lupe.

It was recognizable at once as the old lady across the aisle. He watched her work the kinks out of her fingers like a piano virtuoso about to attack a concert's flashy first piece. Just let her at those one-armed bandits.

Mal stood up and shouldered his carryon and beat her into the aisle and off the bus. In case anyone watched who got off buses, Mal waited at the foot of the steps to help the old lady down and walked with her a ways. A watcher looking for Harry Pace would hardly see him as part of this couple.

They parted politely at the exit, the old lady taking a taxi to a casino hotel and Mal making for the bank of pay phones.

Mal dialed the L.A. area code and his home number. He heard the first ring, then his greeting played. He waited for the first beep after his greeting, then pressed the 3 button. He held pressure on the 3 button till he heard the low tone. The answering machine played the messages. He heard a repeat of Guido Palmieri telling him the number to call about the phony Ajay Richards hit. Mal wrote it down.

170

He held on, just in case. Another beep, and a fresh message played.

"I have the girl. Come on down. See if your luck holds."

Time stopped. The world froze. He did not need to hear the name or to have heard the voice before to know that that had been Ramón Díez speaking.

No further messages.

The line hummed while Mal thought. He caught himself mentally harmonizing "Danny Boy." Shit, the word wasn't "play-ay-ing"; it went, "The pipes, the pipes are caw-aw-ling." He and Ramon weren't play-ay-ing. And Ramón thought Ramón was caw-aw-ling the tune. The tune was Lupe.

To everything a season. A time for surgery and a time for butchery. Mal jiggled the switch and dialed the number Guido had given him.

It answered on the fourth ring. The Irish tenor told him he had reached the number and to leave a name and a message at the beep. Mal hung up.

Mal frowned, then smiled, then fed the slot and dialed the number again.

He waited for the first beep after the greeting and pressed the 1 button. He held it down but no low tone followed. He hung up and tried again, this time holding down the 2 button. No luck. He began to think the guy's answering machine lacked that feature, but kept trying. He went through the motions with the 9 button. Jackpot.

Guido Palmieri's voice. *Get back to me and tell me the burned body in the handcuffs is Harry Pace. If you don't, I'll know it's you, you fucking fuck-up.*

Mal nodded, smiling a thin smile. He couldn't belie his eaves, as Uncle Phil would've said. One way or another, Guido had to pay for setting him up.

A beep, then a woman's voice. *I'm telling you, Tim, this lady is pissed off. You stood me up for the last time. You swore you'd let me know if you couldn't make it, so I waited a whole hour for you to pick me up before I left. And let me tell you, I didn't go home alone. So there.*

Mal hung on, but that was it. He hung up. Thought some more.

Ajay Richards's real name was Tim something. Tim apparently lived alone. Tim definitely would not be returning home. And Mal needed a base.

Mal reached into his pocket and fingered the plastic card he had taken from Tim. For an electronic door opener; just might open Tim's front door. Opened *something* worth looking into, and Tim's place would be the place to start. If he knew where Tim's place was.

He found a Las Vegas directory and cracked it at the white pages. No listing for an Ajay Richards, no Richards at all with the phone number he had called. That would've been too easy. He turned to the yellow pages. Looked up Detective Agencies and learned they were under Investigators. He walked his fingers to Investigators. Display ads connoted greatest resources. He phoned Inquiries Unltd. A recorded voice said it was closed for the day but offered an emergency number. He hung up and phoned Ace Clubb Investigative Associates.

A falsely bright live voice answered, reminding him of Uncle Phil's. It told him it was Ace Clubb himself speaking, it assured him Ace Clubb would be in the office for another hour, asked him who Ace Clubb should be expecting, and it gave him directions from the bus terminal to the office on E. Charleston Boulevard. Under cover of his body, Mal tore out the street-map page.

Through the glass of the outer door the suite looked dark, and Mal thought Ace Clubb had changed his mind about staying or had gone on an emergency call. But when Mal turned the knob and pushed, the door opened and Clubb's voice told him to come right on in.

Mal went right on into the one lighted office and found the

man behind a desk and behind a file folder. The man closed the folder and put it down.

Ace Clubb's jaw was wide and fleshy, a pit bull's. His brow, too, was a pit bull's, but it showed signs of uncreasing as the jaw stretched even wider in a smile.

Clubb waved Mal to the client's chair. "Yes, sir. You're the gentleman called me half an hour ago?"

"I called you eighteen minutes ago."

"Do I have the name right? Ajay Richards?"

"That's the name I gave you."

"I gather you're from out of town?"

"I guess you could gather that from the bus-terminal call and from my carryon."

The pit-bull jaw held its grip on the smile. "How can I help you, Mr. Richards?"

"You have Cole's reverse phone directories for the Las Vegas area?"

Clubb held the smile but gave him a hard stare. "If you're looking to locate a name and address from a telephone number, we have our methods."

"I'd like to look up a number."

"This isn't a public library or a reading room."

"How much to let me look up a number?"

All traces of smile faded from Clubb's face.

"I'm not sure I appreciate the implications of that. If you want a name and address, we can find it for you. We respect confidentiality. We keep our findings secret from everyone but the client. We're bonded. Our integrity has never been questioned."

Could've just said no.

"How much for a minute's private look into the directory?"

"You realize this is a highly irregular way of going about it."

"Figure that in."

Clubb eyed him sourly. "One hundred dollars a minute."

"Fair enough."

"In advance."

Mal took out a hundred and handed it to Clubb. Clubb held the bill up to the light and then folded it and put it away. "I take it you won't need a receipt."

"You take it right."

Clubb got up. A build to match the face. He picked up the folder he had been studying when Mal came in and filed it in the top drawer of his cabinet and locked the drawer.

Mal said nothing about not appreciating the implications of that.

Clubb went into another room and came back with a Cole's for Las Vegas. It looked virginal. "Latest edition. Just came." He set it in front of Mal. "I'll leave you alone with it in here for one minute." He looked at his watch and padded away again into the dim outer reaches.

Mal opened the directory and ran down the phone number and learned the West Bonanza Road address of a Timothy Farrell. As he closed the book, he noticed the fresh crease in the spine that would show he had cracked it at the 555-2000s; he knew that Clubb might raise a print where Mal's finger had stopped and rested. Mal opened the directory again at the same place and rubbed the heel of his palm over both pages to smear any prints and then underscored with a thumbnail the first Bonanza Road address listing he came to on the page facing Tim's—a residence on East Bonanza in the name of an Owen Nellis. Then he closed the book for good and still had time to get up and meet Clubb in the doorway as the minute expired and Clubb came back in.

"Find what you wanted?"

"Yes, thanks."

Clubb nodded and resumed his seat and was tapping his fingers lightly on the Cole's as Mal left.

The elevator car Mal had come up on still waited at the

floor. In the elevator, he got out the street map and looked up Bonanza Road. North of Charleston Boulevard and running parallel. The map did not say whether Bonanza was commercial or residential or a mix, but Las Vegas patrol cops would double-o a guy walking any street at this hour with a carryon over his shoulder. By the time the elevator let him out on the ground floor, he had decided to taxi to Tim's.

He walked to the nearest corner. It took him five minutes to flag down a cruising cab.

The cabbie got going before Mal could give him the destination. "McCarran?"

Because of the McCarryon. "No. The thirty-one-hundred block West Bonanza Road."

"Gotcha." The cab waited its chance and made a U-turn.

Mal did not move his head, just slid his eyes, as they swung past the building he had just left. He did not want Clubb to know he had spotted Clubb.

The pit bull sat hunched over the steering wheel of a black sedan that pulled out of the building's parking lot after the cab had gone half a block and that now made a U-turn to follow the cab.

"Oh, shit," Mal muttered.

The cabbie stiffened. "Say what?"

"Nothing. I just realized I left the lights on."

"Want to go back? I'll wait."

"Keep going. So they burn all night. It's not like I'll be away a month."

"Yeah, what the hell. In this town, you're going to lose money whatever you do."

They turned north, and Mal moved to correct course before they hit Bonanza. "Did I say West Bonanza? I mean East Bonanza."

"No problem. The meter's running, so whatever you say."

The sedan tailed the cab north for a couple of blocks, then hung a right.

Maybe Clubb, having detected the underscored listing, felt sure he knew where his galling client was headed and had knocked off for the night, confident he could satisfy his curiosity at his leisure.

But Mal kept an eye out after they turned onto East Bonanza Road. The cab slowed down as they neared the thirty-one hundreds.

"Tell me when."

They came up on the Nellis address, a garden-apartment complex, and Mal was about to give the cabbie another course correction. Then he spotted the black sedan in a slot of the parking spaces out front.

Clubb had taken a shortcut, beaten him there, and parked with the lights out and his head below the driver's window. But the window was open. Who parked for the night with a window open?

"Oh, shit."

"Don't tell me you want to go back *now?*"

"No. Drop me off here."

The cab pulled up at the curb just past the driveway. Mal paid the cabbie and waited for the red taillights to disappear before he unzipped his bag enough to reach in and palm his .22.

Clubb would be patting himself on the wrinkled back of his neck. *Having anticipated subject's destination and established a stakeout of the Nellis address, observed subject's further suspicious behavior upon his arrival at said address. Subject loitered at the curb after his taxi departed. Subject then proceeded across parking area toward nearest entrance, all the while looking left and right, but suddenly swerved and*

stepped up behind the driver's window and said, "Hello," and when Clubb straightened with a sheepish smile under the pit-bull clothing, Mal shot him in back of the ear.

Mal reached in and pushed Clubb away from the door so that the body would not fall out when he opened the door.

Then he opened the door and shoved the body all the way over to the passenger side. He got in behind the wheel and closed the door.

He made sure Clubb had no pulse, then patted the body down. He retrieved the hundred he had paid Clubb and pocketed it, along with the couple hundred in tens and twenties he found in Clubb's wallet. He drew an FIE .38 caliber derringer from Clubb's shoulder holster and stowed it in the carryon. He had already held on to the .22 too long; it tied him to the S-Bar-T Ranch. Same went for the Uzis, but their usefulness outweighed their taint and he would hold on to them till he could replace them. He wiped off the .22, looked around, and spotted the complex's stack of trash bags in a niche.

But the first-floor window directly above the packaged midden was lit, and human shadows moved across the curtain.

The cough of the .22 had not penetrated the window, but any rustling under the window might make someone look out and see something more than a dog or a rat. Mal nestled the .22 in the holster on the body. That at least got it out of the way for now.

He took the keys from the ignition and went to see if the trunk had room for the body.

Serendipity, Murphy-style. Too much eavesdropping and recording equipment and a large tool chest and a key-duplicating machine in addition to the spare tire. He started to close the trunk lid, then stopped.

He opened the tool chest. Everything from the smallest of steel files to the largest of bolt cutters, with door rams and jimmies in between.

All *right*. He grabbed screwdrivers and pliers and removed a license plate apiece from three nearby cars. Lots of cars riding around all over the place with one plate missing; cops hardly ever stopped you for that even if you didn't trouble to fashion a cardboard temporary replacement for a missing front plate and prop it inside the windshield; he would trouble.

He put the tools back; he slid the three plates in as well—for use outside Arizona, in case the car owners reported the thefts locally.

He closed the trunk and got back into the car and buckled Clubb up to keep him from flopping and pulled out of the garden apartments. He headed west to Timothy Farrell's address.

It picked itself out of the night in blue neon script: TIM'S LOUNGE. The dark apartment over it had to be where Tim lived. A low stone wall edged the street side of the property's parking lot. As Mal pulled into the parking lot, he picked up the throb of a rhythm section and a shrill laugh; Tim seemed to be thriving in the lounge line and should have stuck to it and not branched out.

First, to get rid of Clubb. Mal had parked in the darkest corner of the lot, but the nearest lamppost still shed too much light. He opened the trunk and got out a jimmy and pried a stone from the wall. Took him three throws to put the light out. He waited, but no one had heard the glass shatter or the stone fall back down and bounce off a car roof.

He jimmied open the trunk of the car next to his. Lots of room. He unbuckled Clubb and transferred him to the other car's trunk. The catch had sprung, and he had to give the lid bottom a hard tap to make it jam.

When he returned to his car to close the passenger door, a sheet of paper on the ground just outside the door caught his eye; he felt sure it had not been there when he opened the door. He picked it up and knew what it was even before he raised it to see it by the car's interior light.

One of Ramón's circulars depicting Harry Pace and Philip Oom/Philip Zio.

Must've lain on the passenger side of the seat and got moved to the seat-door interface when Mal shoved Clubb over, then got slid to the ground unnoticed when Mal lifted Clubb out. Thing like that could stop a guy's heart.

Mal pocketed the circular, got in and closed the door, then scooted over and just sat behind the wheel in the dark, thinking.

So it had been more than idle curiosity on Clubb's part. Clubb had made him—or at least had strong suspicions that way.

The word was really out. If a guy he picked at random was onto him, he was safe nowhere.

That meant he had nothing to lose, whatever he did.

Mal stirred himself and shifted the car to the other end of the lot. He got out again.

He wore vinyl exam gloves and carried the jimmy up his sleeve and the .38 derringer in his left coat pocket and his flashlight in his right coat pocket as he walked over to the building.

The entrance to the upstairs apartment stood at the building's near side. The door had a regulation lock, so the electronic card in his pocket stayed in his pocket. He looked for alarm wiring, saw none, then worked the jimmy between the door and the jamb.

The sounds from within the lounge suddenly swelled and he froze. Then, even before the sounds died down again, he jerked the jimmy free and stuck it up his sleeve and made himself part of the building.

A wraparound couple came in sight, making for the parking area.

He waited while they ambled to their car as if they were in a slow-motion instant replay of a three-legged race.

And while they French-kissed in the front seat.

And while they finally backed out and swung away. Too bad their car wasn't the one with Clubb in the trunk.

He worked the jimmy into place again and put his weight into levering it. The door splintered open.

The sounds of the lounge swelled. He listened over and

under the sounds for a second, but if he had set anything off it was a silent alarm.

His flashlight beam flew upstairs to a door that would lead into Tim's apartment. The beam swung back down and swept along a short hall to a door that would lead into Tim's Lounge, either directly or through a storage room. He stepped inside and pulled the outer door shut and chased the beam upstairs.

He forced the apartment door open and made a quick tour of the place, rooms *and* closets, to make sure there would be no surprises.

The lady on Tim's answering machine could have a key and be waiting here to spring herself on Tim.

Mal was happy for her that she wasn't, that she hadn't gone back on her anger, that she didn't have to die. Joy uncoffinned, Uncle Phil would've said.

The floor throbbed to the beat from below. Drive Mal crazy to live over that. He blocked the noise from his mind while he searched. He would know what he was looking for when he found it. Anything that strengthened him, informed him, or furthered him would satisfy him.

He homed in on an alcove that held a locked rolltop desk. He jimmied it open.

Checkbook. Bank statements, latest balance fifteen hundred and change. Two sets of bills with canceled checks neatly stapled to them. One set personal: safe deposit, utilities, charge cards, and the like. Other set lounge business: linens, bar supplies, salaries, and the like.

He riffled through the personal-business stuff, paused at a statement of charges for rental of self-storage space, rubber-stamped PAID IN FULL. The logo stopped him: U casting shadows both ways; matched the one on the card in his pocket. The letterhead spelled it out: U-NIVERSAL U-NIT U-TILITY, SELF-STORAGE AND MINI-STORAGE, 24-HR. ACCESS, CLIMATE-CONTROLLED. The statement supplied the address, right here on West Bonanza, couple blocks farther west. The statement itemized the charge, one 10' × 25' room, #16. He pocketed the receipted bill and the check stapled to it, for an example of Timothy Farrell's signature in case he had to sign in. At a glance, simple enough to forge: block-letter *T* and a squiggle, block-letter *F* and a squiggle.

No sense pushing his luck by sticking around beyond response time.

He raised the beam of the flashlight for a farewell sweep of the walls. He held on a framed photo of Timothy Farrell, a.k.a. Ajay Richards, and moved in for a close-up.

Twenty years younger, in police uniform, shield number 4230.

Knew it. Richards/Farrell had dressed well, but the clothes had not unmade the cop.

The booming from below cut off at the end of a number. Or at what passed for the end these days. Numbers did not have a beginning, a middle, and an end anymore; they had a beginning that went on and on over and over till even the musicians got tired of the whole thing.

Mal raced out and downstairs through the silence as lightly as he could, even though the silence was not absolute. Apparently lightly enough—or the hum of conversation covered him—because another number began before he reached the outer door.

He slowed to a walk but took long strides. Noticed that the car with Clubb in the trunk had gone. Made it to his car without seeing anyone or anyone seeing him as far as he could tell, pulled out of the lot, headed west. Stripped off his gloves as he drove.

None too soon. A block ahead, rounding the corner and coming his way, a squad car flashed its lights but made a silent approach. So his break-in had registered on some sensor after all.

He lightened his foot on the gas, switched on the stereo, punched the tape deck, turned the volume way up on what proved to be country rock, steered with his right hand, reached his left arm out the window to beat time with his hand on the roof.

His arm screened his face from the cops in the squad car as the squad car sped on by toward Tim's Lounge without a second look at him.

Two blocks along, the UUU building loomed on the right, a floodlight washing out the already-faded colors of its sign. Mal pulled into its parking lot around back, glad to get his car off the streets and out of sight while cops were on the Tim's Lounge break-in.

The break-in would probably lead them to make the connection between Timothy Farrell and the burned corpse at the S-Bar-T sooner than they otherwise would've. Mal hoped that was a worthwhile trade-off for what he found here.

He closed the car window and locked the door. Only one other car here, in a RESERVED PARKING slot. Old, rust-edged; replacement fender not yet painted or weathered to match. Safe bet it belonged to the night-shift security person.

Loading platform and delivery entrance back here, but securely locked from inside.

Front way was the best way anyway. He expected a padlock on the door of Room 16, so he took the jimmy. He carried it inside his left pant leg, one curved claw hooked over his waistband. His .38 rested in his left coat pocket, his flashlight in the right pocket. He went around to the lighted front entrance.

He saw through the glass door to a desk with no one behind it. To the right of the desk, a passenger elevator and a freight elevator. He spotted the electronic card slot alongside the entrance and had the plastic card ready by the time he got there.

The card slid in but he heard no click. He took the card out and presented the opposite edge and heard the click. He drew the card out and pocketed it and pulled the door open and stepped into the lobby.

He went behind the desk, hoping to find a chart of room locations thumbtacked or taped to the inner surface of its raised back. Everything but; all kinds of warnings and reminders and guard schedules and emergency numbers.

On the desk itself, a phone and a phone directory, an issue of *American Rifleman,* a thermos jug, and a lunch box. He hefted the jug and the box; they felt full. He pulled the chair away from the desk and looked under the desk and saw an alarm button on the floor. Guard making his rounds or using the john.

He heard the hum of an elevator. The passenger car was descending. He walked around to the front of the desk and waited.

The elevator door opened and a gray man in a gray uniform stepped out. His paunch overhung his gun belt. Looked like a .45 in the holster. The ready smile lost depth as the eyes registered an unfamiliar face. "Yessir, how can I help you?" The eyes slid to the door and back.

"You can tell me where to find number sixteen."

"That mini-storage or room?"

"Room."

"Room, hey? And what's the name, sir?"

"Timothy Farrell."

"Timothy Farrell, hey?" The eyes hooded and the man eased toward the desk.

The man knew. Be odd if he didn't know, Tim's Lounge just down the street.

"I'm acting for Tim. Tim's away on business and he left his entry card with me and asked me to get something from his room here. So if you'll just show me the way."

The man smiled and nodded. Seemed itchy to position himself behind the desk with his foot near the button. Once set for backup, be asking to see some identification, some authorization.

Mal drew his .38. "I forgot to say please."

The man's hands shot up. "Hey, I only work here. I don't own nothing in none of the rooms. I won't give you no trouble."

Mal gestured him to turn around.

The man turned. He clasped his hands and lowered them to cover the top and back of his head and hunched his shoulders. "You don't have to knock me out."

"I won't knock you out. I just want your piece."

"Take it, take it."

Mal took it and pocketed it. "Okay. Now lead me to Room sixteen."

"Sure thing." The man turned to face Mal and unclasped his hands and started to lower them.

"Be nice if you kept your hands on your head."

The hands resumed the position. "Sure thing." He led the way to the passenger elevator. "It's on the second floor."

"After you."

The man stepped inside and Mal followed.

They stood waiting.

"Uh, I can't press the button like this."

"Sure you can. Use your elbow."

"Hey, you're right." The man used his elbow. Awkwardly, but he got the right button.

The door closed, they rode up, the door opened.

"It's on your right."

"After you."

The man led him to the door of Room 16.

Shit. It did not have a padlock, it had a keypad for an electronic lock. With the right leverage, the jimmy could have snapped a padlock. The heavy steel lip of the jamb offered the jimmy no purchase. Clubb's trunk didn't run to a propane cutting torch.

The guy broke in on Mal's thoughts. "Can't help you there. You rent a room, you program the lock yourself. Nobody knows the access code but you." Something in the guy's voice. Mal slid a look at him and caught a smile.

Mal had been leaning toward leaving him tied up and locked in. But the smile changed that.

The man wiped off the smile.

Mal eyed the keypad. A riddle. You could juggle combinations a lifetime and not come up with the right one. The right one would be a number easy for Tim to remember, a number with strong associations.

What the fuck was the shield number in the photo of the dedicated young cop?

Mal punched 4230.

The lock clicked.

"Lucky guess. Push the door open."

The man stared at Mal, then elbowed the heavy door open a crack.

"All the way."

The man shouldered the door wide open.

Both stood staring.

Mal had thought to find files full of filched police records, or a cache of drugs, or a haul of hot merchandise, or untaxed cigarettes, or just cases of liquor Tim had no room for at the lounge. This was none of the above.

An arsenal. Wall-to-wall weapons, street price in the millions. Another sideline of Tim's, dealing in guns and ammo.

Mal's mouth watered. Taurus PT-92AF 9mm Parabellums with fifteen-round magazines, .357 Magnums, TEC-9mms with thirty-six-round magazines, Glock 17 and Glock 19 9mm semi-automatic pistols, Mac-10 and Mac-11 9mm assault pistols, silencers for same, Mossberg 12-gauge sawed-off shotguns, Winchester 12-gauge shotguns, Barrett .50-caliber assault rifles that would take six-inch cartridges capable of piercing armor, speed loaders, laser-sighting devices, combat flak jackets, cases of ammo . . .

"After you."

Mal followed the man in and shoved the door to. Best to take care of the guy right now. First, "Oh, one thing. What you got in your lunch box?"

The guard threw a blank look back over his shoulder, then smiled hopefully. "Lite American cheese on rye with lettuce and tomato, big piece of apple pie, nice banana just starting to speckle, bag of unsalted potato chips, Twix bar, can of Diet Coke. Thermosful decaf coffee, nondairy lightener, sugar substitute. You hungry, you welcome to it all."

"Thanks." Mal shot the guard.

Now he could take a complete inventory with both eyes.

In passing, he found Timothy Farrell's driver's license, credit cards, and ring of keys neatly arrayed on a crate near the door. Before taxiing to Hughes Airport or getting a lift there from Haynes or someone, Tim had stopped here to arm himself for the delivery of Harry Pace to Ramón Díez at the S-Bar-T. Seemed Tim believed in traveling light, in carrying nothing he might lose accidentally that would lead to him.

Mal examined the license and lifted an eyebrow; you never knew about a person. The license had the organ-donor section on the back signed and witnessed. The photo on the front was bad enough and the physical description was close enough and Mal had a handle on the signature, so he pocketed the license and the plastic. Should be safe to use for a few days.

He moved around the room. He made his pick and began to pile stuff near the door. Then he shifted his first load to the freight elevator and took it down. He stopped off at the first floor to wedge the jimmy under the front door, then went on to the basement.

As soon as the elevator door opened, he spotted a hand truck, which he used to move the load from the elevator car to the overhead door that opened onto the loading platform.

He unbolted the loading-dock door and went out and jumped down and brought his car alongside. He opened the trunk and took stuff out to make room. He liked the long-range mike that attached to binoculars and stashed that and a few tools in the glove compartment. The rest of the stuff he put on the dock to leave in Room 16.

The load of weaponry half-filled the car trunk. He slammed and locked the lid, stepped to the dock, loaded the stuff from the car trunk onto the hand truck, rolled the hand truck inside, closed and bolted the overhead door. Into the elevator with the hand truck and up to Room 16. Punched 4230, dumped the stuff from the car trunk, and loaded the hand truck with cases of weaponry.

This load filled the car trunk.

Third and last load he stacked on the backseat of the car and on the floor behind the front seat, where it would be safe till he could rent a U-Haul trailer. Only marking that showed: OTHER SIDE UP.

He climbed onto the dock, rolled the hand truck inside, closed and bolted the overhead door, put the hand truck back where he had found it, and rode the elevator to the first floor. Before he unwedged the jimmy from the door and let himself out, he went over to the desk and grabbed the thermos bottle and the lunch box. Cheese was binding, but this would make one less visit to a fast-food joint for somebody to get a slow look at him.

He pulled out and found his way onto Interstate 15 and headed west, some 275 miles L.V. to L.A., with a disc jockey playing a song the L.V. Chamber of Commerce wouldn't like: about the sun is too hot and the dice are too cold and everything glitters and nothing is gold.

CHAPTER 17

Detective Sergeant Carol Shanley of Metro Dade Homicide stood by the machine in the communications room and watched the faxes come through from the sheriff's office, Pima County, Arizona.

Montage of driver's licenses and coroner's-office photos of three of the dead in the S-Bar-T Ranch Massacre identified as Miami homeboys.

Sheriff, and over his shoulders the Arizona State Police and the FBI, looking for information on the deceased's (plural) kin, friends (euphemistic), and business and criminal (redundant) associates.

All three had on their persons circulars depicting Harry Pace, wanted for questioning in the Felipe Díez homicide, and so Shanley had more than an inkling that the S-Bar-T Ranch Massacre had not gone down over Las Vegas turf but over the Felipe Díez homicide.

She recognized one of the men and took the faxes to her office and made a few calls. When Jack Vogelsang came in, she showed him the faxes and told him what she knew and thought.

"This one I know as Gringo Thrush. One of my snitches says Gringo recently went to work for Ramón Díez."

"Shit. Not opening up the Felipe Díez homicide again?"

"Opening and widening. My guess, Ramón sent the three hoods to get Harry Pace and it backfired."

"You saying it was Harry did all that? One guy?"

"He ganged up on them."

Vogelsang gave Shanley a look. Then he sighed. "It won't get us anywhere to talk to Ramón, but I guess we got to go through the motions." He raised his eyebrows. "Together?"

She nodded. "That way we only get half a heartburn each."

"Too much for you, there's milk of amnesia. Forget the whole thing."

"You know we can't do that."

"I knew. Just something to say."

Shanley looked through him in thought. "First let's talk to Guadeloupe Martínez. Find out if Ramón harassed her for a lead to Harry Pace. *Somebody* told Ramón that Harry would be at Terminiello's ranch. Maybe Harry got in touch with her and Ramón forced that out of her."

Vogelsang aimed a finger at her. "Let's."

The name Marita García was still on the mailbox along with that of Guadeloupe Martínez's roommate, Kathy Frakes. Kathy was there to let them in, though they had to ring long and hard to get through loud music.

She looked put upon. "I'm fond of Marita—I still think of her as Marita—and I feel sorry she went through a bad time. Really. But you don't realize how hard this has been on me. All the publicity about Felipe's death, the media sticking mikes in your face, impacted on my studying and I'm still trying to catch up. And it's not over yet."

Shanley pounced on that. "What do you mean, 'it's not over yet'?"

"You're here, aren't you?"

"We're here to clear up a few things. When do you expect her back?"

"No idea. I didn't expect her to be away this long."
"How long has she been away?"
"Two days."
"Say where she was going?"
"Not a word. She was moody last I saw her; I figured it was her period coming on. She just didn't come back from classes."
"Did you report this to anyone?"
Kathy dropped her gaze to the rug. "No."
Shanley and Vogelsang let silence lean on her.
Kathy looked up. "Like I said, I'm trying to catch up and I didn't want to stir up anything over what might be nothing. Or something purely personal: like another Felipe happened."
Shanley thrust a business card at her. "Here's my number. If you hear from her, tell her to call me right away. Now we'll let you get back to your books."
The music did not start blasting again till they were almost out of the building.

They crossed the causeway and wended toward Ramón Díez's home. They were a hundred yards short of the gate when it opened and a grocer's delivery van pulled out and headed their way. Shanley touched Vogelsang's arm, and he veered onto the shoulder and braked.
The young black driving the van gave them a look as he passed. Vogelsang waited, then made a U-turn and followed. When they had rounded a bend, Vogelsang clapped a light to the roof of their unmarked car and flashed the van's driver to stop.
Shanley and Vogelsang got out. Shanley made for the van driver's window; Vogelsang went behind the van. Shanley showed the driver her shield.
The driver was cool. "Yeah, I wondered about you and the gray boy. So you the Man. What you want with me?"
"You just made a delivery to the Díez place. Like to ask you a few questions about it."

The deliveryman looked relieved, but the face closed. "I don't know nothing about nothing."

Vogelsang came alongside. "Is he being less than a good citizen? Well, stopping him won't be a total loss. Cite him for broken taillights."

The deliveryman looked pained. "Shit, man, you went and busted the taillights on me?"

Vogelsang put up his hands in horror. "You making an unsubstantiated slanderous accusation in front of a witness?"

"I'm just saying I didn't have no busted taillights a couple minutes ago."

"And you won't have a citation a couple minutes from now, give you grief with your boss, if you know something about something. Fair enough?"

The deliveryman looked at Shanley. "What questions?"

Shanley pulled out a photo of Marita. "Did you see this woman on the Díez property?"

The deliveryman's brow wrinkled. "I see her—but not on the Díez property. I see her in the papers and on TV."

Shanley took back the photo and pocketed it. "Like to see your copy of the delivery slip for the Díez order."

The deliveryman found it and handed it to her. The signature space had a scrawl Shanley could not make out. The deliveryman would need the slip back for proof of delivery, so she jotted the items down in her notepad before handing it back.

"Here you go. Any changes you notice from earlier deliveries?"

"Ordering a lot more. But a lot more people staying there now."

"What kind of people?"

"Men. Kind of men take more than two of you to go around kicking in they taillights. They kick *your* taillights."

"Notice anything else?"

"That be enough for them to see me notice."

"Thanks for being a good citizen."

"Yeah, sure. Good citizen, my ass. The taillights still got to come out of my pocket."

Vogelsang took a few steps backward to see the van's behind. "What do you know, they healed themselves."

"Man, you a bigger crook than the crooks you after." The deliveryman shoved the van in gear and pulled away.

Shanley and Vogelsang got back into their car. Vogelsang rested his elbows on the steering wheel and faced Shanley.

"What item on the list made your eyes light up?"

"Very last item: sanitary napkins. Like an afterthought."

"Why is that remarkable? The woman of the house—what's her name? Elvira?—isn't into menopause yet. Unless she's a hell of a lot older than she looks."

"Sure, *could* be for Elvira, and *could* be perks for the female help. But it's a two-ply coincidence, coming after Kathy tells us Marita is having her monthlies. Bet you anything she's on the grounds—or on Ramón's boat."

Vogelsang shook his head, then nodded, then shook his head. "Sanitary pads won't hold water for a search warrant."

Shanley looked icicles at Vogelsang. "I know that. We just have to keep looking for probable cause." She pulled at her nose. "Think Ramón shipped his goons via corporate jet?"

"We can check flight plans and expense vouchers. If they haven't been doctored or lost. And if the pilot tells us the truth."

"Which they have been. And which he won't."

"So we go through the motions again."

"Think of it as dancercise."

"Whose tape we do it to?"

"Sisyphus's."

The deliveryman had it right about a lot more men at the Díez estate.

"Looks like Ramón beefed up security."

"Yeah. I don't see a lot of familiar faces, but I do see a lot of new familiar-*type* faces."

Ramón was home but kept them waiting five minutes at the gate and fifteen minutes in the house. When he strolled into the Florida—a.k.a. sun—room, though, he was the soul of courtesy and hospitality.

They turned down drinks and eats and Shanley showed him the faxes of Gringo Thrush and the two others.

Ramon studied the faxes gravely. "Am I supposed to know these people?"

"You're just supposed to tell us if you know them."

Ramon smiled. " 'Know' is a strong word. It seems to me these men look very much like three men I hired for a time as bodyguards but had to let go because for one reason or another they didn't work out."

"Maybe they didn't have the right tape."

Vogelsang said it softly, and to Shanley, but Ramón picked it up and his face darkened.

"What did you say about tape? Are you hinting that my dealings with these men have been recorded?"

Shanley shot Vogelsang a wink hidden from Ramón, then a reproving look. "He shouldn't have said that."

"But he did. And *I* have nothing more to say till I have spoken with my lawyers." He handed her the faxes with a turn of his wrist.

"Then we'll thank you for your time and go."

They ran into Elvira Díez being chauffeured in as they were driving out. Elvira wore a dreamy smile and patted bright red hair with one hand and rested the other on the pile of packages beside her.

Shanley waved to Elvira and Elvira saw them and waved back.

"She doesn't look like she's having her monthlies."

"How can you tell?"

"I can tell. But she did have her hair done. Changed from blonde to redhead."

"That so? I knew there was something different."

There seemed to be no satisfying Ramón. Here she had rushed home so he would not slap her for being late for dinner, and here he looked ready to slap her for being too early.

He seemed too furious to notice her hair change. "I tried to reach you on the car phone, tell you to stay away for another hour."

Elvira blinked. "We didn't hear any ringing." Uh-oh, she had as much as called Ramón a liar. "Maybe that was while we were both in the boutique. Lázaro came in to carry the packages out to the car."

"Maybe, maybe. Well, no damage done. You weren't here for them to question you."

"Oh. The police. I *thought* they looked familiar."

Now he noticed the hair change. He stared at it and she grew afraid. It had not occurred to her that he might hate it. She had been redheaded before and he had always liked the spice of the change.

He stared now at her face and then ran his gaze down her body, as though sizing her up.

"While you're still dressed for shopping, and while the stores are still open, go back out and buy a black wig."

He did not sound angry, merely thoughtful. Definitely no satisfying Ramón.

Running on the guard's coffee, Mal crossed into California and reached Barstow before dawn. He had meant to put more miles between himself and Las Vegas, but he caught himself nodding off. He left I 15 for a dead-end street, where he parked, rolled up the windows, locked the doors, and snoozed.

He got up with the sun. He had found an electric shaver and a bottle of Lectric Shave in the glove compartment; he disinfected the shaver blade with the Lectric Shave, plugged the shaver into the cigarette-lighter jack, and shaved. Touched up his face with the liquid tan.

He finished the guard's dry sandwich and cold coffee and was ready for the business day to begin.

Yellow pages directed him to a U-Haul dealership, but when he saw that the dealership also offered self-storage, he changed his mind about renting a trailer and leased a storage room in the name of Martin Garfunkel and stashed the bulk of his weaponry right there.

He found a tailor shop—CUSTOM TAILORING & EXPERT ALTERATIONS—and had the tailor fashion a pair of deep canvas pockets and sew them inside his jacket.

The old man had shaky hands but his stitches were straight. He helped Mal on with the jacket and tugged at the bottom and smoothed the lapels. He had a shaky head but his gaze was direct. "I take your money and do the job, but I got to tell you: it's the first place they look."

Mal looked into his eyes. "Don't worry. I'm not a mule. The pockets aren't for drugs. They're for guns."

The old man smiled. "That's good." Then he took a step backward. "Oh."

Back in his car, Mal fitted an Ingram M-10 into one inside pocket and its skeletal stock and a pair of spare thirty-two-round magazines into the other. The Ingram M-10 fired 9mm rounds at the cyclic rate of twelve hundred rounds a minute, or some twenty rounds a second, so you had to use a light trigger finger to keep from emptying the weapon in one burst. He already had a Glock-19 9mm semiautomatic strapped to each leg.

He stoked up at a drive-through, gassed up, and drove to Pasadena. He bought shirts, slacks, shorts, and socks, then checked into a motel and slept the afternoon away. He showered and changed, checked out, stoked up again, then went on into Los Angeles.

Mal drove slowly, but not too slowly, past his apartment building. His apartment overlooked the street.

He had left the venetian blinds slatted downward on the inside to let sunlight sift in.

Now they looked slatted upward on the inside for a view down at the street.

He parked two blocks from his apartment building and got out. He wore his jacket with the M-10 in the inside pockets. He slung his carryon over his shoulder; it held his jimmy and his remote-sound amplifier. He walked to the building across the street and down the ramp at the side to the basement entrance. He jimmied his way into the basement, rode the elevator to the top floor, and jimmied his way onto the roof. He knelt at the parapet and unzipped his carryon and took out the remote-sound amplifier. He put on the earpieces, held the binoculars to his eyes, and aimed the long-range mike at his window with the best view of the street.

Nothing more than a hum at first, then a yawn and a man's voice, the sound loud enough but fuzzy. "Could be doing better things with our time. He ain't dumb enough to come here."

Another man's voice. "He's smart enough to think we think he ain't dumb enough to come here. That might make him dumb enough to come here."

"For what? We took the place apart and ain't found nothing for him to come back to."

"We got orders to stay; we stay till we get orders to go."

Another yawn. "Speaking of orders to go, time to check with Angelo." A click, then, "Hey, Angie, stop scratching your ass." A big laugh. "Fuck you right back. So I guess you don't see nothing neither, huh?" A pause, then, "Frankie is gonna go down and cover while you get pizzas for everybody. I hope this time you remember no fucking anchovies for me. Lotsa pepperoni, lotsa cheese, *no* anchovies."

Mal hadn't heard dialing, so this had to be a walkie-talkie exchange; Mal couldn't hear Angelo's end. The two hoods in Mal's apartment watched the front, so Angelo had to be at the ramp entrance.

He listened another minute, heard the door open and shut, heard a yawn or two, then nothing. He put the mike-binoculars combo back in his carryon, went in from the roof, rode down to the basement.

When he came out and walked up the ramp to the street, a battered fedora covered his head, his jacket had its collar turned up and hung unbuttoned, ashes from the incinerator and grease from the oil burner smeared his face and his shirt and pants, his carryon was in a trash bag under bottles and cans, and a Glock was in the left pocket of his jacket.

He shambled up the street to the next building, went down its ramp. Waited two minutes, then went back up to the street, crossed to the other side, and shuffled to the rear of the building next to his own. Waited another two minutes, went back to the street, and shambled to his building's ramp. Heard a whisper as he neared the basement door.

"Yeah, the bum's coming. I'll roust him."

The door opened; a man stuck his head out. "Beat it, bum."

Mal put a wino's whine into his voice. "Just picking up the empties they leave for me. Take a minute."

The door opened wider and the man stepped out. The walkie-talkie was clipped to his belt. Frankie. "Fuck off, you bum. Don't make me use muscle."

Mal drew the Glock and shot him. Pocketed the Glock, stepped over the body, rested the trash bag on Frankie's chest, and dragged the body inside.

Spotted a hand-printed sign taped to the laundry-room door. LAUNDRY ROOM SHUT FOR REPAIRS TILL FURTHER NOTICE. THANK YOU. Opened the door. No surprise to find no repairs in progress. Dragged the body into the laundry room. Transferred the walkie-talkie to his own belt, took a .45 from Frankie's shoulder holster, pocketed it, opened one of the big dryers, emptied his trash bag's cans and bottles into the drum, and then the bag itself when he got his carryon out, closed the drier door, and slung the carryon over his shoulder.

The walkie-talkie spoke. "Problem with the bum, Frankie?"

Mal thumbed the switch. "No problem."

"Then what the fuck— Hey, is that you, Frankie?"

"No, it's not me." That should bring him storming down.

The elevator cab stood at the basement from Frankie's descent. Mal got there just as the UP arrow glowed green. He pulled the door open before the cab could move. Leaned in to press every button, then let the door close and the cab go up empty. It would take the guy to the top before the guy could express it to the basement.

Mal took the stairs. He left the walkie-talkie behind at the first landing so that the guy would not hear his own squawk. Padded upward to reach his cache under the stairs below his own floor. Reached it while the elevator door was still taking its time opening and closing at the second floor. Heard the guy try to raise Frankie on the walkie-talkie, heard him bad-mouth the elevator.

He felt with his fingertips the outline of the little door to his cache. But somewhere along the line, maybe when he loaded or unloaded the boxes of weaponry, he had worn and torn his fingernails to the quick; he had to dig into his pocket for a plastic card, but it tended to buckle on the point of leverage; took him a good bad minute to pry the little door open.

Got a shock when it seemed empty. But that was because he had taken the .22 and the cash for the car trip to Miami. The Woolf letters were there. He pocketed them and closed the cache door.

He heard footsteps above, descending. Could be another

resident, but the footfalls sounded swift and soft. Had to assume this was the ambush guy; had to suppose the guy had got off at the first stop to keep the elevator from carrying him all the way to the top floor.

Mal did not move except to take out Frankie's .45. He stood looking up at the turn of the stairs.

The guy hurried down on his toes. He had his hand thrust inside his coat, ready to draw his gun. The guy recognized the bum, knew now for sure that the bum was Harry Pace, died with that knowledge.

Mal heard no stir in the ringing silence after the shot, but that did not mean somebody might not now be dialing 911. He took the guy's gun, another fucking .45, and traded it for Frankie's, which he wiped to smear possible fingerprints before dropping it beside the body.

He raced downstairs to the basement. No sirens yet. But the nearest pizzeria was only a block and a half over and he had to foresee running into Angelo.

And he foreheard the footsteps down the ramp as he reached the basement door.

Angelo would have his hands full, so Mal opened the basement door for him. Angelo stepped inside. Mal reclosed the door to muffle the coming shot.

"Hey, Angelo. Something from Frankie." While Angelo stopped dead with his mouth open, Mal blew him away with the third guy's .45. So he lied that it was from Frankie; just that he didn't know the third guy's name.

Mal hauled Angelo into the laundry room and stretched him beside Frankie. He smeared the third guy's gun and dropped it next to Frankie—so in a way, that made what he'd said true.

He took Angelo's gun, still another fucking .45, and pocketed it. He left the Glock that had done Frankie for attribution to Angelo. He felt a pang as he gave up the Glock; a bad trade. But the best of guns was only a tool and tools were to use.

Took a half minute to ditch the battered fedora in the dryer, put his coat collar down, brush ashes off his pants, button his jacket to cover the soiled shirt.

On his way out, he picked up the three pizza boxes.

Up the ramp and down the street. Now there were sirens. As he neared his own car, a squad car tore past, and he turned to watch; the cops saw only the pizza boxes and didn't give him a second glance.

Mal opened the boxes and examined the pizzas only after he had driven well out of the neighborhood. They were still warm and had survived their fall with only a slight shift of their toppings. A few slices had jumped their fault lines.

But that Angelo. All three pizzas had anchovies.

Mal put away one whole pizza while he read Al Woolf's letters more hungrily and more thoroughly than he had aboard the *Queen Mab*. Now he had more time and more cause to take note of the payoff venues. He could not get at his own money without alerting Guido's and Ramón's snitches. He could get at Guido's money and hurt Guido's operations by sticking up Guido's bagmen.

A trip to New York.

First, unfinished business here with Freddy Friday.

He found a parking space around the corner from Freddy's building.

An old building with low security, so he went right in without buzzing ahead and took the stairs to Freddy's floor. He listened at Freddy's door, heard nothing but what could have been refrigerator hum. He wrinkled his nose at a bad smell that seeped out of Freddy's place. He felt he knew what the smell meant: Someone had beaten him to it. But it would nag at him if he went away without making sure.

He jimmied the door open. The smell blasted him back. He clapped tissue over his nose and mouth, went in, and shoved the door to. Ran past the body of Freddy Friday on the floor to raise windows.

They were stuck, and he held his breath while he jimmied them open. He leaned out and breathed in.

The guard in Room 16 and the private eye in the car trunk would be stinking around now, too. Though their deaths were cleaner. Someone had slit Freddy's throat, and the bluebottles and their maggots had lots of blood and gaping flesh to feast on.

On the quark level, Uncle Phil said, *nothing is filthy or disgusting or obscene or nauseating. But that knowledge didn't keep me from throwing up when I watched an autopsy.*

Mal looked around. He would like to use Freddy's phone and fax machine, but he didn't operate on the quark level, either, and he had to get rid of the stink first. He found a spray container of Pine Magic in the kitchenette and sprayed the body and saturated the air. He still had to hold tissue over his nose, but he could stand the adulterated stink.

He rang his own number. See if a cop lifted the receiver and asked who was calling. Find out if they had tied the three dead to his apartment. Not that he meant to return there. Harry Pace was gone for good.

His greeting answered.

He waited for the beep and said, "Hi, Harry. This is Fred. I just blew into town. I'll try again later."

No one took the bait and came onto the line. He hung up, satisfied the cops had not made the connection yet.

Then he thought to find out if anyone else had left a new message. He lifted the receiver again.

He followed the remote-access s.o.p. and heard the old messages he had saved, then a new one from Ramón.

"I thought you might like listening to some sound effects." A woman's scream. Shook him a bit, but could be any woman. Then a woman's voice he knew had to be Lupe's. "He's trying to make you come. Don't, no matter what he does to—" A long-sustained scream, then Ramón again. "Too bad you don't have a fax machine, I'd send you the pictures go with the sound." Then a click.

Mal held on till he heard "Hi, Harry. This is Fred. I just blew into town. I'll try again later." He hung up. He wiped his clammy hand on his jacket.

He felt cold and hollow. New York, for the looting of Guido, was out. Miami was in.

But he could at least give Guido a long-distance reaming and Ramón a preliminary scare.

Ramón first. Mal dialed the information operator and got Metro Dade's Homicide Division number. He dialed the number, said he was Detective Lieutenant Thursday of the L.A.P.D. and asked for Homicide's fax number.

Then he dialed that number and faxed Al Woolf's pages on how the Palmieri family and associates routed soiled money to Ramón Díez for laundering. Before he fed the last page in he added in block letters at the bottom: YOU OWE GUADELOUPE MARTINEZ ONE.

Between feeding pages to the machine, he withdrew to the nearest open window to gulp air. Looking back into the room, he could see bare spots in the wall display of Freddy Friday's porno shots. Had the killing been over that? If so, so what? Other people's motives for giving someone the business were none of Mal's business.

His business was to focus on the matter at hand. When the good folks at Metro Dade saw the footnote about Lupe, they would call L.A.P.D. back to ask Lieutenant Thursday what that meant. When they found there was no such animal as Lieutenant Thursday, they would try to trace the send. Mal figured he could risk a few more minutes here.

Take us the faxes, the little faxes, that spoil the grapevine. Now, that was something Uncle Phil might've said.

He found out the fax number of Guido Palmieri's real estate office.

* * *

Funny, Guido happened to be in the real estate office and was just thinking of Al Woolf, and of how he had had that fucking Harry Pace lay Al Woolf to rest, when Al Woolf's words manifested themselves on the office's fax machine.

Guido liked to come in a few afternoons a week, play the legit businessman, sit behind the desk and dream. Mostly of the past. The past was known, safer, nonthreatening. The past was set in concrete, deep-sixed.

The machine was strictly for exchanging stuff with fellow agents and with managing agents and with the Bureau of Buildings and other city agencies, but every once in a while some smartass muscled in on the machine with an unsolicited offer of some service or other, using your paper, your ink, your electricity, your phone time.

The girl got up and went over to the fax machine when it came to life, and the stuff materialized slice by thin fucking slice on the cut-sheet plain-paper laser fax.

"*Queen Mab,*" she said. "Do you know what that is, Mr. Palmieri?"

Sure he knew. Boat Al Woolf sailed on and died on. For a second, he thought she had read his mind.

Then he swiveled and saw her standing at the fax machine and staring at what scrolled out.

He got up and went over. *Queen Mab,* all right, and now a ship logo, and now a handwritten date—went back to the time of the cruise—and now a jerkily handwritten letter to the D.A.

Guido elbowed the girl aside and bent to read it as it ran.

He straightened and screamed, "Stop it! Stop it! Turn it off!"

But when the girl moved back in to switch the machine off, he pushed her away again. Pulling the plug at this end wouldn't keep the fucking words from flowing to the intercept point; the Feds would still get it all on their tap, and if he stopped receiving he would be the only one not to know everything Al Woolf was spilling.

With his eyes big, he watched the shape of his doom grow. He patted the pocket over his heart. The bottle in that pocket would keep him from ever going on trial. His family doctor had prescribed medication to fake a heart attack. At the rate his heart was going now, he would not have to open the bottle.

The faxes were waiting for Shanley when she returned to her office.

The lieutenant was proud of himself. "Nobody knew what the hell to make of this or who to hand it to when it came in. Handwritten letter on a ship's stationery. All about money laundering. And to Homicide? We checked with L.A.P.D. and there is no Lieutenant Thursday. We began to think hoax. But there was an Al Woolf, Big Apple borough president died aboard a cruise ship—the *Queen Mab*—I remembered hearing about it."

"I remember too."

"Yeah." The lieutenant pointed to the bottom of the last sheet. "This printing at the end—our handwriting expert says it's in a different hand—ties it to your Felipe Díez case. I'm setting up a meeting with U.S. Internal Revenue, with the State Banking Department, with D.E.A., and I want you to be there to brief them on Homicide's involvement. I'll let you know when."

Shanley's eyes shone. "Speaking of Guadeloupe Martínez, does this letter give us probable cause to search Ramón Díez's estate and yacht? Vogelsang and I think he may be holding the woman against her will."

The lieutenant's face hardened. "Are you nuts? We don't want to jeopardize one of the biggest-ever money-laundering cases by alerting Díez now. We're part of a team. The team has to nail down the facts before anyone from Homicide makes move one. You and Vogelsang will stay a mile away from Díez."

"But—"

"That's an order."

Shanley's eyes went dull. "Yessir."

CHAPTER 18

Discountoutletmotelusedcardruglumbershoemovieba-rcomputertoyclothingbeautyrealestatestationerydentistopitic-iantelevisionfurnituregasburger. The transcontinental hero sandwich with oil-and-rubber relish.

Mal had reequipped himself at the self-storage in Barstow. Might never come this way again, so he took all he thought he would need, and more. Weapons, ammo, bulletproof vest.

As he drove, ate, relieved himself, and rested, he thought back and ahead.

The Al Woolf letter about money laundering should focus heat on Ramón, preoccupy him to some degree. Ramón would have heard of Guido's heart attack—real or faked—and the reason for it. Ramón would think Guido had turned snitch, had made a deal with the Feds.

Mal had thought briefly of trying to make a deal with Ramón—the letter for Lupe. But both knew neither trusted the other to keep any such bargain.

Dumbest thing Mal could do now would be to rush in, all muscle and no brain. Smarter to stay a shadow, a haunt. A scared ghost, even. Uncle Phil always said to set your own pace.

After five, six days, Ramón would think that Harry Pace had not heard the messages or that Harry Pace had heard them but had punked out.

Either way, Ramón would give up on Harry Pace. But then Ramón would have no more use for Lupe and would do her like the show girl at the S-Bar-T. Have to hit Ramón when he let his guard down but before he did Lupe.

Because he could do nothing about how Ramón treated Lupe in the meanwhile, Mal wished her luck in toughing it out and put that part of it out of his mind.

Discountoutletmotelusedcardruglumbershoemoviebarcomputertoyclothingbeautyrealestatestationerydentistopticiantelevisionfurnituregasburger. The transcontinental hero sandwich with oil-and-rubber relish. He saved the empty Coke bottles that went with it.

Ramón returned home from Banco de los Inocentes shaken. Bank examiners who seemed to know what to look for had shown up for a surprise inspection of the books. Right after the S-Bar-T Ranch Massacre, Miguel Luqué had broken their truce by hijacking, or condoning the hijacking, of a shipment. Now this. The jackal had smelled the lion's sickness.

Once inside his gates and out of his limousine, Ramón did not take himself and his dispatch case—heavy with records and documents he had just smuggled out of the bank—into the house. With his two bodyguards, he walked around to the back and then to the side, to the fence along the property line.

Newly transplanted bushes masked a new gate. He was good neighbors with himself; under another name, he had bought the place next door for cash.

They passed through and crossed the grounds to the contaminated house. The sound of fans ventilating the house overrode birdsong and insect whir.

Ramón unlocked the rear door. One of the bodyguards went in first to scout, then Ramón and the other bodyguard entered. A bodyguard scouted the basement, then Ramón and the other bodyguard joined him. One shoved a heavy steamer trunk full of junk to one side, uncovering a freshly installed in-floor safe. Both bodyguards faced outward while Ramón dialed it open.

It held suitcases stuffed with eleven million dollars, plus three passports bearing Ramón's picture but different names. He pocketed the passports. "*Bueno*, we will take the bags to the yacht."

The bodyguards turned and lifted the suitcases out. Ramón closed the safe door and twirled the dial. One bodyguard shoved the trunk back over the safe. They all climbed the stairs and went outside, Ramón locked the door, and they passed back through the fence.

They walked down toward the docked *Medallion*. An armed man stepped out on deck and stood ready to cover them. They boarded the *Medallion*.

Ramón looked back at his house. Elvira passed the windows of her room from left to right and right to left, weary and forlorn as a prisoner. She did not have to act. She had directions to pace around the clock, with few breaks. With her dark wig on, she could pass at this distance for Guadeloupe Martínez.

And in Ramón's eyes, she was just as expendable. Everyone was but Ramón Díez.

The bodyguards with the bags stood waiting.

"Let's go." He led the way to the master stateroom. Once inside, he gestured for them to set the bags down and wait outside.

He locked the door and slid a wall panel from in front of a vault embedded in the bulkhead. He dialed it open, stowed the bags and the briefcase inside, and locked it. His hands felt sweaty and he washed them. He unlocked his door, went into the dining saloon, and sent one of his men for the Martínez woman.

Two heavily armed men stayed with her at all times. The three men brought her from the cabin.

Ramón crooked his finger at her from across the *Medal-*

lion's saloon. Her eyes were dull, but she saw him beckon and came.

He pushed her hair back from her brow, then thumbed her face as though modeling clay. She stood for it like a statue. His hands fell away and he stepped back to study her. "Elvira's prettier. What does he see in you?"

She answered dully. But she answered. He had taught her that stubborn silence brought pain. "He does not see anything in me. I have told you, he does not know me, much less love me."

Ramón cocked his head to one side. "You may be right. He seems to have abandoned you. I have not heard from him. Or of him. Not since the shoot-out in Los Angeles. The police call it a shoot-out, the three men canceling one another, because the police do not know the three were business partners doing me a favor." Expendable, all three. "But it has his signature. Like what happened at the S-Bar-T." Quick emendation: "Like what I *understand* happened at the S-Bar-T."

His face darkened. He stepped close again and his fingers bit into her arms. He whispered into her ear, "I will have to cut my losses all around. My operations here, many of my possessions, you." He gave her a shake, then let go and stepped back again. "You. You cost me my mother, my brother. You and this man of yours." His mouth tightened and his eyes burned.

She seemed to feel she had to fill the silence with an answer. "I have told you, he is no man of mine. There was no plan. I did not set Felipe up. I took hold of the steering wheel and swung it hard right. I was trying to hit the causeway guardrail. I wanted to kill myself." A flash of fire. "Yes, and Felipe too."

Ramón slapped her face absently. At best, she was untrustworthy bait. Hence, Elvira. He had already held her too long after the black woman detective sergeant's visit. But of course he could not let her go free. "Take her back to her cabin." In his mind he added, "When it is night, she will swim with the sharks."

Mal woke from a dream. In the dream, a dog trotted around inside a fence, pausing at the corner posts to mark out its turf. Uncle Phil was right: Dreams toward morning had to do with pissing.

He had his piss and washed up and checked out and got under way. The homestretch. He had overnighted in a Tallahassee motel, having switched from I 10 to U.S. 27 to shorten the run. He stopped for a light brunch and a leg stretch in Ocala.

At high noon in Winter Haven, he found an Army and Navy store that carried firemen's fallout coats and bought one a size too big. He said it was for a part in a farce. He also wanted a fire helmet or a fire captain's white cap, but they had none in stock. The clerk suggested a costumer or a uniformer, but Mal said he thought he knew where he could get one.

With just ten miles to go, he stopped in Hialeah to rest up at a motel. He bolted the door, tilted the blinds to darken the room, lightened his body of his weapons, hit the sack. He fell asleep almost before he could tell himself not to think, not to dream, just to pound the ear he would play it by.

It was still day when he left, still business hours when he crossed the causeway to Key Biscayne and cruised the waterfront.

He knew what he was looking for when he found it. The watery notion of some small craft to reach the Díez place by sea crystallized when he spotted a Kawasaki Jet Ski for sale.

"Yessir, just like a motorcycle, with a skid instead of wheels." Padding under the guy's skin stretched, and stretching paled, the tattooing on the guy's bare chest. The guy demonstrated. "If you can handle a motorcycle . . ."

He could handle a sickle.

The price was right. And a discount and a full tank thrown in for cash. The guy also sold him a good-as-new life jacket and a secondhand boat trailer. The guy wrote Mr. Garfunkel out a sales slip. "Where you staying?"

Mal gestured vaguely thereabouts. "Like to put it right in the water, get some practice."

"You have to hurry, it's nearly dark."

"It doesn't work in the dark?"

The misty mermaid on the guy's belly got laugh-tossed. "Just that it's against the law to go out on one at night."

"I'd try not to get a ticket."

The guy's hand stayed on the money in his pocket while his eyes shifted. "I don't like to keep too much cash on me, so I'm closing up and going down to the bank depository and then home to supper, but you can park in back and manhandle the Jet Ski right down into the water and then out again. It isn't all that heavy." He looked Mal over. "Think you can manage?"

"I think I can manage."

"Yeah, I guess you can. *You* don't worry about carrying lots of cash."

"Maybe I'm just too dumb to worry. Or maybe too trusting."

"Yeah. So I hope you don't mind me warning you to lock your car. And I hope you understand I'm not responsible for your car or what you leave in it."

"If you want me to sign a release . . ."

"Hell, no." The guy stuck out his hand. "Well, pleasure doing business."

The guy didn't know how much pleasure. The guy stayed alive. Sure, the guy wanted him put while the guy verified the cash wasn't funny or hot; but it simplified things, the guy providing a staging area for the amphibious assault.

Mal shook the guy's hand, watched the guy lock up, waved bye-bye as the guy drove off. Then Mal swung the car and the trailer with the Jet Ski on it around to the back, which sloped right down to the water.

The building in front and the high wooden fences at the sides gave him privacy here on land, and the car shielded him from eyes out on the sea.

He opened his car trunk. It became his workbench. He had already rolled a .50-caliber Barrett assault rifle and four magazines of six-inch cartridges in the fallout coat; he stuffed this bundle inside one heavy-duty plastic trash bag. He rolled up his jacket with the disassembled M-10 in the deep pockets and stuffed that in another trash bag. He taped the mouth of each bag shut with duct tape, then put the two mouths side by side and taped the two mouths together. Heaved these trash-bag saddlebags over the fairing forward of the Jet Ski's seat.

His carryon held silencers for the Glocks. It also held a dozen disposable lighters still in their blister packaging—*one* of the little fuckers had to come through in working order. His carryon also held, packed upright in an insulated plastic six-pack holder with a zipper-closed lid, Coke bottles filled with gasoline siphoned from his car's fuel tank and plugged with strips of linen shirt.

The long-range mike and attached binoculars went into a third trash bag; he taped the bag's mouth shut and worked this bag into the carryon. Took off his shoes and socks and stuffed them in. This stretched the zipper halves apart but he forced them to interlock at the zipper tab as he pulled it shut. He stuck a strip of duct tape over the zipper as final waterproofing.

Rolled his pant bottoms up to his knees. Drew the Glocks from the belly holsters in his waistband, wrapped each in a vegetable bag, taped the bags shut, then reholstered the pieces. Put on the bulletproof vest, the life jacket on top of that, then slung his carryon over his shoulders.

Closed the trunk lid and locked it. A struggle to pocket the keys with all that stuff on him. Felt fat and stiff as he manhandled the Jet Ski to the water's edge. Gravel and sand bit into bare soles. Shoved the Jet Ski afloat, mounted it. Started it, wrung power out of the handlebars.

Headed due south along the seaward shore of Key Biscayne, held parallel about two hundred yards out. Ducked his head below the windscreen, leaned sideways against the breeze and the swells, into the stain of night spreading swiftly west.

He had only about a mile to cover, so he throttled down to just above stalling; synchronize the passage of darkness over him with the spotting of his landing point. He looked for his seamark: the *Medallion*.

All this was fruitless if Ramón had taken it—and Lupe—out to sea.

Saw the *Medallion*. Pair of guys on deck, one leaning against the seaward rail, the other standing and gesticulating. Neither had the configuration or attitude of Ramón. Hoods.

Mal kept going, past the Díez property, past the polluted house where Benny Sánchez died, past the property next down the line, without, as far as he could tell, having drawn their attention. Powerboats and sailboats—dozens of them scored the water. As long as he seemed to be minding his own pleasure, he should not stand out.

Once out of sight, he let the engine idle. As he shifted the carryon around to his chest and peeled the duct tape from the zipper, lights came on in the house.

Timer to make burglars think someone was home, because he saw no moving shadows in any of the windows, none on the grounds, no craft moored to the pier.

He unzipped the carryon. It took both hands to wrestle the bagged amplifier-binoculars combo out without jostling his shoes and socks into the drink. He rezipped the carryon.

While the coasting Jet Ski bobbed, he ripped the wrapping off. The breeze-whipped plastic beat blindingly at his face before sailing away. He fitted the headphones of the long-range mike to his ears and brought the binoculars to his eyes. Holding the combo with one hand and steering with the other, he glassed the dusk-dimmed property and swung the Jet Ski in toward the pier. Still no movement, no voices.

He gunned the engine to get way, then coasted to the pier. Caught hold of pilings and worked the Jet Ski in under the pier and beached it. Found big, loose rocks and concrete chunks down there to chock it with. Unslung the carryon and took off the life jacket. Lifted the saddlebags off the Jet Ski's fairing and draped the life jacket in their stead. Crept out from under the pier, shouldered the carryon and the saddlebags, waded along the shore back up the line.

Rounded the fence where it played out in the water, squatted in the lacy foam, and brought mike and binoculars into play again.

The polluted house looked dark but emitted sound: a wheezy, rattly hum. Couldn't place it at first, then figured it for the noise of ventilating fans. Denise Kay's idea to make the place salable sooner? He grinned. Sorry to think the fire would do her out of a sale but pleased to think the fans would spread the flames.

Swung the combo toward the floodlight aura of the Diez place. Picked up salsa from the servants' quarters, then voices and figures nearer at hand. Spanish too rapid and regional for him to catch anything but *"el patrón"* and *"yate,"* but two forms moved midway along the fence on that side of the grounds, almost lost in tall new shrubbery that all but hid a new gate in the fence. Looked like, sounded like, the boss had sent one hood to pull another hood off sentry duty at the gate and back to the yacht.

Mal watched them vanish, heard the gate latch after them. He padded across the grounds and up to the fence and the amplifier tracked their footfalls down to the dock and onto the yacht. There, because the mike reached only two hundred feet, everything drowned in the sound of the sea.

He turned and padded to the rear of the polluted house. Set the saddlebags down, unzipped the carryon, took out his socks and soft-soled shoes, wiped his feet dry with a handkerchief, put the socks and shoes on, pulled his pant legs down. The pant legs were damp with sea spray and clung clammily but would dry soon enough.

Tore the paired trash bags open. Unrolled the fallout coat and snapped a magazine of six-inch rounds into the .50-caliber Barrett assault rifle, stored the three spare magazines in the coat's pockets. Set the Barrett down on the fallout coat. Lifted out his jacket with the M-10 in the deep pockets, put the jacket on over the bulletproof vest.

Drew the six-pack chest from the carryon, stood it atop the fallout coat on the stone patio. Took one of the disposable lighters out of the carryon, freed it from its bubble, tested it. It worked. Placed it atop the six-pack chest. Stowed the combo back in the carryon.

Picked up the Barrett and walked around the house to the side away from the Díez place. Smashed six windows with the butt—salsa should cover the tinkle.

Walked back to the patio, stuffed the fallout coat and the Barrett in his carryon, shouldered the carryon. Picked up the disposable lighter and the six-pack chest, cradled it in his right arm, unzipped the lid of the chest. Pulled out a Molotov cocktail, lit the linen fuse, hurled the bottle through a pre-smashed window.

Whoosh. Moved right along, lighting and tossing the rest. Threw the empty six-pack chest in after the last one.

The ventilating fans, until their power cords melted, fed oxygen to the flames. The fires licking out of the windows became one big fire engulfing the house and erupting through the roof.

Still no stir on the Díez side of the fence. Just when he thought he would have to go to the fence and holler *"Fuego!"* he heard shouts of alarm from the Díez grounds. About time.

Took a silencer from his carryon, fitted it to one of the Glocks, held the Glock ready.

The prevailing wind kept the flames from jumping to the garage, so he kicked the garage's side door in and waited inside the empty garage. Kept the door open a crack and watched two hoods come running through the gate in the fence to stand on the patio and gape at the fire. It lit them like demons, and shadows writhed over them.

He took aim through the crack and popped them. Got the second before the second was aware the first had fallen.

Went out and dragged them into the garage. Waited again, but no more came. Too spooked. Maybe they guessed Harry Pace was here.

Just when he thought that Díez's people would let the house burn to the ground without doing anything about it, and that he would have to break into the house on the other side to dial 911 himself, he heard the sirens. About time.

He took the belts off the bodies and ripped one's shirt off. Tore strips from the shirt. Laid these things aside.

Donned the oversized fallout coat over the carryon. It covered the carryon when he shifted the carryon to the front. Gave him a chesty look. Mr. Universe.

Through the dusty glass panes of the garage door facing the drive, he saw flashers, headlights, and spotlights of a pumper and a hook and ladder that pulled up outside the front gate.

He waited patiently while fire fighters, and now police, shouted and milled and got little done till somebody with bolt cutters opened the gate. Then fire fighters, dangled breathing masks bouncing, fallout coattails flapping, poured in, dragged hoses across the lawn. He spotted a white helmet and lifted the garage door halfway. Crouching in the opening, he called and beckoned. "Captain. Over here."

The fire captain hurried there and bent down to look past Mal. "What is it? You find accelerant here?"

"No. A couple bodies."

"What?"

"See for yourself." Mal moved aside.

The fire captain stared at the bodies, then ran his eyes over Mal's fallout coat as if looking for insignia. "Who the hell are you?"

"Arson squad."

"Arson squad, hell. Who the hell *are* you?"

"Your replacement." Mal brought the Glock around front. With his other hand he grabbed a fistful of the fire captain's fallout coat and pulled. The man lost his balance and fell onto the floor. "Come on in."

Mal brought the door all the way down; it just cleared the man's heels. Before the man could do a push-up, Mal lifted the helmet off and knocked him out with a pistol whip to the back of the head. Gagged and bound him with the cloth strips and the leather belts.

He took the man's breathing mask for himself, hung it to conceal the lower half of his face, clapped the helmet on. Sweaty work, fire fighting. He was already soaking.

Walked out the side door of the garage, around to the patio. Nodded and waved encouragement to the gallant men and women who fought a losing battle. Made for the gate in the fence, stepped through, paused in the shielding shrubbery to case the floodlit grounds.

Looked toward the *Medallion,* thinking like Ramón. Place to keep Lupe as bait for Harry Pace, handy for deep-sixing both. Looked toward the Díez house, still thinking like Ramón. Place to position hoods as bodyguards for the Díez family, handy for trapping Harry Pace in cross fire.

Locked his gaze on a second-story window overlooking the fire. A woman leaned out to watch the action.

Lupe.

He stepped out of the shrubbery into full floodlight and waved to make himself register in the corner of her eye. She turned her face his way. He waved again. She straightened and stood staring. He looked around, then lifted the helmet off his head and pulled the mask all the way down, just for a second. After a beat, she waved back.

His chest swelled. Inch more and the fallout coat would pop open. Lupe knew him, knew he had come to save her again. He raised a gladiator's palm and moved briskly to the nearest door.

Ran into the cook sneaking out. She jolted to a stop. The wild look in her eyes faded as she took in the coat and the helmet.

"They tell me stay in my room, but how I can stay in my room when is a big fire next door?"

"You're right, ma'am. Exactly why I'm ordering evacuation. You hurry on around to the road. Wait—before you go, who else is in the house?"

"The lady. But she can't go. Is two men with her."

"Are they all on the second floor?"

"One is up the stairs outside her door, one is down the stairs by the front door."

"*Bueno.* Go now. Save yourself. I'll take care of . . ."

She was gone.

He worked the silenced Glock from his waistband, held it under the overlap of his coat. Drew a deep breath, stepped through the door.

They were waiting for him.

The one supposed to be at the front entrance fired at him through the archway at the right. The .45 burst stitched across his chest, slammed him to the floor. That saved him from the .45 burst the one at the head of the stairs triggered a fraction of a second later. This burst stitched the space Mal had filled a fraction of a second before. But he lay too stunned to roll aside; they had to think they had got him.

He felt outraged, wanted to say, "Hey, come on, you guys. Can't you see I'm your friendly helpful local fire fighter?"

But they knew he was Harry Pace. How? Lupe couldn't've, wouldn't've, tipped them off. Had one of them looked out another window, seen him—big ham—unmask himself? All of that went on in the part of him that took notes while the part of him that acted acted.

Fast, before they wondered at the lack of bleeding. He overrode the pain from the pounding he had taken through the bulletproof vest. As they closed in on him, he moved his head weakly from side to side and rolled his eyes vaguely to distract them from his slow draw of the Glock from under the fallout coat.

"Why . . . shoot . . . me? I . . . come . . . warn . . . you . . . wind . . . carry . . . sparks . . ."

Their eyes flickered and they looked at each other.

Now. Without having to think, he steadied his head, steadied his eyes, steadied his hand, fired till they fell.

Took him ages to get onto his feet; cracked rib or two, by the feel. Took him longer than he liked, though probably less than it seemed, to put a fresh clip in the Glock and give each man the shot to the back of the head. Took him aeons to pull himself upstairs.

Made for Lupe's room, held the Glock ready, stepped stiffly but swiftly in and to one side. She was alone.

She huddled with her back to him, but the fire had turned smoky and he could see her reflection in the window. She held her hands over her ears.

He unscrewed the silencer and holstered the Glock. Stood looking at her. She wore something filmy and clingy.

She took her hands a little away to listen, lowered them, picked up a lighted cigarette from an ashtray on the windowsill, and held the cigarette to her mouth with trembling hands.

He frowned at her. "You ought to quit smoking."

She turned from the window, eyes wide. The cigarette fell to the carpet.

He took two long steps to grind it out under a heel. "You have to be careful. That's how fires start."

Her hands still cupped her face, but in wonder now. Her gaze fell to the bullet holes in his fallout coat.

He smiled. "I'm okay. You're okay. You can walk out the front while I go down to the boat and settle with Ramón."

"The boat," she whispered. "Ramón." Full of fear. She ran to the window that faced the dock.

He frowned at her dress. "You ought to put something on before you go out."

"The *Medallion* sails." Her voice sounded funny, hysteria welling up.

He moved to look out past her head. First time they had stood this close together. So close he sensed his breath rebound from her hair, perfumed.

Two hoods were casting off the yacht's lines.

He tensed, then relaxed. "So I'll settle with him another time. Right now, let's both go out the front."

There'd be rubberneckers, fire buffs. He could commandeer a car—hell, take the fire captain's official car. Forget the Jet Ski; it had done its part. Drive to the dealer's, pick up his own car. Plant Lupe where Ramón couldn't get at her, then go after him and finish him off.

Mal put his hands on her shoulders. Smooth. Soft. Warm.

She shivered out from under his hands, moved aside. She yanked off her black wig, threw it to the carpet, stamped on it, cursed in Spanish.

He stared. Redhead. He grabbed her and turned her around. Her face had twisted ugly with fury. Ramón's woman, Elvira.

Her eyes and lips suddenly glistened with pleasure in his pain. "He goes away with her."

Mal gave her a shove that knocked her to the floor. He ran downstairs, outside, down to the dock.

Got the Barrett out of the carryon on the run. Rounds had pierced the carryon, banged up the Barrett's stock but none of the vital parts.

The *Medallion* pulled away from the dock, making southeastward. Looked and sounded like engines at half-speed ahead. Mal made out Ramón himself at the wheel.

The hoods coiling line looked back across widening water, spotted Mal coming. They yelled to each other, dropped the ropes, braced Uzis on the rail, kicked up turf where he had stood.

He had thrown himself flat, to the right, into the line of shrubbery along the fence. Grinning with pain, he broke off a branch, removed the white helmet, poked the helmet out of the greenery, prodded it forward along the ground to give them a target while he wormed through the screening brush, the Barrett assault rifle cradled in his other arm.

By the time their fire had bounced the helmet out of reach of the stick, he had reached the greenery's edge. He braced the Barrett. The two had moved to the stern. Mal raked the stern rail, blew them away. Hurried to change clips.

Before the *Medallion* pulled out of range, he poured the fresh clip of six-inch rounds into the hull below the waterline. Chunks of splintery debris bobbed up in the yacht's wake; he had holed her.

The *Medallion* did not head in toward shore; held course into deeper water. Either Ramón did not yet realize the yacht was slowly sinking or Ramón did not care if he went down as long as he took Lupe with him.

Mal did not stand gaping. Changed clips, ran down to the water, plodded along the shoreline, struggled out of his fallout coat and carryon, ditching them as he went.

Detective Sergeants Carol Shanley and Jack Vogelsang had heard the radio call about the fire next door to Ramón Díez.

They recognized the address, looked at each other, responded unofficially.

And ran into D.E.A. Agent Eamon O'Keefe.

They looked at each other again, hung their badges from their breast pockets, joined O'Keefe on the road out front, and helped him watch the house burn down and the fire fighters keep the flames from jumping fences.

Before they could trade lies about how they just happened by, they heard a small-arms firefight out back, down by the water. The cops who had responded officially were hundreds of yards away, diverting traffic. The three hopped over hoses, ducked under streams of water, then stopped to peer around at the patio.

A fireman stood beside a smoking timber he had hooked out of the ruins. He turned away from the ocean, glanced at their badges, pointed.

A yacht without lights angled out to sea. The remains of the fire spread an ashen glow over the water, and Shanley thought she saw a couple of crumpled forms at the rail. The *Medallion*. With the Martínez woman aboard?

Another form ran doggedly along the shore. Bareheaded man with an assault rifle.

"It's him, it's him!" O'Keefe had his .357 Magnum out and drew a bead on the man.

Vogelsang breathed heavily after the short trot. He was always talking about he was going to cut down on junk foods. "It's who?"

"Harry Pace."

Shanley felt just as certain as O'Keefe. "You sure?"

"I'm sure. Don't distract me. I'm going to bring him down before he gets onto the next property."

Shanley felt torn. She should be drawing her own piece, be calling out for Harry Pace to halt and drop his weapon. But Harry Pace was the only one doing something to save the woman. And O'Keefe wasn't giving the man a chance to surrender.

She took a step, tripped herself, and bumped against O'Keefe just as he squeezed the trigger.

The shot went wild.

The man turned and fired their way. Heavy metal sang past O'Keefe's ear, whizzed through the shell of the house, slammed hard into something solid. Then the man was gone.

O'Keefe regained his balance and whirled on Shanley. "Stupid black bitch. You spoiled my aim."

Vogelsang outroared him. "You moron. I saw the whole thing. You ought to be kissing her black ass. She just saved your lousy life."

Mal reached the Jet Ski under the pier, unchocked it, launched it, and mounted it without stopping to don the life jacket. Left the life jacket draped over the fairing—he would snatch it if the Jet Ski went under.

Cost him a minute to regain sight of the *Medallion;* it was now well out of the glow from shore and moved without lights, black on black.

The *Medallion* had a big lead, sent back the sound of full speed ahead. But it seemed lower in the water and sluggish. He led the target. One job, one thought: Reach it before it foundered.

The Jet Ski could fail first; it was not made for these swells. Mal needed both hands for hold and for balance, so he jettisoned the Barrett. Felt a twinge, but he still had the M-10 in the deep pockets.

He held to his job, to his thought. And the *Medallion* changed its note, lost way, wallowed.

Sharper black on black. Definitely closing on it. He throttled down. Came up alongside and caught the ladder, holding the jet Ski off to keep it from thumping the hull.

Stepped up on a rung, and with a hard pull and a twist

hooked the Jet Ski's handlebars inside the ladder's frame. The Jet Ski rode with the yacht.

Heard feet on the deck, heard grunting, heard swearing, heard a rubbery scraping, close by and coming closer.

Hooked himself to the ladder with one arm, took the M-10 from its pockets, assembled it. Edged up for a look.

A life raft waddled his way. Two hoods wrestled it toward the ladder. Probably never had lifeboat drill, but doing their best to get it overboard and shove off, with or without Ramón and Lupe.

Be a shame to riddle the life raft, be a worse shame to pass up catching two hoods with their hands full. He held his fire till he knew Lupe was not behind them. Then fired.

He ducked down again on the ladder, changed clips, waited to see what the firing brought. Nice if it brought Ramón from the wheelhouse.

Nothing.

Glanced at the foot of the ladder. Ocean creeping up on it. Jet Ski still hanging on. Couldn't wait while everything drowned.

Slid up on deck, moved in a crouch, shifted the torn life raft from the torn bodies. They carried Uzis. He took these, but hung them on and went with his M-10.

Glided toward the wheelhouse, paused to see if shadow moved across instrument glow, saw no presence or movement, swung in.

No one at the helm.

Had Ramón already abandoned ship, in a life raft all to himself? Left his hired guns to save themselves, left Lupe to drown?

Mal swung out the other door, made for the companionway, eased on down. Stepped into a foot of water.

It swirled, with a cold, oily feel. Liquid leg irons he had to drag along.

The only light came up through the water from under two doors.

Mal kicked in the nearer.

Ramón turned from an open wall safe, in the act of lifting out a suitcase. Stood frozen, eyes big, till the weight of the suitcase pulled it down to stand beside another suitcase already on the flooded floor.

What Ramón valued enough to risk his life for Ramón had to lose before he died. Mal blasted the suitcases to bits with the M-10.

Ramón screamed when exploding water splashed his face. Put his hands to the wetness on his face, looked surprised when his hands came back unbloodied.

Shreds of thousand-dollar bills floated upon the water.

Ramón raised his eyes to stare into Mal's. "What have you done? What have you done?"

"Laundered money, looks like."

The yacht had a noticeable list. Mal felt the slant.

He leveled the M-10 at Ramón's chest. "Enough chitchat." He squeezed the trigger. A short burst ripped across.

Ramón flew backward, splashed flat. An island chain: nose, belly, toes.

Mal raced out into the corridor, sloshed to the other light from below. Kicked the door in.

Lupe lay on a bed. Mouth, wrists, ankles taped. Eyes open, taking him in.

He wondered how he could ever have mistaken Elvira for Lupe.

Found space for the M-10 and the Uzis at the foot of the bed. Moved to the head of the bed.

Pulled the tape from her mouth, his own mouth twisting, then picked at the ends of the tape around her wrists and ankles and unwrapped them.

She sat up. Worked her mouth, but only raw croaks came out. She put a hand to her throat, smiled weakly.

He put up a hand. She could thank him later. They had to get off the yacht before it sank.
Her eyes looked past him, widened.
He made a grab backward for the M-10.
It slid away too swiftly; another gun was already poking hard at his back.
"Wearing a bulletproof vest too? So I know not to make your mistake."
Ramón.
Mal whirled with a Glock from his waistband in his hand, but Ramón fired first, point-blank at Mal's thigh. The .357 hammer blow knocked Mal off his props, threw Mal's return shot off.
Ramón fired again, at the gun arm. The Glock flew out of Mal's hand, splashed. Ramón shot again, the other thigh. Mal toppled bedward, onto Lupe.
His shattered arm weighed a ton, might've pulled him off the bed if Lupe hadn't held him from slipping.
Ramón kept them covered with his Magnum while he screeched his rage.
Mal did not listen to the words. Under cover of his body, his good hand put Lupe's hand on the remaining Glock in his waistband. He felt her pull it from the holster. "In the face," he whispered. Then he rolled off Lupe, fell to the flooded floor. Only the list saved him from drowning.
Heard a shot.
The Glock, not the Magnum.
Sat himself up with his good hand. Proud of her. Got Ramón between the eyes.
She dropped the Glock, swung her feet to the floor, knelt beside Mal.
Mal eyed her with nostalgia for an untasted future. He would never learn the answers to all the questions he wanted to ask her. Such as, "Why 'Guadeloupe' and not 'Guadalupe'? Was your mother French?"

Said, "If it hasn't worked loose, there's a Jet Ski with a life jacket on it hanging to the ladder. If you don't mind. In the dark it's against the law. The switch . . . the handlebars . . . Oh, shit, work it out yourself."

She stared at him. "But what about you? You're bleeding." *The situation is precarious and calls for fluoride toothpaste.* How right you are, Uncle Phil.

He was fading in and out. In sync with the spurt of lifeblood. The first shot had nicked his femoral artery. Every time his heart beat, it pumped blood out. Blood rose and sank through the threads covering his thigh.

"Bleeding? No shit?" Then, furiously, "Get the fuck out of here, you stupid cunt."

She stiffened, then slapped his face.

They stared at each other.

Good, he thought. Now maybe she'll get off the boat before it takes her down, too.

The world darkened even before he closed his eyes. He heard nothing but the creaking of the yacht and the lapping of the water and the blood beat in his ears. Alone in the flickering light and the rising water with his last kill, Ramón.

Uncle Phil, his first kill, would've laughed like hell.

The sound of ripping made him open his eyes. He willed sight and focus.

She was still there, and she was tearing her bodice, splitting her dress from the V to the hem, as if ungirding herself to cry rape.

Against which corpse, the poor crazy bitch? Because she had to have been driven psychotic to be still here, doing this witless thing.

Then, as the tearing kept on, turning the dress into strips, he saw her purpose. He read with growing wonder her compressed lips, her whitened nostrils, her narrowed eyes.

Easy, Mal. Bad to let the heart beat with too much feeling, only pump the blood out faster.

He studied her intent face as she rolled strips into pads and tied them in place over his wounds with other strips.

When she had done the best she could to hold the bleeding, she got behind him, caught hold under his arms, pulled him through the water.

Dragged him to the door, out into the corridor. Even half-floating, he could not have been all that light. Slipping, sliding, she splashed backward. Stopped.

He twisted his head to see why she had stopped. Her heels had hit the foot of the companionway. Never get him up those steps.

She seemed to realize this; her grip loosened in his armpits. But it was to freshen her hold; her fingers bit into his flesh once more.

Felt bumping. Heard groaning; his, hers, or both.

The world darkened again.

Shanley, Vogelsang, and O'Keefe stood in forced chumminess at the taffrail of the police harbor-patrol boat.

The boat stood alongside the *Medallion*—or alongside what little showed of the *Medallion*. Too much of the yacht was below the surface for there to be any good tying lines to it. Best the harbor patrol could do was watch it go all the way down and then set a buoy to mark the spot.

"Job for the divers," Vogelsang said.

Shanley tired of looking at the sinking *Medallion* and wondering what divers would find aboard it. For all practical purposes, as far as she and Vogelsang were concerned, it was Case Closed. She looked away from the yacht, scanned the sea horizon, then the shoreline. It was going to be a fine day for those who liked to be out on the water to be out on the water.

Seemed to be a lot out already. One craft, though, if you could call a Jet Ski a craft, was already heading in.

A mile to the east, it worked awkwardly in toward shore. Maneuvering it, a speck of woman in what looked more like panties and bra than a swimsuit. What made it hard for her to steer the thing, something bulky lay folded over the fairing. A man?

Shanley stepped away from the others, tapped a water cop who had binoculars resting on his chest.

"May I borrow your binoculars?"

"Sure." He lifted them off and handed them to her.

She found the Jet Ski and brought it and the woman and the man riding it near.

Either she said something or her body tensed.

Whatever, Vogelsang picked up on her sudden absorption.

"What you looking at, Shanley?"

"I'm not sure."

Vogelsang reached for the binoculars. "Let me."

Shanley pulled the binoculars from her eyes and held them out to Vogelsang. Before he could take them, they slipped overboard.

Vogelsang eyed her in disgust. "Christ, Shanley, you sure got a bad case of the clumsies."

Shanley put her hands on her hips. "That's right, Vogelsang. Blame me."

Vogelsang put his hands on his hips and his face in her face. "Damn right I blame you. You're not sticking me with losing the binoculars."

O'Keefe weighed in. "Hold on, Vogelsang. You're the butterfingers. I saw the whole thing." He turned to Shanley. "What *were* you looking at?"

Shanley shook her head. "I'm not sure." She waved at the vanished Jet Ski. "And it's too late now."